THE OTHER WORLD

THE OTHER WORLD

K.N. Proctor

ISBN 978-1-7357469-1-3

Printed in the United States of America

CONTENTS

CONTENTS (CONTINUED)

CHAPTER ONE

RETROSPECTIVE

Is an early glimpse into the shape of human nature the necessary for the readiness that is all?

Two boys skipped back and forth in front of Nadine tossing her shoes in the air.

"Give me back my shoes", Nadine, mortified, barely managed to raise her voice enough to be heard.

Laughing, they ignored her, and continued tossing the shoes back and forth between them. A shoe fell in the snow and Derek looked to see her face. Nadine avoided looking at the boys. Would they give the shoes back once she arrived home or would they carry them off she wondered. Many uncomfortable and interminable moments later they dropped the shoes in the snow in front of her house and ran off.

What a relief. They were gone and she had her shoes. These funny shoes, which she quite liked were expensive leather Oxfords that her mom had bought because it was important while her feet were growing to have sturdy shoes to support her arches. After the relief, Nadine felt something else, the injustice of it. It was wrong to take someone else's things. Why would someone taunt and tease another person? One thing was certain she wasn't going to put up with it. Something inside her welled up in a fury against injustice. She would not ever take someone else's things, neither would she taunt and tease someone. Nor would she risk damaging another's belongings. She would not accept this behavior.

She imagined those two boys in her mind's eye, especially Derek as he had started it all. She wished she would not ever see him again, that he would disappear. This wasn't the only time Nadine focused with all her might on someone who was being nasty to her. There was a girl in gym class who would throw the ball extra hard at her or purposely bump her in soccer. Nadine knew that Kathy Walker envied her. Nadine, slender, with beautiful thick shiny auburn hair, and a happy smile, got top marks.

One day Kathy Walker bumped Nadine so hard that she fell onto the gravel scraping her knee. Anger rose within Nadine and as she got up, she knew that this was the last time she was going to be bullied. Standing and brushing herself off, she looked up. There was Kathy Walker sneering, expecting to see tears. Instead she met in Nadine's eyes complete determination. Kathy was suddenly very uncomfortable. The girls she picked on were smaller than her and she was used to them cowering. Nadine however was not cowering. She said, "Fat Kathy Walker you are never going to bully me again." Kathy's sneer disappeared. Nadine's voice, strong and determined, rang as fact. As Nadine spoke she walked slowly toward Kathy. As Nadine drew closer Kathy took a step backward. It was like the ground was giving out where Kathy stood. She stumbled and fell on one knee. She picked herself up and backed away again. She fell again this time on the other knee and scraped herself. All the while Nadine held her gaze steadily upon Kathy. Kathy began to mutter something about her mother being away and her sister being mean to her. Her eyes were moving every which way, she could not look at Nadine who had stopped advancing and stood her ground. Kathy turned and ran. She kept running all the way across the playground and out of sight. That was the last bullying Nadine ever experienced.

About a year after the shoe tossing and teasing incident Nadine heard that Derek had disappeared. He'd been out hiking with some friends and had gotten lost. They never found him. This was disturbing to Nadine and she thought about what power one can have if one focused on something very hard. Also she vowed to be very careful for what she wished.

Will Hamlet was the boy in the neighborhood that too many parents wanted their children to emulate. He was the best soccer player. He played hockey superbly, no one could out skate him. He aced his classes, from physics to history. His parents never had to urge him to study, to get up early for a game, or coax him home early from a party. He was mature relative to his peers. This was saying something because he was at least a year younger than his classmates.

In tenth grade Will's physics teacher, Mr. Nelson, asked Will if he would like to help him in a physics experiment he was conducting. Will eagerly agreed to help.

"This is going to work!", Will exclaimed as he stood by his bench in the school lab and lifted off his eye protection goggles.

"I think you've done it. It looks like we've found an effective way to remove oil from water. You may soon be hired by Chevron", Mr. Nelson said, smiling.

"Does this mean we are going to the World Conference of Physicists?", Will's enthusiasm was contagious.

Mr. Nelson, laughing, replied, "If they are willing to stick to their principle of merit over age and position, yes."

In the end, the school gained permission from The International Association of Physicists for Will to attend their conference and help present the findings. While at the conference Will met an old inventor Bartholomew Fenfrew. Over the course of the next two years through many conversations and a few meetings to work on ideas they had become good friends.

"Will, you should seriously consider Edinbridge. Their new department of technology is superbly outfitted with the best professors and the latest technology and equipment. Furthermore, Hale Paslan is someone you will want to meet and get to know", Professor Fenfrew said.

"Is Professor Paslan in the department?", Will asked.

"No, better than that, he is my oldest and dearest friend and a man of such character that you would wish to have him as a friend for life," Fenfrew replied.

Will looked serious and then responded, "If he is your friend it would be a privilege to meet him in hopes of knowing him."

"David, would you answer the question please", the teacher asked for the second time.

"Oh I'm sorry Miss Peepcorn, what did you ask?" David replied.

Miss Peepcorn sighed and asked again, smiling to herself though not to the class. She knew that David was day dreaming. She also realized that those day dreams were far more fruitful than her classes or most probably than any class in any classroom in the country could be.

"What author and book did you choose and please

pick one key area of learning that you would like to high-light for us", repeated Miss Peepcorn.

"Oh . . . yes . . . I chose Ayn Rand's *Atlas Shrugged*. Her novel is her philosophy of life woven into a story through the character of her protagonists and speaks to the impact on lives and life that individual character has."

Someone in the back of the classroom cleared their throat and someone else snickered. David Solomon rose to his feet and began to speak to the philosophy.

"Miss Rand draws a clear picture of the dollar, as a representation of our time, energy, and talent, and what this means when the value of the currency is properly understood and when it is not. When for example government apprehends our earnings, usurping the authority of those who earned the money, the lack of understanding of the source of the intrinsic value has serious consequences. For example it results in significant damage to people's motivation, corruption of their motives, and in the long term Rand demonstrates how destructive this is to society. The key concern I had about Miss Rand is that she left out God", David concluded.

"Thank you David", Miss Peepcorn smiled apprecia-tively.

"We can help create the world we really want", David said with boyish enthusiasm.

"What world are we creating then?", asked his good friend Sam Barts.

"What is most important? Why do you come to school every day?", David asked.

"I have to", replied Sam.

"What do you think is most important?", prodded David.

"I don't know. But I know what I want. I want to get up when I want and do what I want when I want."

"Who do you want to be in the end?", David went a little deeper.

"How do I know!", Sam squirmed.

"You do know, you just haven't uncovered it."

"What do *you* want then?", Sam retorted.

"I need to know who I am, be the best I can be. How else can you know what is most important? What else will bring your best life forward for the living?", he asked.

"Oh come on", Sam said with a sigh as he picked up his glove, "we'll be late for batting practice."

CHAPTER TWO

EDINBRIDGE UNIVERSITY

The broad old oaks, green pine, spruce and heavy walnut trees spread themselves above and across the lawns. The tallest and broadest trees grew along the river, always getting all they needed to drink. Still wearing their leaves, they shaded the new life walking with purpose along the lawns.

Will Hamlet strode along the path which edged the campus taking in this shimmering September day. He was brimming with excitement for this meeting. Above, the sunlight fingered the clouds dancing on the rich blue of the sky. Surrounded by the green of lawns and trees nature spoke inviting you to enjoy her beauty. The trees, hundreds of years old, spread their arms magnificently upward and outward as a crown of glory for the lawns, and as a guard of honor for the classical architecture. This architecture housed the halls of learning where students made their home for four or more years. The ivy wending its way up the stone of the buildings, whispered around the windows with stories from more than four hundred years. As Will crossed the great lawn he had the sensation that knowledge and wisdom oozed from the bark of these great trees. He followed the arms of the oaks toward Chartwell Tower and felt their long kinship with the centuries old architecture.

If the stone of the buildings could speak what would it say he asked.

"Within these walls you will be privileged to learn from masters of many subjects and a few who understand the true tools of learning. You will go where many have gone before who have left behind pearls for wisdom if you can reach out, touch, and hold them. You will have to choose wisely where your time here will bring you. There are many paths to take along the way. What will you choose when the path forks?"

"Where did that come from", Will exclaimed aloud.

Then to himself he said, whose voice was that? He had paused under a particularly tall oak whose branches seemed to spread a full block over the great lawn. As there was no answer, not that he expected one, he moved from the lawn to the sidewalk leading to the tall ivy covered tower.

Chartwell Tower stood at the end of an expansive lawn in the center of the Chartwell quadrangle. His heart raced as he anticipated meeting Professor Paslan. The introduction had been arranged by Bartholomew Fenfrew, whom he had met three years ago while attending The International Association of Physicists conference. Professor Paslan was famous. He held a senior position in the governance of Edinbridge University, one of the oldest in the english speaking world, and was renowned as the only expert, on the area of study he had created, History of the Known Universe.

As Will walked up the steps of Chartwell Tower a few students were coming out of the door. Two girls smiled at him. Will was tall and lean with broad shoulders and a thick head of blond hair. A relaxed wave kept his hair back from his face in a permanent wind swept effect. His structured facial features; the strong jaw line, straight nose, and broad forehead, reminded one of a Greek God.

"Hello", smiled the blond girl who was probably a first year too.

Will looked directly at her and responded with his warm smile, "Hello", he said, and held the door as the two girls passed out.

He quickened his pace climbing the stairs towards Professor Paslan's study. Will was bursting with questions. Yet he also just wanted to listen to this man of whom Fenfrew thought so well. Slowing up as he reached the third floor he looked around. A long hall extended before him with only a few doors off either side. There at the very end of the hall was a great solid dark oak door with an enormous brass knocker in the center. Will passed the other doors making his way to the one at the end. This must be it he thought as he arrived at the end of the hall. The door seemed to be set in an ancient metal. Was it brass, like the knocker, Will wondered as he stood before it. He shook his head. Wanting to touch the metal, though feeling somehow irreverent, he leaned in a bit to look more closely, was it gold? He removed himself from the question and took hold of the knocker. Before he could strike the door a voice from within, strong and warm said, "Come in Will."

The room was a large rectangle with an alcove at one end and an enormous picture window looking out over the lake. Everything was in browns and deep reds. It felt warm and comfortable, the deep comfort that comes only from time in one place, a very long time. A huge oak desk with more than a dozen drawers held the prominent place in the alcove. Bookcases of deep dark wood, completely filled with books, floor to ceiling, were apparently purposefully designed to the measurements of the walls. As Will stepped further into the room instinctively he turned to the light. Two enormous floor to ceiling windows on the right end of the room brought the outdoors indoors. In the middle of the wall a magnificent stone hearth fireplace crackled with a fire. There stood the Professor.

Will was struck by how young Professor Paslan looked. As he stretched out his hand to greet Will a warm full smile lit the professor's face. Will gapped and then pulled his mouth closed. The professor looked in all respects a fit and healthy man of thirty years.

"Will come and join me in my favorite place here", Paslan beamed and welcomed Will with a gesture to the armchairs in front of the fire.

Will's eyes were riveted on Paslan. What was it about this man? He was tall maybe six foot two, long of leg, slender of form, with broad shoulders. He radiated power and vitality. Instead of grey hair and a beard he had a full mane of dark brown hair that swept back and away from his face revealing a firm jaw, high cheek bones, and a long straight nose. In place of the more typical drooping shoulders and thick glasses of a learned professor, Paslan stood straight and tall looking out from clear dark brown eyes arched in thick dark brows. Those eyes seemed to twinkle right into Will. He doesn't look that much older than me, thought Will. He is a handsome man, but it was not his physique that struck Will. It was his presence.

Paslan leaned forward to the little tea table between them and offered Will a plate of plump scones and chocolate biscuits.

"They are very good, Jane makes them each day", he said.

"Thank you", Will said as he helped himself to one of the scones. Then he asked, "Who is Jane?"

"Jane studied here three years ago for one year and wasn't able to complete when the funds her grandfather left her ran out, she had to withdraw. Jane has become our chef. Once a week when I am here she comes to my study and we continue the conversation", he said in a lively tone with a warm smile.

"These scones are very good", Will said, as he munched appreciatively, finishing the scone he'd covered with strawberries, jam, and double cream.

"Well then help yourself to more", said Paslan with a grin.

Paslan was studying Will. His eyes seemed to dance over his guest and take him in, all of him. Will had the feeling his very soul was being uncovered.

"Bartholomew has told me that you are an inventor", the enthusiasm in Paslan's voice was enough to stir the fire. For a moment Will's attention was drawn from Paslan's face to the hearth where a starburst of sparks shot upward to the chimney.

"What are you interested in now?", Paslan asked.

"Fenfrew got me going on the pollution magnet", said Will and Paslan nodded knowingly.

"That got me thinking about how opposites behave. If you draw together the opposite sides of something what does this mean for the sides that are opposite, that share elements in common? Then once you've got them closer what could this mean for the parts that are not opposite? What might the possibilities be?", Will had easily taken up the story that he shared with Paslan's old friend.

Paslan was listening and smiling.

A bird flew to the open window and perched himself on the sill.

"Ah, Chaffinch . . . come in", spoke Paslan and the bird hopped inside and down onto Paslan's knee.

Chaffinch cocked his head to the right to take a look at Will, rolling his eye back and forth over him. He opened his beak and chirped sweetly for a moment looking at Will.

Then his attention was drawn to the plate of scones which was now covered in crumbs. Paslan stroked the back of the bird's neck with his forefinger and said with a smile,

"Yes alright then go ahead."

Chaffinch fluttered down to the crumbs and had a right little feast as Will watched, amazed by the exchange Paslan had just had with the bird.

"He's been coming since July", Paslan said. "Oh I almost forgot, this is the one class I teach." A bell rang in a distant corridor. "I will be late if I don't get along."

Will looked bewildered by the sequence of what had just occurred.

"I'm sorry to interrupt our tea together. I have a feeling we are just getting started", Paslan said as he stood up, looking very fit in his pale blue oxford cloth long sleeved shirt with a deep red tie and dark brown trousers. His shoes were Oxfords, brown, an old style that suited him well.

"You are welcome to stay", he said to Will who was now standing. "As you see there are a lot of books here and you may just find something that will spark your interest", he gestured to the wall on his right.

"Well. . .", Will hesitated. I'd love to stay and search the books here he thought to himself. The atmosphere here is as breathing in knowledge but I don't want to impose, I really want to be invited back.

Before Will could speak his thoughts Paslan said, "It is not an imposition. Would you enjoy being here?", Paslan asked simply.

"Yes, yes I would", Will responded.

"Good. I'll see you at dinner then, in the Great Hall. There are a couple of people to whom I'd like to introduce you". He picked up a book entitled *Where the Stars Meet Your Eyes* and walked to the door. "When you are ready to leave the door will close behind you", and with a twinkle in his eye suited the action to the word, and so did the door.

Will looked about. Chaffinch was watching him. He gave a chirp, flew to the window and out to the lawns below. Will took in a deep breath.

"What an unusual man!", he said aloud.

The air was filled with the smell of old books. What a wonderful smell thought Will as he took another deep breath.

What was it about Paslan he liked so well? It was a quality in particular Will had not seen before. He let his mind travel as his fingers wandered along the spines of the books where Paslan had gestured. Only in a public library had he seen so many books. His finger stopped. *Life and The Mind*, by Bartholomew Fenfrew.

"Bartholomew", Will exclaimed. "I didn't know of this book."

As he turned the first few pages his eye fell on the publishers notes, "First published in 1902 Bartholomew Fenfrew." "1902! But that would make him well over a hundred years. The Bartholomew I know is fifty, maybe." Will turned to the beginning of the book and began to read…

> What is your mind? Simply it is your think-
> ing and being by which you live each day
> and understand, or fail to understand,
> yourself, others and life. With understand-
> ing comes a step to meaning. From your
> mind comes your life. To see that you help
> create your future and should understand
> our human nature is thinking that leads to
> a life worthy of the gift. To see life as a

struggle for power, position, gain, to accrue comfort, or adapt to the will of others is to give up real life and deep living to a shallow shadow of what could have been. What regret to have had life in your hands and to let it slip away because you would not face the mirror of reality. Our language sources from our thinking. As our means of communication we would be wise to consider our language for itself and for the thinking to which it points. What is the condition of your mind? . . .

Will continued to read for some time and finished off at...

What is the music for the mind? What thinking will play portamento for you and carry one forward into the life with the greatest meaning? Do you play rubato and allow for a libretto that holds you back? What mind are you in? What mind do you carry into your everyday? Your every day amounts to your life over a life time.

Will sat in the embrasure of the picture window looking out over the lake. What a mind had Bartholomew Fenfrew. What a privilege to have the chance now of also getting to know Hale Paslan. He felt excited, happy being here at this university, in this room where such a fine person lived, someone he really wanted to get to know.

The afternoon light was streaming through the trees and playing along the sides of the buildings below. In this light the stone of the building and the leaves of the trees appeared to have changed color from earlier in the day.

Now the stone of the building across the quadrangle looked a light browny red where earlier it was a light tan color. The leaves looked almost silvery. Students were walking along the lawns and paths in all directions. As Will watched he noticed that something seemed out of synch. The sky was overcast yet down below on the lawns sunlight streamed through the trees. Where was the sunlight coming from?

Will went over to a window further along the room. He could see part of the lake and the sun playing on the water. The sky was the same overcast grey. Will looked at the pane of glass in the window, was it tinted in some way? It was a leaded pane, without tint. Sunlight was pouring into Paslan's office and playing along one shelf of books. One book trimmed in gold glistened in the light. He reached for the one gleaming in the light, *Light and The Other World* by Hale Paslan.

As Will opened the book he felt a breeze over his shoulder. The pages rustled and a few leaves of the book turned forward. He looked around to see the open window where Chaffinch had entered. The breeze disappeared and the pages rested quietly. Will read,

> "What is our passage in time? Is it the passage of time that has us see the value of time? Does this passage have us see with a different light? If we will register the greatest value of time will we understand life?"

Somewhere a clock chimed 5 O'clock. He returned the book to the shelf. Will walked toward the door and stopped in the middle of the room. Standing there for a moment, he realized that he felt at home here. He wanted to stay and sit in one of the big chairs and read these books but his stomach told him that he was hungry. He remembered Paslan was to introduce him to two people at dinner.

The sunlight continued to play upon the books. And what was that . . . music? He listened. No he must have been mistaken. Will opened the heavy door and before he could pull it closed the door began to close on its own. He was reminded of Paslan's words "When you are ready to leave the door will close behind you."

"I'm not sure I'm going to like my professors and classes", Nadine said to David. The two friends sat across from each other in the Great Hall on the huge old oak benches.

"Why do you say that?", David asked.

"It is a sense I have. Something has changed since the spring. This new term doesn't feel like last year. Something's wrong", she responded with a frown.

David noticed his friend's furrowed brow. He was pretty sure he knew what she meant. Rather than worry her he said nothing about his own serious concerns. Instead he replied,

"Paslan is going to introduce us to his old friend's friend Will, who is just starting his first year at Edinbridge. Let's welcome him cheerfully", David smiled. Nadine nodded.

Will stood at the entrance of the Great Hall wondering where to sit. The Great Hall was filling with students making their way to dinner. They were seating themselves at the dark oak tables arranged in rows which stretched almost the length of the Great Hall. Well worn wood benches matched either side of the tables. Then he saw Paslan smiling at him from the center table as he sat down to join two students. As Will approached Paslan gestured for him to sit in the seat beside him.

"Let me introduce Nadine Redwood", Paslan smiled upon the pretty young woman with shining long auburn hair sitting across from him.

"David Solomon", Paslan gestured to a man with extraordinary sparkling brown eyes who now sat on her right.

"Hello", Nadine said brightly, her eyes twinkling and her warm smile shining out at Will. She offered her hand and Will noticed her firm grip. David stood up, he was about six feet tall, dark haired, slender and elegant. A smile creased his mouth and as he offered his hand and leaned toward Will Will met deep dark brown eyes mirroring a great intelligence.

David said, "We are glad to meet you and that you are joining us for dinner. Food is very good here. Tonight we're eating roasted chicken with a vegetable casserole and fresh green salad", and he gestured to the wee feast before them on the table. Will sat down beside Paslan and took the plate David offered him.

Nadine said, "David tells me that you are friend's with an old friend of Professor Paslan", and smiled.

"Yes, Barthlomew Fenfrew. We have shared a lot of ideas on inventions that we're both interested in, he's a great fellow", Will responded with enthusiasm. Nadine and David smiled.

Paslan said, "Will is starting classes in our new Department of Technology. You will have a brilliant new professor who joins us from China this year, Su Su Rong. Do tell me your experience with her Will. I invited Professor Rong for tea in my chambers last week. She said very little. As I prefer to listen we ate a lot of scones", he laughed from a place deep inside.

Will and Nadine laughed too. David smiled. Paslan's eyes twinkled.

CHAPTER THREE

CLASSES

Nadine looked around the classroom as she sat prepared for her Literature in History Through The Ages class, waiting for it to begin. There were about forty students most of whom looked to be second year's like herself. Edinbridge was known for its literature and history department, her major. The lecturer, Alison Herd, sounded very learned based on her blurb in the university calendar. However one never knew what kind of teacher anyone was until encountering them in the classroom.

Professor Herd entered the room from the first floor door at the bottom of the round. She was tall and slender with browny greying hair piled up neatly but not perfectly on top of her head. She wore modern small black glasses, a long charcoal skirt just above her ankles, and a crisp white shirt with a grey and red vest. Having put her laptop down on the desk she looked up at her class.

"Good afternoon class", she addressed them in a precise even toned voice. "Our major focus this term will be female authors of the 19th century", she started in immediately. "The bulk of the mark for the course will be based on an essay of ten to twelve pages, the topic chosen from a list you will find on-line at my website. Please make a note", she paused a moment for people to ready themselves. "It is www.herdonthestreet.com. Please let me know via email which topic you have chosen by 1 October."

Nadine turned to her neighbor who was still fumbling in his bag for a pen so she could not catch his eye. A girl in the row above was looking her way and raised her eyebrows in a 'hmmm not sure about this one' look. Nadine wrinkled her nose in response.

On the way out the girl from the row above said to Nadine, "She didn't waste time with niceties."

"Isn't the course Literature in History Through The Ages? What about all the male authors?", Nadine asked her classmate.

"I'm with you", she said. "I've had it up to here", and she touched her hand to her forehead, "with women's studies. I'd like to learn something of literature - the best - whoever wrote it", she said with enthusiasm. "I'm Sarabeth by the way."

"Hi . . . I'm Nadine, glad to meet you. Funny name for her website", Nadine commented and they smiled at one another as they turned down different corridors.

That night at dinner David and Nadine sat together over beef stew, steamed broccoli, and cucumber salad.

"Alison Herd you said?", David asked.

"Yes she is our Literature in History Through the Ages lecturer and I don't like her", Nadine replied as she squeezed a slice of lemon over her broccoli.

"Go on", David was listening.

"She walked into her first class, her first contact with us, with something else on her mind. When she did look up it was with a phony smile."

David looked at her sideways and with affection, "Come on now . . . you know you can jump to conclusions."

Nadine looked over her juice glass, "And I'm usually right", she said firmly.

". . . yes , yes you are . . . Herd, I think she is a new teacher and is under Avaricis Bale, head of the history department. He and I have butted heads more than once."

"Over what?", Nadine asked as she helped herself to another serving of stew.

"My second year I had him for American History. His book list was entirely of new works every one of which was a rewrite of history. I remember one afternoon class a few of us got into an argument with him over Patrick Henry's famous cry which happened to be part of what was being read aloud. "Is life so dear or peace so sweet as to be purchased at the price of chains and slavery? Forbid it, Almighty God! I know not what course others may take, but as for me, give me liberty or give me death!" In his friend's book 'Forbid it, Almighty God!' was left out. Bale couldn't get off the hook because there were three of us who knew that one by heart. One fellow had been reading ahead in a book Bale had us buy. He pulled it out and quoted passages full of fact omissions, twisted interpretations, and plain lies. He pointed to the preface where the author had thanked the support of the Carnrock Foundation which is behind all sorts of organizations where its leaders can further promulgate their power. That fellow was a history buff and his family had taken part in forming both the original American and British historical societies. He felt strongly that the current American and British historical societies had abrogated their responsibilities by blatantly ignoring the founding principles and writing their own purpose for the societies. And that their purpose was to steer history and guide our education to suit their interest rather than for the sacred purpose of education - to bring us forth to be the human beings we are and to learn to think for ourselves. Bale was steaming and after that class he withdrew from us. He didn't encourage debate he just assigned the readings, essays, and tests. His class was my lowest mark that year and if I hadn't had A's in my other classes I would have missed getting into graduate school."

Nadine had stopped eating and was listening intently to David.

"Herdonthestreet didn't wait for descent she plowed us right under with her dictated homework before any conversation could begin", Nadine frowned.

"If she was hired by Bale she's working for him not her students", said David.

"Sounds like a spy operation", Nadine said with gusto.

"In a way it's much worse," David said, looking around the table. Paslan was away for the week and the seats at their table had a few different faces.

"Let's go for a walk", he said.

Nadine finished off her juice and got up. David rose and they walked out into the light. They headed for the lake. David had not spoken since his last words at the table and he began slowly, "Paslan has brought the case to Andrew McLellan and McLellan agrees."

"What case exactly?", Nadine asked.

"The rewrite of history case. As principal of Edinbridge McLellan is concerned that a large number of lecturers and some professors here have formed a group to concentrate their efforts on steering and guiding their classes away from the traditional tenants of education to their own idea of education led by Bale. Avericis has done his homework. His ambition has been his guide for decades. His mentors were like minded and now he's cultivated his own followers. As a result he has made huge inroads into academic life. Because this is one of the oldest universities in the world he has parlayed his strength here into a springboard for spreading his beliefs and work far and wide. He has been at it for years. Bale has influenced the board of academicians at the Global University Forum, and the UN Forum on Education. This is to say nothing of his being the lead Board member on the Triumvirate for World Peace. He has got himself appointed director of the new body, The New World Order Commission. That commission is a political body made up of those seeking worldwide power in whatever their area of interest. Recently some of McLellan's supporters jumped ship and swam over to Bale's boat. Paslan has been spending more and more of his time", David paused, "elsewhere."

CHAPTER FOUR

ELSEWHERE

Nadine sat at her desk where she was supposed to be studying. Instead she was day dreaming. As she gazed out the window to the trees and park below a robin landed on her windowsill. He was a big fat robin, an older robin Nadine thought. He had grizzled light colored feathers beneath his chin, if robins have chins. He kept sitting there, snuggled she felt, in the corner made by the glass of the window and the stone of the building. He had been looking out in the same direction Nadine had been looking and now he turned his head to the window. He tilted his head to the left to give his right eye perspective, then he moved his head more to the right to look directly at Nadine. His eye tilted up and down as his head remained steady. A ray of sunshine caught his eye and glinted off directly at Nadine. It was as a spark of fire meant for her. She hoped he would not fly off. And he did not fly away. He sat looking at her. As she studied him instead of her books she began to sense the communion. If he were to fly off why could she not go with him? He turned to look straight at her. He had his head bent to one side a bit so his eye could be right upon her. He opened his mouth and said, "You can."

He was flying close beside her on her left side. She felt

that he was helping keep her aloft. They seemed the same size. She wasn't sure if she was smaller or he was bigger. It didn't matter. This was another world. How wonderful to be experiencing another world. They flew over golden meadows and past lush green trees. The sky was azure, and green mountains and hills in the distance seemed to play along its edge. Wisps of white cloud appeared to be smudged on the sky with a painters thumb. Nadine felt one big warm smile fill her face.

"Where are we going", she asked her friend.

"Ahh ... you'll see when we get there", he answered. It was a 'he' for his voice was deep and rich and rang as though in song.

"Wheee", she heard herself sing out as she tilted her arms, feeling comfortable enough to try a new position in the air. Robin picked up speed and flew ahead and then across her path to the right. She followed close on, picking up speed too and wondering as she did how she had done so.

"There below, do you see the lodge?", he asked her.

"No . . . where?", Nadine replied.

"Over in the valley, in the clearing," he said.

"Yes I see it now", she said. "Your eyes must be very good."

"Practice", Robin responded.

Robin descended and Nadine followed.

"I will land on the bushes. You must land on your feet", was all he said.

She slowed herself down, consciously pulling her legs down from the air pushing them out in front of her. All the while Nadine was flapping her arms and moving her hands wildly as rudders. She was on the ground running, and then came to a halt near the bushes.

"Here we are", Robin chirped warmly and looked toward the lodge.

"Go on", he encouraged her, "go in."

She looked at him, "Who lives here?"

"You'll see."

Just then the door opened and in the doorway stood Professor Paslan. He did not look much like a professor, rather he looked like . . . . well he looked like . . . himself, thought Nadine.

"What!" . . . , Nadine spluttered.

"You made it!," Hale Paslan exclaimed with an enormous grin. "I knew you would", he said happily.

"What?" . . . , was all Nadine could utter as she stood rooted to the spot.

"How was the flight?", Paslan turned to ask Robin.

"A very good flight I'd say", Robin cocked his head at Nadine to confirm. She nodded and beamed.

"Come in. I have tea ready for you", Paslan said, gesturing them inside.

The room was very different from his study at university yet she could tell that Paslan lived here. All the books that lined the walls were great old books and they had that wonderful smell of years of history about them. The big windows for day dreaming were very familiar as were the tea and scones, Paslan's special scones.

"I'm hungry. Thanks so much", she said as she took the plumpest scone from a plate Paslan held for her.

"Of course you are hungry, you've just had your first flight", he said with boyish enthusiasm, . . . "What was it like?"

"Wonderful. Another world." Nadine's smile was full and bright. Paslan laughed from deep inside.

"Robin was there on my windowsill and then we were up in the sky together flying off . . .", Nadine burst out. She paused. Nadine was about to ask how it all happened and sensed that that question would reduce the wonder.

Somehow that wonder was related to being there with Paslan and in this new place and she was very happy for it. Then they all just started talking comfortably about all sorts of things. Robin had a few suggestions for Paslan's garden. Paslan asked about the robin population and the bird population in general this year. Robin was perched on the edge of the third chair and enjoying the plate deep with scone crumbs Paslan had placed before him.

Then Nadine asked, "Will you tell me about this place?"

"Yes. Though not today."

The grandfather clock chimed 5 O'clock.

"Ahh it is time for you to return", Paslan said to Nadine.

She wasn't sure what made her but she immediately stood up, surprised not to feel hungry. When she had taken the first scone she was so hungry she was sure she'd eat them all. Having just finished the one she was perfectly full.

"Would you like me to take you back . . . or would you like to go on your own", Robin asked her.

Nadine paused, "Can I find it on my own?", she asked them both hesitantly.

"Yes," Robin responded.

Then he said after another pause, "I will take you this time."

And with a little chirp he cleared his throat and said, "Thank you Paslan that was a very good scone."

"Buttery Butter Scones", Paslan said with a smile.

The next thing Nadine knew she was back at her desk and there was a knock on her door.

"Yes", she inquired as she went to the door.

"It's me", it was Will's voice.

She opened the door to see the ever energized bright face of Will Hamlet.

Will said, "I was just in Paslan's rooms. He asked if I would drop by and ask you to pop in to see him."

"Now?", Nadine's voice was uncomprehending. "How did he get back before me . . . and wait a minute", she wondered aloud to Will . . . "Were you just there . . . with him?"

"Yes, I had some questions about what I've been reading in his library."

"Just now?", Nadine asked.

"Yes . . . what is it"?, Will asked, wondering at her seeming astonishment.

"Ohh . . . uh . . . I'll go right away."

Will said a little uncertainly, ". . . I'll see you at dinner", and went off down the corridor.

Nadine struck the knocker of Professor Paslan's door firmly three times. The solid old oak door made a deep reverberating sound that rolled within the interior room.

"Come in my dear", a deep, warm, and resonate voice called from somewhere inside.

Paslan was sitting by the hearth with his feet up on a huge burgundy and green firmly stuffed ottoman with a book in his lap. As Nadine entered he stood up. She stared at the calm ever present professor.

"Come and sit with me here Nadine", he looked directly into her eyes in that warm, welcoming, and reassuring way he had of being present right where you are. He gestured to the huge arm chair across from him. Nadine plumped herself down into it's comfy recesses. She loved sitting here across from Paslan. Whenever she sat here she felt like all her insides were tingling ready for anything, she felt very alive and happy.

"Have some tea", and he handed her a cup and saucer with the steaming brew.

This tea tasted quite different, a little bitter, stronger than the tea she had just had or was that some time ago... He was looking steadily at her. She burst out with questions.

"You were still there when Robin and I left. How did you get here before me? In fact ... Will said he'd already been talking with you . . . Will you explain? What does this all mean?"

"Time . . . is very interesting . . . is it not?", he said simply and had another sip of tea.

She was staring at him blankly with her mouth open.

"Drink your tea it will get cold my dear", he encouraged. A moment went by.

"Present Time". . . , he said in his warm deep voice, carrying her with him . . . , "is with you and being very present in the here and now you are positioned to be ready for the future, another time and place. That time and place is related to you, and who you are in the present."

Nadine was listening with every element of her person.

"So" . . . she attempted, "if you are very present in the present you can give yourself the present of the future?", she asked with exclamation in her voice.

"Yes", Paslan laughed, "you are getting it."

"There is something else", he said in a serious tone. "Your intention has to be pure."

" . . . pure?", she repeated the word, inquirying.

"Pure in the sense of coming from the deepest place in your heart and at the same time sourced beyond yourself."

"Hmmm" . . ., Nadine responded.

'Yes", and Paslan took another sip of his tea.

"There was something about Robin", Nadine began.

"Yes . . ." , Paslan said encouragingly.

"I was so interested in watching him. And as I did I became so interested in understanding him. And as he gave me more opportunity to observe and learn, I felt close to him.

"Yes", said Paslan assuringly.

They looked at one another and their eyes became focused together in one place. In this moment Nadine was reminded of the place that she had gone with Robin. Did the fact that she was able to focus on Robin afford her the connection with Robin that then notified him that she was there within his world? Did Robin make a choice or was it a natural occurrence that she, having made the choice, allowed them to move together to another world? Now in this moment there was a difference. This time it wasn't just Nadine it was both of them. Paslan and Nadine were focusing simultaneously on the same thing. What was it? An element of life, something elemental to life, to being in life in the fullest way. In the wink of an eye they were flying together . . . High above the clouds into the blue and the sunlight.

"Flying seems to be simple for you", Paslan's voice strong and deep and rich came from beside her.

She saw him close beside her and somehow he didn't look funny with his arms out from his sides, he looked his complete self.

"Oh I love it", she heard herself say. Yes I love it she said to herself.

Then she said aloud, "It's not just the flying there is something else . . . it is a state isn't it, a state of being."

Paslan smiled and said in reply, "This way", and

veered to the left toward the hills on the horizon. She followed. Beneath them were a few houses scattered along the hillside and in the valley, maybe a dozen homes set privately with land not visible to each other from the ground. They were cozy looking homes, with big windows, well painted, with flower gardens, and Nadine guessed vegetables too in the back.

"Who lives here?", she asked.

"It's a small community called Windsor Port. It sprang up the spring after the big financial crisis in our world", he said.

"Our world", Nadine repeated, "This really is another world then?", she asked.

"Oh yes my dear", he replied. "It is another world all together."

He began to descend and she followed closely. He had chosen a green and yellow field of grasses near the scattering of houses she had seen from above. Paslan had landed up ahead and moved aside to give her plenty of room. She pulled herself up and this slowed her down quite well. Her feet touched the ground and she found herself having landed, running forward until she came to a stop. She turned to Paslan to find him smiling broadly at her. He said, "You are taking to this like a bird and a graceful bird I will add. Now come along there is someone to whom I want to introduce you."

They walked toward the edge of the trees where the houses seemed to begin. It was a beautiful neighborhood if you could call it that. There weren't planned out streets with houses all in a row. Rather each house seemed to be perfectly individually positioned for quiet, privacy, and beauty. The first house they came to was a charming old gingerbread looking house. Nadine wasn't sure how old it was it just seemed to have been built in another time. It was a white bungalow with huge picture windows, dark green awnings, and with enormous trees flanking it. There was a cobbled path that wound up a little hill to the house. Beautiful trees of a few varieties marked the path and a lush green lawn greeted you. The large overhanging branches of the trees seemed to frame the exterior of the house in a warm and mysterious way, letting the light flood into the windows yet providing privacy at the same time. Paslan led them up the path. As they walked towards the house there was a delicious smell of sweet peas. The lawn was a rich deep green and the many colored flowers played beautifully against the fresh white of the house as they nestled in their beds. The pink and purple sweet peas frolicked with abandon in and out of the white and pink peonies and multicolored stock. The best thing about the garden was its unplanned playfulness.The cobbled path led directly to the large wooden front door, made of a beautiful blond oak. The door was framed on either side by a large oval window. As they arrived, the door opened.

There stood a magnificent looking woman. It was impossible to tell how old she was. At first look she had a radiant energy of youth and vitality. At second look in her long auburn hair one could notice streaks of white. At third look her posture held her tall frame completely erect and she seemed more than six feet in height. It was her eyes that gave you a feeling of ageless wisdom and under-standing. Then she spoke.

"Paslan. Please come in", her voice was as magnificent as her bearing. The tone was deep and rich and joined the words as ingredient to her meaning. As she said this she included Nadine with her eyes and gesture. Her magnificent body glided back from the door and with a deep warmth invited them to be with her inside her home.

Paslan spoke, turning to Nadine, "This is Nadine Redwood. Nadine this is Terhaven."

Nadine stood in the entryway completely taken in by the eyes of this woman. A dancing hazel of green and brown her eyes lighted upon you and they seemed to play music as an introduction to seeing you. A strong and extraordinary energy exuded from her eyes that was like a warm and wonderful fire and at the same time like a refreshing flowing river.

Nadine managed to keep this woman's gaze and found herself feeling very happy to be here. Terhaven took Nadine's hand and led her inside. The strength and warmth of this woman seemed to flow through her fingertips into Nadine's palm. It was the kind of deep warmth that Nadine had felt sitting beside Paslan at his fire.

Nadine was standing in a large open room with high ceilings filled with light. This was a home not merely a house. The light seemed to play along all the walls, without any shadows, it reminded her of Paslan's study. There was a massive bowl filled to overflow with sweet peas on a pale wood circular table that sat in an enclave near a large picture window. Many paintings rested on the walls. The floors were wood and in many places were covered with simply and beautifully designed carpets.

"Nadine please feel free to wander", Terhaven spoke warmly.

"Thank you", Nadine replied.

Nadine was drawn to a painting on the wall by the window. The painting sat in a simple wood frame and as she stood before it the light from the window seemed to brighten and illuminate the canvas. The scene was of a countryside in summer, of a great meadow of grasses and flowers, with hills in the distance covered with trees. A stream wound through the center of the scene, with trees covering the area close to the banks. Looking more closely, she could see two young boys sitting on the bank of the stream. Were they fishing? She couldn't quite tell. They were certainly engaged with each other laughing. The sun's rays rested upon the boys at the edge of the steam. She looked more carefully. One face seemed familiar. My goodness she thought have I seen that face before? There was a robin singing in one of the larger trees. Nadine thought to herself why do I think he is singing? She leaned in a bit. His beak was open. Perhaps he was singing. She leaned in a bit more and . . .

They say that a great painter stops time and allows us into that time. The robin had turned his head to look out at Nadine and invited her in . . .

She heard Paslan's voice calling to her, "Will you join us in the garden?"

She stumbled as she landed on the wood floor in front of the painting in Terhaven's home. Nadine tugged at her skirt to straighten it and ran her hand through her hair. She must have gotten rumpled when she helped them bring in that fish . . .

"There you are", Paslan said as he came around the corner into the room. He glanced just for an instant at the painting and back at Nadine. Was that a grin she glimpsed before he said,

"Come join us, the garden table is set for tea."

As they walked through the French doors which were wide open to the garden, he said to her, "May I suggest you set your watch seven minutes ahead of time", and before she could say anything he'd moved ahead to pull out a chair at the table for her.

The back of the house was completely open to a large expanse of lawn that backed onto a forest. The size of the lawn one would not have expected from a view of the front yard. They sat at a large circular table covered in a white linen cloth. An enormous tea pot of a design she had never before seen sat in the center of the table. It was designed as a huge, faintly orange cabbage with great green leaves winding themselves in the form of the spout and handle. There were three cups each different. One was as a huge purple plum, another a great orange, and the third a big red apple. An elegant silver dish held numerous large fluffy scones. Everyone who knows Paslan must appreciate his love of scones, thought Nadine. Beside the plate of scones was a pot of white devon cream, three pots of different jams, and a dish of rich white yellow butter.

"Help yourself", Terhaven said as she noticed Nadine eyeing the scones.

"Are you wondering about your . . . being here?", Paslan's eyes twinkled.

"Yes!", Nadine cried as she plopped butter on the warm scone. "Yes I am."

"You see, you were able to get here", he paused, "some are not."

"What does that mean?", Nadine wondered aloud and sank her teeth into the warm scone.

"What were you telling me about being with Robin? Why were you able to connect in the way you did?", he asked her.

"I don't know exactly", Nadine replied through her munching.

Paslan was smiling as he watched her trying some of the blueblackberry jam.

"I remember being very interested in Robin . . . I wanted to know more about him, I wanted to understand him."

"That's it, you wanted to understand him. This meant you had to get to know him. It meant being with him in the real sense. That is, you had to be truly interested in Robin."

Nadine looked at him quizzically while nodding.

"That's all you wanted, the motivation was pure or as pure as it can be given that we are human."

"Why can we live in two worlds at one time?", she asked.

"It has to do with one's relationship with life. It is like your connection with Robin. You were able to join his world because you were very present with him", Paslan began. "There is relationship. And there is Time. And they are related. Have you ever experienced when the day comes to a close and you've worked hard trying to get everything done, you suddenly realize that all is done for that day and you have some time, some simple unstructured time before sleep?", Paslan asked, offering another angle.

"Not often. Though yes I think I know what you mean. Yes I have experienced that though it's usually the other way around. I don't seem to have enough time", Nadine said in anticipation.

"What if you could take the time you found and place it elsewhere when you need it. Like at lunch time when you're hungry and need to stop to make something to eat. If you stop you will break your concentration. Whereas if you finish up you can start afresh on something else after lunch. Then it would be better if you could have it both ways . . . you can if you've stored time."

"How do you do it?", she asked.

"It's all related to one's understanding and appreciation", he said simply.

Nadine caught Terhaven's smile, a wonderful warm calm smile that made the space around them, and inside too, feel like home.

" . . . understanding . . . and appreciation . . . , like the interest I found in Robin?", she was thinking aloud.

"Yes", Paslan said simply. "Because you appreciate you are saving Time. Remember that in one sense time is life. In saving some life you are storing or giving yourself Time."

" . . . I don't understand what you just said", said Nadine her brows furrowed.

"Well for example if you save money, you have some to spend somewhere down the road. If you appreciate your dog you give him more care and attention, perhaps you save him from running into the road and being killed. They say", Paslan looked at Terhaven, smiling, "that if you talk to your plants they are healthier and grow better", he finished enigmatically.

Nadine was looking out to the magnificent garden listening and day dreaming at the same time. She absently took up the napkin to pat her sleeve. For some reason it was wet.

Paslan smiled to himself and continued, "Only in appreciation can we create. Criticism acts in the opposite way, it is destructive. Living in appreciation we create room for the energy of creation. Within this energy is a great power. The source of this power is the source of all good. With appreciation comes a deep respect and understanding. The powers that live in the world are very different than the power at the source of creation. Recognizing this makes a world of difference."

Terhaven observed Nadine's interest in the garden and said, "It is a happy place when one appreciates life and the gifts of life", she paused to take in a fragrant breeze that wafted by the tea table. "If you are focused on being in the moment, appreciating every moment, you gather more beauty than data, gain more understanding than fact, and in learning in a deep way open your life to greater and greater meaning. When you truly see the beauty of life you help create the future. Life is relegated to the mechanical when one pursues power and things and one in essence leaves real life behind", she finished as she took up her tea cup.

". . . and some people, especially ambitious or proud people, can not accept being left behind", said Paslan rather mysteriously.

Chapter Five

Class

N adine decided to sit in the second row in Professor Herd's class. The first row was a bit too close, the second made the statement she wanted to make, she was interested in learning about history through literature. There was only one other person in that row a boy, or he looked like a boy. Maybe he is a first year Nadine thought. He wore a scruffy brown sweater and grey corduroy pants. His hair was brown and shaggy and though not long looked like it needed a cut. He wore googly glasses and seemed to keep to himself.

Herd entered the classroom and plunked her laptop down on the desk. "Good afternoon", she said without looking at them.

"Most of you have emailed in your term essay topics. For those of you who have not please see me after class. There were two topics which I received that were not on the list. George Hand and Nadine Redwood, would you please see me after class also."

Herd's lecture was on England of the 17th and 18th century. As there were few female writers to whom she could refer her focus had shifted somewhat. The note she kept playing was the affection the Brits held and still hold for their justice system. Her note was discordant as she found this affection to be a significant barrier to any change to the law. The awe inspiring confidence the British held for their justice system based on common law seemed to irritate her. She announced that this fervor resulted in an inability to adopt foreign modifications that would improve the law or suit the times better. Nadine was about to ask what change was she thinking may have been an improvement when the boy in her row put up his hand.

"Is it an assumption that change with the times is an improvement? Is not a similar argument raging in the United States over judges legislating from the bench and jurors not being properly informed of what the constitution is on the matter at hand?"

Nadine had turned to look at her neighbor as he spoke and when he had finished she turned back to see Herd's face. There was a pause and Herd's mouth hardened. With effort Herd asked slowly, "What is your name?"

Without hesitation he responded, "George Hand." She paused again and said with a little release of breath, "You are staying after class regarding your essay topic we can speak then", and she continued her lecture.

As most of the class was getting up to leave Nadine turned to her boyish neighbor and introduced herself.

"Hi I'm Nadine Redwood", she said and smiled as he looked up from something he was reading, "I like your questions."

He looked at her for a few moments and slowly a little smile creased his lips. He put out his hand and when she took it his grasp was firm.

"I guess it's you and me after," . . . and he nodded to two other students who were now talking with Herd.

They both rose from their seats and exited the row to walk the few steps down to where Herd was engaged with the students. Nadine noticed that Herd seemed much more aware of George and herself, and that they had been sitting together, than she was of the student with whom she was talking. She wondered if George noticed this too.

When their classmates had gone, Herd looking at the two of them asked, "Why did you not choose one of the topics on the list for your essay?"

George looked to Nadine to give her the chance to speak first.

"The topics about women not only do not interest me they do not offer opportunity for substantive learning in history and the others were like the topic today, with an underlying theme of what went wrong back in British or American history for which we are still suffering today. Rather than any detriment to us I believe we have gained enormously; economically, educationally, and morally, from our British and American heritage", Nadine finished firmly.

Herd gave her a long cold stare and seemed to decide to wait, perhaps to cool her temper, she turned to George reservedly.

"I could say about the same", George said simply and held Herd's glare.

"Alright then", she said, "go ahead with the topics you've chosen", and she picked up her laptop and left the room.

They watched Herd leave. Nadine's brow was furrowed and George's mouth was pursed.

"I bet she'll ignore us the rest of the term", said Nadine as they walked out together.

"Forever you mean. I wonder if she will even read our essays", George asked rhetorically. "I bet we get a minimum pass, no matter how good our papers are."

"It's really important that you put up your hand. Even

though she robbed the class of the opportunity you offered for dialogue or debate, at least they heard your questions", Nadine said.

"I guess if it's not 'heard on the street' it can't be valuable", George said.

Nadine laughed and with feeling said, "It's great to know that you are in the class."

"Thanks, likewise", he gave her a simple smile, one that reflected a real warmth.

"What else are you taking?", she asked as they walked down the corridor.

"I graduate this year. I missed a history course and this is the only one that fit my schedule. I've heard about Herd and didn't want her as a lecturer. However I think that we'll learn a lot about the infiltration of those who would and are rewriting history to suit not the truth, rather their imagined ideals or personal ends ... and those who would wittingly or unwittingly support them."

"Which category do you think Herd is in?", asked Nadine.

"I think she is unwittingly following Bale. She wants to be in Bale's camp. He is pretty powerful and puts on a good show for any intellectual", said George.

"When I first saw you in my row I figured you were a first year, you look, well, really young", Nadine smiled.

He laughed, and this was so unexpected Nadine jerked her head to see his face as he walked beside her. "I'm twenty eight", he said. "Thanks for the compliment."

"You look eighteen, if that", Nadine returned, surprised. "What have you been doing these last ten years? It sure agrees with you", she said with laughter in her voice.

"I've been working. My dad died when I was twelve and Mom went to work. My brothers and I have been working at one thing or another ever since."

"Do you have a plan for after graduation?", she asked.

"A little one. I'm going to work for a magazine as a copy editor and hopefully will get to write some articles. Also, I've been hired part time, I've just started, at a think tank where I help out with everything and can meet and listen to the regulars and the guest speakers."

"Congratulations", Nadine offered.

"Thanks", he said shyly and looked happy.

They were quiet for a few moments as they passed out of the building onto the Great Lawn. Then George asked, "What classes have you got with other than the Herdonthestreet type?'"

"I've got English Literature II with Professor Yumara. He's an old fellow who seems devoted to his subject and that's usually a straight forward raison d'etre."

"Yes", George agreed.

"Then there is Philosophy 201 with Yarnick ... I don't know yet. His first class was pretty vanilla, a review of the course. Last week he was away", Nadine said.

"He is pretty close to Hil Gore ... Gore sits with Bale on the Global University Forum. What are you doing to ensure you actually get an education here?", he asked seriously.

" ...Well ... what would you suggest?", she inquired.

"Did I see you sitting with Professor Paslan?", George asked.

"Yes", Nadine said surprised again.

"Time with Paslan is the best thing you can do. I've got to get going. I'll see you next week in class", and he was off.

CHAPTER SIX

CHANGE

The breezes had picked up since the beginning of first term. Some of the leaves of the trees of the Great Lawn had begun to turn. A little bit of yellow and a touch of red had appeared. Most of the passing students did not notice the change.

Will, Nadine, and David, received a letter in their mail box from Hale Paslan. It was hand written and asked them to come to his study that evening at 8 O'Clock. Nadine ran into Will in the courtyard between buildings after her English Literature class.

"Will", she called, and waited while he said goodbye to another student. "Are you coming tonight?"

"Of course", he said emphatically. "I'm really looking forward to it. It sounds like Paslan wants to talk about something in particular."

"Yes . . . I think so too", she replied thoughtfully, as they began walking. "I'm glad he's back. Are you coming from a class then?"

"Yes, I have a software development lab once a week here", he pointed to the building, now behind them.

"How do you like your lecturers? Are they open to you and your ideas, to conversation with you?", Nadine asked.

"Yes they are. We're all sort of in this together trying to take technology another step forward", he said keenly.

"Yes, that would make a difference", she said almost to herself, she smiled at him. "See you tonight then."

"See you", he replied as he paused to watch her go.

As Nadine walked down the long hallway towards Paslan's door she heard footsteps behind her. She turned around expecting to see David or Will. And there was someone she did not know.

"Hello Nadine", she said. "I am Professor Rong, one of Will's professors."

"Oh . . . . hello", Nadine surprised, had nothing else to say.

"Good evening", Professor Rong said, and opening a door on her left, left the hallway.

Nadine paused, where did that door lead she wondered. She hadn't noticed it before, but then she hadn't been looking for anything but Paslan's study before. She waited a moment and then went over to the door. It didn't look like an office door. Was it a stairwell? She pulled it open. It was a stairwell. What was Rong doing in this hallway?

Nadine knocked on the big oak door.

"Come in", she heard Paslan reply.

At the sound of Paslan's voice she forgot her trepidation about Rong and her having been nearby.

She entered the study to a crackling fire ablaze in the hearth. Paslan stood to greet her as did David and Will who had been seated by the fire.

"Thank you for coming this evening", Paslan said graciously. "There is something I want to talk with you all about. However first let's have some dinner."

A long table had been set for them with all good things. A large white linen table cloth hung to the floor and the table was laid with silver dishes and crystal goblets. David and Will moved to the table to appreciate the feast. Paslan, having anticipated both their curiosity for the food and their hesitation to be the first to uncover the dishes, did so for them.

"I'm going to start with one of my favorites, lentil soup." He drew a bowl from the side table and filled it from the tureen of delicious smelling broth. "Help yourselves."

David took a heaping plate of lamb chops, mint jelly, and vegetables. Will wanted chicken and pasta. Nadine helped herself to some vegetables and asked about the dish no one else had yet tried.

"That is guinea fowl and Jane does it very well", Paslan said encouragingly. Nadine decided to try it.

They all helped themselves to slices of wonderfully warm fresh homemade bread with butter. The goblets were already filled for them with what looked like red wine. They brought their plates back to the fire.

"I've been away and as you may know", he looked at David, "or have sensed", he looked at Nadine, "or been wondering" and he looked at Will, "I've been in the Other World."

David was nodding, Nadine uttered "Oh" under her breath, and Will looked confused.

Everyone was listening.

"I'm not usually away for as long as a week. However it was necessary and I will be gone more often now. There are changes about to take place everywhere", he said simply.

"Andrew McLellan is to be replaced by Avaricis Bale as principal."

"No", David exclaimed as though he wanted to change the fact with his word.

"McLellan has lost supporters in the last year while Avaricis has garnered a lot of strength", Paslan continued. "Avaricis will try and take over as quickly as possible. He will however come up against a stubborn barrier of tradition that not even he will be able to change. A changeover takes place only at the end of the sitting principal's watch and that will be in April of next year. It isn't long but it gives us some time", Paslan paused on his last word.

"All the tradition here is as a mighty fortress and comes down only a few stones at a time. They began falling years ago and you have been experiencing the onset of the final destruction as evidenced in some of your classes. Although even now, most will not see or understand what is happening around them. It is a funny trait of ours to never learn from history", he said this last bit slowly in his deepest voice. "While we can muster our own strength to lessen the damage Bale will do, we must also be ready for the longer term", he stopped and the air hung expectantly with what would be next. Paslan did not continue. He looked at each of them in turn, his eyes moving into them giving them some undefinable sense of the future.

"I have been away preparing in the Other World. There are many who have already left and made homes there. You met one who did so many years ago", he looked at Nadine who nodded slowly.

"What?", Will blurted out as he gave Nadine a bewildered look.

Paslan rose and stood closer to the fire.

"I have been a governor of this University for thirty three years", Paslan said. "When as a full time professor I was asked to join the Board all the members were dedicated to the education of their students. They invested time thinking about and discussing not only the curriculum, also the value for the students of the overall education they would receive in their four or more years here. Over the years as members retired or died and new members filled their seats the atmosphere in our great study where we held our meetings began to change. It was gradual at first. Our old members would gently coax new members on our founding principles. For a few years the new members did come around. As time passed however it became harder and harder to successfully encourage new board members, let alone teachers, to look to the founding purpose. In recent years each new member has had their own agenda. Our old group started to get together to discuss what to do about the dissonance between the new and old members. For the most part the new members had little or no interest beyond their own ambitions. In truth they had too often convinced themselves that their interests were best for the larger whole and that their intelligence was superior and would win out. It is a great and dangerous arrogance that thinks it knows better what is good for another", he took another drink from his goblet.

"They were ambitious for themselves and often lazy in their thinking about the whole picture of life. They had not a thought for the founding principles of Edinbridge. In effect, as the number of non-principled members grew and our numbers dwindled, the founding purpose was being destroyed and a few of us knew that over time then so too would be the University."

Paslan paused, his three young friends, silent, kept their eyes and ears upon him.

"Bartholomew Fenfrew had been a Board member for a very long time", Paslan looked at Will. "He is another who moved to the Other World some time ago. I remember the last Board meeting he attended. Avaricis

Bale had just taken a seat on the Board and at his first meeting within the span of two hours he had lassoed most of the new members and corralled them. He was subtly rewriting the constitution for the Board, writing out any purpose directed to education as we knew it and replacing it with his own directives. These directives, which were in essence Bale's ambitions, were not so clear then to the other Board members. After sitting with Avericis for two hours they were clear to Barthlomew and myself. Following the meeting we two went for a walk along the lake. That evening Bartholomew decided he was leaving Edinbridge. Paslan paused as he held the burgundy drink up to the light of the fire and gazed into the reflection of the crystal.

"You see it was Bartholomew Fenfrew who helped create the Other World and then founded it with a few others."

There was a release of breath from Will as they all listened attentively.

"The way we choose to live our life is more important than we may think. It will determine, whether we know it or not, who we will be in the end. Do you recall Fenfrew's book *Life and the Mind*?, Paslan looked directly at Will.

"Yes . . . but how did . . .?", Will spluttered.

Paslan went on, "In that book he shares with the reader the essence of what is required to create another world. That is, to think, to think for yourself about what is most important, this of course requires a classical liberal education, to imagine another world, and allow yourself to believe in it, and to believe whole heartedly, most importantly to believe in the creator. It is that whole heartedness and belief that then makes you fully present with the world you are imagining, that actually brings it alive",

Paslan looked at Nadine. "It is easier for those who will go there now as those who live there can help bring another, if that other believes, as Robin did with you", Paslan smiled.

Will, his mouth open, looking completely bewildered, turned to Nadine for explanation but Paslan continued. "While only Fenfrew and I understood the consequences of Bale's pursuits and his plans at the time, Bale's ambitions have been more than clear for some time now. His ambitions are clear for all to see if they have the will to see. For anyone who has a love of the truth and freedom, Bale's pernicious pursuit of power is an anathema. He has been undaunted in his efforts to rid the Board of all the long time members and to fill the seats with his own followers. I am still on the Board. He has been unsuccessful in ridding himself of me."

"Why?", Nadine suddenly asked.

"I'm not sure that I know", replied Paslan. "It has something to do with a lasting remnant of the old school, a tie to tradition. This school was founded in 1483, one of the oldest universities in the English speaking world. It has been a great irritation to Avericis that I have not been removed", he said with a smile. "When I am there in my old seat, closest to the fire", Paslan's voice was deep and rich and full, "Bale's face is set with anger the whole meeting because he is thwarted in his direction. When however I have been away he has been able to push through measure after measure. So that these past several years he has done immeasurable damage. You are feeling the effects in your classes", and he looked to all three of them inviting them to share their experience.

David began. "I am writing my dissertation and so work mainly on my own. However I have a doctoral adviser, Jeremy Grimble. When I was pulling the research together and before I started writing he was less involved. Lately he's been popping in to see what I've done and unasked is offering me advice. I think that he is getting direction from above. He knows that I come here", David looked respectfully at Paslan who nodded. "I have a sense that he's been told to watch me so that my philosophy thesis is within their parameters of acceptability for their doctrine."

Paslan said slowly, "You know..., there is a doctrine. Avericis had Ginbreste, who is head of the law school, write it. And it includes ... 'Any written document, manuscript or other material where publication is a possibility will be approved by the committee for upholding university standards.' There is nothing in writing that specifically outlines what those standards are because they are not technical", and he paused, "they are of opinion. Avericis hand picks the committee for approval of any thesis." Paslan turned to Nadine.

"I'm uncomfortable with my literature in history class with Herd", Nadine began. "She is interested in some agenda, not in the students. She gave us a restricted list of subjects for the main class essay, so restricted that I decided on my own subject."

Paslan beamed across at her and asked, "What did the other students do?"

"The student in my row did the same thing. Herd called the two of us to see her after class. She asked us why we had chosen our own topic. I said I wasn't interested in the other topics nor did I believe in their underlying direction. She seemed to let it rest. This reminds me I just saw Professor Rong in your corridor on the way here. It was odd. She seemed to know me."

"Where exactly did you see her?", Paslan responded immediately.

"About half way down the hall from your door. She left the hall through a doorway to a stairwell", Nadine explained.

Paslan was silent for a moment as he looked into the fire. Then he turned to Will, "What is your experience in your few weeks of classes", he said with warmth.

"Well ... I've been enjoying classes and have gotten pretty quickly into the work."

"Yes ...", Paslan said. "I am glad. Your area of study is transparent. The effects of the permeation of the doctrine are not as easily seen through technology. It can however", and he leaned forward ever so slightly towards Will, "be felt. There are people who would carry your work into hands that care nothing for you and your love of original thinking. That is, people who discourage freedom to think for oneself because it interferes with their ambitions for power. And because their ambitions are for power, they place themselves in position to effectively discourage such freedom. Remember what an ambition for power truly is. It is a desire for power over other people. When you are with such people if you are aware, you will feel it. Once you do you can begin to see how they go about their objectives."

Paslan's voice became quite serious, "I would ask you to think about what you would like to see for the outcome of your work Will and what you would not accept."

Will had been listening very closely and nodded his head.

"Have you met Su Su Rong yet?", he asked Will.

"She came into our Lab last week for the first time", Will said with some excitement in his voice. "Professor Rong came over to where I was working with another student on the Opposites Magnet and asked a couple of questions. She has been coming in most days now. Professor Rong is certainly interested and seems very bright."

"Oh yes she is very bright", Paslan said slowly. Let me know anything else, anything at all with regard to your contact with her", Paslan said.

"I will", Will replied.

Paslan leaned back in his huge chair and seemed to relax into another place. The atmosphere changed and the three students spontaneously began chatting back and forth. It was wonderfully comfortable to be close to Paslan in this way, sitting in his study, by the fire.

Their world was changing. There was a sense in this space together that the change would bring them to a wholly different place, a place within themselves, with life itself. Each of them sensed in this moment that this new place was necessary if they were to be wholly themselves, their very best. The conversation had stopped and for many minutes the three of them sat in silence. Paslan's eyes were closed. Then a quote from long ago came to the minds of the young people who sat quietly by the fire . . .

"There is a tide in the affairs of men which, taken at the flood, leads on to fortune; omitted, all the voyage of their life is bound in shallows and in miseries. On such a full sea are we now afloat; and we must take the current when it serves or lose our ventures."

Paslan opened his eyes and said to Nadine, "I know Yumara includes Shakespeare in your Literature course. I hope you read Julius Caesar, it is one of my favorites."

CHAPTER SEVEN

PERSONAL GIFT

Nadine stood before the mirror in her room as she tried to adjust her shirt and jacket. Her room was one very big square with a fourteen foot high ceiling, and an enormous rectangular window looking south over the Chartwell quadrangle. The loose fitting shirt was hanging below the blazer jacket the weather now demanded. She snatched another jacket from her closet, a long burgundy blazer. No that didn't look right either, too long and besides it didn't button up and there was a cool breeze outdoors. She dropped it on the bed and changed shirts. This pale blue shirt was just right with her jeans and it tucked in properly. What jacket? The brown thick corduroy one might work, it buttoned. She put it on. It sat a little too low over her hips. She placed her fingers just below her waist and imagined the jacket sitting right there. Before her eyes the bottom of the jacket shrank upward to the place where her fingers rested. She stood staring in the mirror. As she stared she saw and then felt the material shrink inwards to snug in at her waist. Nadine looked down at the jacket. Sure enough it had changed shape. She looked in the mirror. It fit just as she had imagined. She heard the bell tower clock chime the hour. Nadine snatched up her packsack and locked the door behind her.

Yarnick's philosophy class was smaller than any of Nadine's other classes. There were only twelve students and they sat together around a circular table with Professor Yarnick. Yarnick was a short man with a spindly build, horn rim glasses, and sparse greying hair. When he smiled, it was more of a crease across his lower jaw, his bad teeth showed and distinctly detracted from any possible friendliness. Today they were discussing Friedrich Nietzsche.

Yarnick began, "Are there any questions from last day?"

Nadine put up her hand.

"Yes, Ms. Redwood?", the professor asked.

"I would like to draw a link between Nietzsche's Apollonian and Dionysian concept and that of his concept of Perspectivism and show a conflict between them."

A frown furrowed Bernard Yarnick's brow. He cleared his throat and said reluctantly, "Go ahead."

"I was watching The Philadelphia Story on the weekend." As she said this an ever so slight sneer appeared on Yarnick's lips while he said ever so encouragingly, "Yes go on."

"Tracy Lord says in comparing her new fiancé to her ex-husband that they are as Damon and Pythias and her general meaning is as light like Apollo and dark like Dionysius. Later on she learns through her own foibles and mistakes to recognize her own humanity. In so doing she also better appreciates her ex-husband and his human faults. Her fiancé, who is trying to be something he is not, she feels can not really love her and she breaks off the engagement."

Yarnick said with impatience, "How does this relate to Nietzsche's concept of Perspectivism?"

"Culturally at the time of the Philadelphia Story a man of the people which the fiancé represents was assumed to be a good man and that a C.K. Dexter Haven, her ex-husband, born to the purple could not be as fine. When in fact the character of the former was much influenced by temporal popular opinion and that of the latter was solid, uninfluenced by outside fluctuations or trends. In other words a person is who he is and chooses for substance and character or no, whatever the culture may dictate."

"I don't see how all this relates", Yarnick had raised his voice. "And do you mean to say that we are not affected by the culture?", Yarnick jabbed out at her with his words.

Nadine responded, "Whether we will recognize it or no we make our choices. Certainly the weak thinking fiance was affected. Tracy Lord was affected . . . although in her case it was not the culture that affected her, rather it was her own ideas that were the current for her actions. When she learned more of who she was she was able to change her perspective."

Another student piped up, "I've seen the movie and remember that Jimmy Stewart's character says that he learned something. That the guy for whom he assumed little respect because he was born to wealth and social standing, C.K. Dexter Haven, actually turned out to be the better man."

Nadine added, "If we turned Nietzsche's concept of there being no ethical or epistemological absolutes, to there being no absolutes about culture as the transcendent factor in forming or designating what is, then perhaps we'd be closer to the truth."

"The truth Ms. Redwood", Yarnick blasted out, "is never absolute. The rules of politics, of education, and of life, are ever changing. If they were not we would be stuck in the dark ages, never learning nor growing. We would be as the beasts, cavemen."

"Could it be Professor that we are not cavemen

because some great men have thought for themselves, known what they believed, and why, and were willing to give up their own comfort or social acceptability and even fight and die if necessary for what they believed to be true, right, and good?", Nadine said this in a low gentle voice as she was a bit worried about Yarnick. He had gotten up from the table with his outburst and was pacing as he spoke. He stopped and took a handkerchief from his pocket and was mopping his brow. The bell in the corridor rang and the students got up and packed up their bags. Nadine was looking at Professor Yarnick as she put her book away. He was glaring at her, rooted to the spot. She felt sorry for him. As she was about to leave she said, "Miss Redwood please Professor, I am unmarried."

Will knocked at Paslan's door. There was no answer. He tried again and this time the door opened. Will leaned inside.

"Professor Paslan?", he called.

There was no reply. Will stepped inside. The door closed behind him. There was no one there. He remembered Paslan's words, 'the door will close when you are ready to leave'. It appeared the opposite was true too. Will had a feeling that getting inside depended upon what your motives were. He had come to ask to borrow Fenfrew's book and now felt compelled to make the most of the library.

The library was as last time, filled with natural light and that wonderful smell of old books. Will smiled as he went to the shelf where he had found Fenfrew's *Life and The Mind*, pulled it down, sat on the carpet by the hearth and began to read. He had finished his labs early. Su Su

Rong had been there again today. She had been coming to see them more frequently of late and in the back of his mind he realized that she made a point of visiting him more often than the other students. She was particularly interested in his Opposites Magnet. As he turned the pages of Fenfrew's *Life and The Mind* these thoughts about her rested there in the back of his mind.

It was Fenfrew's thinking that had started them off on the Magnet. Will was reading . . .

"Being present in the moment, affords the mind an ability to respond in that moment. Time acts with us. We are pulled in time so to speak. Here is where the greatest power is effected. It is as the 'magnetic moment', one of two measures of a material's magnetic properties. The quality of 'time' involved may be described this way. If we are in the moment, wholly present, we are 'in time'. This means we are maximizing time. We are without need to return to fill or complete a moment because it has already been completed. With practice we can be ahead of time. If we will keep in mind that an equation can be made between time and life, Time=Life, although it does not work in reverse, we can better help create the future."

Will recalled the last time he'd been reading *Life and The Mind* where Fenfrew spoke to thinking. Will was sure that Rong wanted to understand something of Fenfrew's thinking. Why didn't she ask Fenfrew herself? Maybe it had to do with Fenfrew being in the Other World.

Will went to the picture window and looked out at the lake. What was it Rong wanted to know? His mind moved to his Chinese friends, the ones who had come from the mainland who had a different concept of time. They might be late for appointments, though rarely for class. Rather than a watch to gage time they used the encounter, the moment, to determine when something was finished and when they should move on to the next engagement. Did this difference have anything to do with Rong's insatiable curiosity about his Lab? Probably not he thought. It was something else.

Will watched the little ripples on the water as they caught the light. There were patches of blue with bits of white. In the sky there were patches of an azure blue with snatches of white clouds. Some grey clouds were gathering. As he stood reflecting on Rong he could see that the section of grey was moving this way. He went back to Fenfrew's book.

It must have been a couple of hours that he'd been reading when he looked up and stretched. The sunlight was playing, as it always seemed to here, along the shelves of books. He stood up and walked over to the window again. The grey clouds had covered the sky and it looked like the pavement below was wet. Will leaned into the window and his nose touched the glass, the pane was slightly warm. It would be he thought with all the sunlight shining in here. But where was the break in the clouds? Below him a student had her umbrella up. Curious very curious thought Will. That made his mind skip back to Rong again. Why was she so curious about his Lab? He let his thoughts play over everything he knew of Rong. She had popped into his Labs, not to guide him, to learn from him. He had passed her in the corridors once and when he saw her she had been looking at him. Now as this scene was recaptured in his mind he felt that she had been watching him. He had smiled at her and said hello as soon as he'd seen her and she had smiled back. But he saw now that she had not been smiling while she watched him unseen. Will had a photographic memory and like a reel he could play back what had occurred. Why hadn't he registered her behavior in that moment? He would in the future. Somehow now he did not look forward to seeing her. What was she after?

David was holding a tutorial for eight philosophy students in Keenan Hall. Francis Keenan had been Principal of Edinbridge in the 1500's and a philosopher. This had been his favorite room. It had become David's favorite place too for conversation on thinking.

"Sam why don't you begin?", David looked at Sam Parker and smiled.

"Thanks", Sam said and pulled up his notes. Sam was a fourth year philosophy major. While he was not the brightest in the class he was the hardest working. "We were addressing Heidegger's view on technology. I'd like to raise a question related to his thinking that technology transforms the way we know and think and will." Sam paused in a moment of hesitation, and when no one broke in he continued, "Is it the nature of technology that makes technology's transformation of the way we know and think in some way pernicious or negative?"

There was silence for a moment and then Jack Cinolla spoke, "Technology is here. We must accept it or be so impractical that we forfeit our place as an individual in the world, as a nation in society."

"Is there something more than 'practical' that we should be looking at", replied Sam.

"More . . . , what do you mean?", Jack responded.

"I mean that if we are only practical beings do we not miss what is most important in life?", offered Sam.

Jack's face was blank, if he had not been such a polite fellow he would have rolled his eyes.

Walter Sparks spoke, "Perhaps Sam is speaking of the

essence of technology when he refers to it's nature", he looked at Sam. "Why I ask, could the nature of technology be pernicious in any way when technology is not alive? That is, technology does not have a nature, rather we imbue it ourselves with any attribute of nature dependent upon how we use it."

"Perhaps how we use it is dependent upon our own nature?", Mary Haber spoke up.

Addressing Walter, Sam said, "Heidegger would say otherwise and so would I." This was the boldest Sam had been in David's experience with him. Sam continued, "I think that we can see all around us each day the effect technology is having upon us and our lives or", and Sam looked at Mary, "that we allow it to have on our lives. I would suggest that we look down the road and gain the benefit of foresight. Then we can make changes now so that technology will not have primacy over our lives, rather we will have technology in hand and use it wisely to help create our lives to our benefit."

Donna Druep immediately jumped in, "Why is this even a question for our conversation?", she asked rhetorically and with disdain. "Technology is the reason for our economic advancement and as Jack said, it works. What else do we need to know?"

Jack's ears perked up at the mention of his name.

David asked Jack, "Do you agree with what Donna has just said, that if it works, what else do we need to know?"

"Well. . . did I say that?", Jack replied.

"No. Actually Donna took it a step further from your vote for practicality to a pragmatic premise", said David. David turned to Donna, "And many steps away from Heidegger I might say to Machiavelli's pragmatism."

"Well if it works?", she flirtily replied with a shrug gesture of shoulder and hands.

Sam came back strongly, "Why do we not think enough for ourselves and of ourselves?", he asked of each person at the table, looking at them in turn. "We sit idly by and let the person down the hall forever email or text us without eye to eye contact and succumb to his cowardly choice by emailing or texting him back. We let our relationship with our parent survive across the miles by phone when with visits in person the relationship might thrive. We sit before the screen for hours experiencing life vicariously because we would not summon the courage to be vulnerable and contact a human being in person. Where will this lead us?"

There was no response.

"Is it by nature that technology's transformation of the way we know and think is in some way pernicious or negative?", Sam repeated his question. "I posit that it is most pernicious because we don't think about it. Technology is benign until we stop thinking about it. I'd say that we began our slide away from thinking around 1950 with the advent of television and stopped thinking about it back in 1995 when we started to use technology all the time. To employ a word Heidegger used with regard to technology, we have become intimate with it. It has penetrated our psyche. It has infiltrated our thinking. So that this machine that we use everyday, the laptop, the iphone, the smartphone which is not really a phone anymore, is managing our very language, our communication. Therefore as Heidegger said in taking our language under its management it is mastering the essence of the human being."

Donna's lips had curled up into a snarl, Walter's into a frown. Jack looked befuddled.

Mary Haber spoke again and to Sam, "I had dismissed Heidegger because of some of his thinking, in particular about the Nazis. You have made me rethink. He sounds like he does have some intelligent things to say."

"There is a note for us here", David said. "What are the consequences of not stopping to think, and in particular about the impact of something we use, involve in our lives, everyday? Why do we not stand back and look to the whole picture, the biggest picture? What can it show us? What is your homework, individually", and he paused to look at each of them, "that you may increase your awareness of the life you are leading and living?"

Donna slammed her book shut and scraped her chair against the floor as she noisily left Francis Keenan Hall.

"What are you doing for your weekend?", Sarabeth asked Nadine as they were leaving their Friday Literature and History Through The Ages class.

"I don't have too much planned. I'll work on this essay", Nadine looked up to where Herd was erasing what she'd had on the board.

Sarabeth followed Nadine's line of vision and said, "I heard that they are having a meeting tonight in the Board room."

"What meeting?", asked Nadine.

"I don't know exactly. It's a meeting they've been planning for a while though. My locker is near the lecturer's lounge and I've heard them referring to it. Herd for example and your professor of philosophy will be there", Sarabeth said.

"Yarnick?", Nadine offered.

"Yes", said her classmate, "and a few others whom I don't know. The thing that is different is that the heads of politics and law have been in the lounge lately to make sure their department people are going to be there tonight."

"Do you mean Hil Gore?", Nadine asked.

"Yes Gore and Libby Ginbreste. Did you know that Ginbreste was a Supreme Court judge in the United States?"

"Was?", Nadine asked.

"Yes . . . I'm not sure how that worked but he's on the faculty board now of the law school here. Avaricis Bale is holding the meeting", Sarabeth said.

"Maybe it's to do with Bale taking over from McLellan as Principal of the university", suggested Nadine.

"Maybe", said Sarabeth rather hesitantly.

Nadine looked at her classmate, "What, what are you thinking?"

"I don't know. It's obviously an important meeting with Bale being there and the professors calling each other together. It just feels different, it feels like a faction, like they are joining together as a force of some kind." She paused and then picked up her knapsack, "Well I've got to go I'm going home for the weekend."

"Have a good visit", said Nadine.

As Nadine left the classroom she found herself walking towards the east exit. She was heading over to the Arthur Zembley building, home to the Department of Technology. She had to find Will and tell him what she had just learned. Zembley was the newest building on campus. The architects had considered the fit with the old architecture of the university. They had chosen stone and an older style roof. The windows were more modern yet the overall look of the building which was the maximum height the city of Edinbridge permitted, five stories, was a structure of character from a former time.

Arthur Zembley was now almost empty of students. A couple who had stopped near the entrance door stood close together in a tete á tete exchange. Three male students were engrossed in conversation as they exited the main doors and came towards her. Nadine was the only one entering the building. Instinctively she mounted the stairs to the second level where the labs were. It was quiet now. Where would she find Will? Nadine popped her head inside one of the classrooms. It was a big open room with work stations, lots of computers, and a huge flat screen that took up the front wall. Otherwise the room was empty. She continued down the hall and the sound of something ahead made her stop. It was two people in conversation. She heard,

"You must be there," said a strong female voice.

"I'm interested in my work, not your politics", responded a male voice with conviction.

"It is not politics, it is purpose. What value will your work have without the support of others? And why not choose the strongest? Avaricis is now Principal and is connected everywhere including the UN Forum for World Peace", uttered the woman.

"This work stands on its own. It will be valuable to many and for many years to come. It is a building block for the future. And Bale is not Principal."

As he said this last bit his voice trailed away as though he were moving away from the woman. There was a momentary silence and then the woman spoke again and her voice was colder,

"You will be sorry Harry. The future you speak of is now and we are making it."

"We?", said Harry and now his voice held indignation. "That is an insult. I am not a supporter of Bale's. He has treated McLellan abominably. He couldn't care less about this work. He is only interested in himself."

A cold hard laugh rang out, "And who is not interested in themselves? What is the purpose of anything if

70

not to advance oneself and be respected by others and others with power to help you along?", she asked rhetorically.

"That's right. You wouldn't know the meaning of fulfilment in one's work, of doing one's best, or doing something because it's the right thing to do, or the satisfaction of being of service to others. You will never know self respect", he said in a note of finality.

Nadine started. She had been stalk still and on that last note the man had moved towards the door. She stepped back as the door was only a few feet in front of her. A man of medium height and build came out into the hallway and turned toward her. His mind seemed to be elsewhere and then he noticed her. A warm kind smile came naturally to his whole face.

"Good night", he said to her simply and kept walking.

Nadine wasn't sure whether to walk forward or turn around. She didn't want to meet whoever it was who had that cold hard laugh. She walked forward and past the door. She couldn't tell whether the woman had seen her or not. Nadine was thankful for the soft rubber of her heels and was sure she had not made any noise. There was another lab ahead on her left, she went right in. There was Will looking out the window. He turned as she entered.

"Hi", he said with a big smile, "glad to see you."

"I'm glad to see you", she said with relief.

"What?", he turned full upon her sensing that something was wrong.

"Are you about to leave . . . I'd like to talk with you", she said and looked towards the door.

"Sure let's go", Will walked directly to the lab table, took up his bag and followed Nadine out the door.

They had just turned right into the hallway and there

in the center of the hall stood a woman. She had been listening. Though as Nadine's mind traced back in an instant there had not been anything important to hear.

"Hello Professor Rong", said Will in an even tone, not his usual friendly one.

"Hello", she returned, looking at Nadine. Her voice was almost sweet now though her eyes were hard and cold, like the voice Nadine had heard a few minutes before.

"We're off for the weekend", said Will in a way that meant we're not stopping.

"Yes, goodnight", she said mechanically and they passed her by.

Once they were outside the air seemed clearer and they took a deep breath simultaneously, turned to one another, and laughed.

"What was that?", exclaimed Will with relief and curiosity combined.

"Oh, yes, that's your professor", said Nadine.

"She is the new chair of the technology department, Su Su Rong", Will replied.

"I hope you have little to do with her", said Nadine firmly.

"I've recently decided that that is a very good idea", he said.

"I was coming to see you because there is some sort of meeting tonight in the Board room that Bale is chairing with a lot of the professors attending", Nadine said. "In fact I heard your department chair trying to persuade another professor to join."

"In the Board room did you say? McLellan chairs meetings in the Board room", Will said.

"Somehow I doubt McLellan is going to be there", said Nadine. "Paslan is right, Bale and his group are on the move. Tonight I bet Bale is asserting himself."

"It looks like the time has come", said Will.

They looked at one another and simultaneously said, "And we're going to be there."

Will and Nadine, walking fast, headed for Paslan's study.

"Do you know what time the meeting is?", Will asked.

"No, but I've got an idea how to find out. Robin could look out by perching outside their offices and listening."

"What!," Will gapped at her.

"It's Robin who took me to the Other World where I met up with Paslan", Nadine informed him.

"What?", Will said bewildered. . . . "Oh yeah . . . when are you going to tell me all about that? . . . and . . . where is Robin? . . . how do you communicate? . . ."

Nadine interrupted Will's questions, "That's just it I'm not sure. I've been thinking about him just in the last few minutes. I think he'll show up."

"Nadine this is not sounding very logical", Will spluttered, "we can't count on. . ."

Just then on a bush up ahead Nadine caught sight of Robin waiting for them.

Nadine's face broke into a smile and she turned to Will aglow, "Here he is."

"Robin, thank you for coming", Nadine smiled at the bird with the beautiful red bib.

"Of course. Are you wondering what Bale is up to?", he asked, cocking his head.

Nadine smiled and nodded.

"I flew up to Bale's office, he has a window near his desk. I have not heard him mention the time of the meeting. I'm about to go to Libby Ginbreste's study to see what I can learn."

"That's great", enthused Nadine.

"Robin I'd like you to meet my friend Will. Will this is my friend Robin."

Will instinctively put out his hand and as he did Robin fluttered up from the bush and alighted gently on the back of Will's hand. Will's first expression was of surprise and then his face broke into a happy grin.

"Pleased to meet you", they both said.

"See you later", and Robin flew off to the law school building.

'He's great isn't he?", Nadine asked Will rhetorically.

Will nodded, his eyes still fixed on the direction of Robin's flight.

Will raised the knocker of Paslan's door and let it drop three times. There was no response.

"Is Paslan here this week?", Will turned to Nadine.

"We hadn't thought of that. He's got to be", she said anxiously.

"If he's not here then it's all the more important that we know what goes on in that meeting", Will said. "Even if Robin could listen from the window it wouldn't be the same as the two of us being there."

"What about David?", Nadine continued.

"David is at a conference in Washington", replied Will. "What would Paslan do?"

Just as Will finished these words Paslan's study door opened for them. Will and Nadine stepped inside, and the door closed behind them. They stood silently in the entryway, and then stepped inside and turned to the chairs by the fire where they would normally join Paslan. Instinctively they moved towards the hearth and sat down. Sunlight glinted off the golden metal grate around the hearth.

"What is it about the way you communicate with Robin?", Will asked.

Nadine looked at him and was quiet for many moments. Then she spoke slowly, letting the words arrive,

"I was free thinking at my desk the first time we connected, day dreaming. As I did he alighted on my window ledge. As I watched him quietly I imagined flying with him."

"And this time . . .?", asked Will.

"This time I didn't see him. I kept thinking of him and our need for him. Then he arrived", Nadine finished.

Will noticed on Paslan's chair a book open with it's spine up. It was *Life and The Mind*, Bartholomew Fenfrew's book, the book he had been reading when last here. He picked it up and turned it over. His eye caught a sentence that read:

'In interest lives a presence that can move one in time.'

Will continued to read.

'Inside this time one is invisible in current time.'

It took just a moment and then Will said, "We can be in the Board room tonight. We can hear everything they have to say, observe them. Just like you flew off with Robin we can be in that room because we really want to know what Bale and his group are up to. They won't know that we are there."

Nadine was looking hard at Will. He continued, "It's like Paslan's door, the door opens when we really need to be here. We will get into the Board room because we need to be there and we will not be seen because we need not to be seen", Will finished speaking.

The door to the study opened and they got up to leave.

Nadine said, "Robin will be waiting for us outside", and the door closed behind them.

Robin informed them that the meeting was at 8:30PM in the Board room.

At 8:15PM Will and Nadine were sitting on the stairs in the north stairwell of Freedom Hall.

"I think it will happen like the door of Paslan's office. We will get into the room and be invisible to them", Will said to Nadine and added with a smile, "I think we're going to understand more about this as we experience it."

"Will Hamlet", Nadine beamed a broad smile upon him, "You amaze me. You know more than I do, in this moment."

Will blushed. Together they moved out into the hall to the Board room.

As Will tried the door he said, "It's as I thought the door is locked and someone is going to come to open it." They stood before the door.

"Let's just hope they don't arrive before we get in", said Nadine.

She had barely finished speaking when Will disappeared through the door. She just managed to stop herself from shouting out. Then she heard Will's voice from within the room,

"Nadine, concentrate on being in here with me. We have to witness this together so that we can share as much as possible with Paslan", Will spoke to her firmly from the other side of the door.

It was Paslan's name that helped her. She had to be there so she could help Paslan. She felt herself pulled forward and squeezed tight. It felt like she was moving in slow motion as through thick jelly. Then she was beside Will. They were sitting on the ledge made by the dental molding encircling the room near the ceiling. She grabbed Will's arm and squeezed it tight.

"Well . . . it's a little different than Paslan's door", Will said.

A long board room table with twelve chairs was in the center of the room several feet below them.

"We'll have a great view from here", Will was looking down at the chairs which surrounded the table beneath them.

"That's the fireplace Paslan mentioned. The first chair at the head of the table must be the one he used to sit in", said Nadine.

"Yes, but there is no fire now", said Will.

Chapter Eight

Avaricis Bale

A key turned in the lock and the door opened. A man of medium height and build strode swiftly into the room directly to the far end and head of the table and sat down. From his position he would be able to see everyone. Nadine looked at Will, inquiring with her eyes as to whether they could speak. Will gave a small shrug and kept silent. Next arrived a sturdy stocky man of maybe sixty five with an uneven gait and small piercing blue eyes.

"Avaricis", said Libby Ginbreste in a strong assertive voice.

Nadine and Will looked at one another - the man at the head of the table was Avaricis Bale. Bale nodded and gave a gruff noise from his throat but did not look up, intent upon his laptop. Then two people came in together, Hil Gore and Su Su Rong. Nadine felt Will move slightly beside her and she saw him studying Rong's face. Ginbreste had seated himself on Bale's right hand side. For a moment it was uncertain as to who would get the spot on Bale's left. Rong was faster. Gore continued around the table to seat herself beside Ginbreste.

A group appeared at the door and hesitated uncertainly. Bale must have sensed this for he looked up from his laptop for one instant and spoke to the group as one.

"Come in", he said and returned immediately to his focus.

Alison Herd, Bernard Yarnick, Thomas Turner, Snatch Devolve, and Mally Framer, bustled in and hastily took a seat. Another group came in behind them and sat themselves at the other chairs at the table and along the walls. Bale closed his laptop and pushed it to one side. He took the group in in one efficient look, as with a long intake of breath. Then he spoke,

"As you know I am now the Principal of this university", his voice was unwavering in it's authority and each note was as incased in steel. Will let out his breath with a sound that made Nadine glance at him. They both looked down to see if they had been heard. All eyes were on Bale and he continued. It was as though Will and Nadine were not there.

"Therefore we can now move more swiftly and effectively in implementing the change that is needed. Libby Ginbreste understands the change better than anyone but myself, his voice held a tone of arrogance and at the same time cold confidence. It was the confidence that held the room in rapture and all failed to hear the arrogance.

"We have not been idle", Ginbreste began in his assertive voice. "We have been working for years beyond the doors of this university. The progress here is symbolic of our accomplishments worldwide. Rong has helped us from China, Gore within our system here as have I in the United States. As an American attorney and then as a Supreme Court justice I have been able to help implement the change we needed there. For too long the justice system in the United States was hostage to tradition, the Constitution. It was outmoded, intolerant of the changes in culture and the trends of society. Over many decades we and others before us have been able to untether the justice system from the Constitution, set it free", his smile was skin deep but his arrogance ran to his core.

"Free from the wisdom of the Founding Fathers?" Nadine's words shot daggers at Ginbreste. "Moored to what? To be set free to float with the wind of the moment? To be tossed upon the waves of change for the sake of change? Do you not hear the hollowness of what he is saying?" Nadine's voice rang with anger like a clarion bell sending a message to any who would hear, as she directed her words to those around the table and those sitting against the walls. She had responded to Ginbreste's words with her own, and they came fast and furiously, and were filled with the wisdom that would not toss tradition for trend. But below they could not hear.

"Now we are ready to make our move", Ginbreste finished.

Bale began to speak again, "We are all", and this time he looked around the table at each of them, "positioned to make the full change", he spoke as though this were a code word.

"You in your classes", he looked at Herd, Yarnick, and Devolve who were squeezed in along the table to his left, sandwiched like peanut butter and jelly.

"You", he looked at Mally Framer, and a mousy haired woman who sat beside her, "in the administration of the university." Mally opened her mouth and tried to smile which was hard because her perfectly capped teeth stuck out too far. But Bale had already turned away.

"You Tiny can help us at a moments notice and with great impact given your position in the media", Bale bayed.

Turner cleared his throat and began to speak, "Now

that we have the conservative radio stations blocked, the newspapers bought up, and the networks in our pocket we are ready."

Bale glared at him for interrupting but Turner was basking in his own pride and missed it. Nadine almost laughed. She had never seen Turner before. He was about 5 feet zero and other than being somewhat on the stocky side he was tiny all over. He had a small nose, beady eyes, little elf shaped ears, and his hands were more like those of a small girl.

The meeting continued for an hour and then Bale dismissed them. Herd, Yarnick, Devolve, Framer, Turner, and their entourage jumped up on cue and filed out. Ginbreste, Gore, and Rong left at their own pace. For about fifteen minutes Bale was writing in his laptop, completely focused, and did not look up once. Will and Nadine watched him. The room was very cold. Nadine buttoned up her sweater. Bale didn't seem to notice the cold. Then he got up as quickly as he had sat down, left the room, and locked the door.

"Let's get out of here", said Will. They found themselves in an instant on the other side of the door in the hallway.

"Whew! I guess I wanted to get out of there as much as you did", Nadine burst out, as they arrived outside the door in the same moment. "What do we do?", she asked, determined to act. "How do we fight them? Their postmodern thinking combined with their ambition and need for power is destroying Edinbridge, what it stands for, the systems upon which civilization is based", she said with vehemence.

"Apparently it takes too long for most people to see and understand who people really are", Will replied. "Paslan showed us this when he shared his experience of the first Board meeting with Bale. The other Board members instead of ousting Bale were taken in by him. Paslan isn't here. . . so it would seem that Paslan is not fighting Bale...here", Will said as he sought a complete thought. He mumbled, "When you are ready to leave the door will close behind you."

CHAPTER NINE

THINKING

A s she swam her laps Nadine reflected on yesterday's meeting in the Board room. Where was McLellan when Bale was holding a meeting in the Board room? If Paslan was in the Other World at such a time then it was too late to delay Bale any longer. Paslan had told them that Fenfrew had left to prepare the Other World years ago, back when Bale had first arrived as a Board member. Bale and his group were more than a menace, it would be nice if they all just disappeared.

Nadine's mind went back to a moment in her childhood. She could see the street where she lived in fifth grade. The snow was thick along the sides of the streets and sidewalks where it had been shovelled and piled. Two boys were running along the street tossing her shoes back and forth between them and laughing. When they finally dropped them in the snow and ran off she had for a moment been relieved and then she had been angry. This is when she had last wished that someone would disappear. Some time later he had disappeared.

At the same time Nadine was doing her laps Will was speeding down the hockey rink in the sport pavilion. He and a few others were having fun while practicing for their games on the varsity hockey team. He'd just scored for the third time when Roger shouted at him, "Hey Will give somebody else a chance."

"Hey . . . sorry . . . I was preoccupied", Will replied as he passed the puck to Roger. I'm preoccupied alright Will said to himself. He skated up and down the ice handing off the puck to his team mates. What is Paslan doing he asked himself. He's got to be in that Other World Nadine is talking about. I think we've got to go there. Is there some big plot Bale is hatching? I can sure see why Paslan would choose to leave. What a bunch of egotistical, prideful, glad handers, and worse in Bale's case - power mongers. Then there is the inscrutable Su Su Rong. What is she up to? I for one would like never to see her again. She wants something from me. What is it? It would be great to talk to Fenfrew again. Why hasn't Rong been talking with him? He knows more than I do on almost everything that interests her. Maybe he *won't* talk with her. She does not answer me straight forwardly when I ask her about Fenfrew. He probably doesn't want to have anything to do with her either. Paslan said he's been living in the Other World. What's going on? Where is David? When is he back? He probably knows more than Nadine or I do. From somewhere in the recesses of his brain Will heard a voice, "Are you coming for a beer . . . or are you going to skate to Alaska?"

Will looked in the direction of the voice. It was Tim Brand calling from behind the boards. Will was alone on the ice. He could see the others leaving the arena.

"Thanks Tim. I've got stuff to figure out."

"What stuff?", Tim asked.

" . . . I've got stuff to . . . thanks for the practice. . . see you." What was Rong up to?

David had been invited to The Conference of Philosophers in Washington. Ten graduate students had been invited to join fifteen professors from around the world for two days of conversation on philosophy. The students were asked to give a brief talk on their thesis topic and then to encourage conversation by the other participants.

David sat waiting for everyone to take their seats. He was excited about giving his thesis work its first airing. His thesis topic, Plato and God, was controversial. He had barely gained approval for the topic in his own department at Edinbridge and when he had submitted it to the conference he had received flak and wasn't sure they'd accept it. Yet here he was about to present to some of the most knowledgeable people in his field. The room was now quiet and the host introduced David Solomon from Edinbridge University. David rose and began.

"Thank you for this opportunity to present to you my thinking as I write this thesis, 'Plato and God'. Your conversation on this topic is an anticipated privilege." David began and was a few minutes into his presentation when a panelist interrupted.

"I'm at a loss to see Plato and God in the same frame. Also I'm wondering about your thesis adviser and your choice of topic. You are at Edinbridge aren't you? Isn't that where Avaricis Bale is Principal?", she asked her question to the rest of the panel ignoring David. Most of them nodded.

"Andrew McLellan is Principal of Edinbridge", said David firmly. "My thesis adviser is Jeremy Grimble and you are right to wonder about the connection between Plato and God", and he looked right at the professor who had interrupted.

She had been whispering to the panelist beside her and now snapped her head around to David. "Who is Andrew McLellan?", she asked with arrogant cynicism.

"Principal McLellan has held the office of Principal of Edinbridge University for twelve years", David said in an even tone.

Someone on the panel cleared their throat. The chair said, "Please continue Mr. Solomon."

"Of course you are right", David addressed the woman who had interrupted, "that as Plato lived on earth and God as Father has not, one might not look at Plato and God in the same frame. However from another perspective one could look at them in the same time frame if as I argue there is a close connection between Plato and God. As time is eternal for God there is the possibility of time being eternal for Plato, given a relationship between God and Plato", David looked at the woman to see if she was comprehending. She was not even listening. She was still whispering to her neighbor. David spoke for another five minutes on Plato's preflection of God when simultaneously two professors began to speak.

The chair said, "Yes Gertrude, what is your question?"

"This topic seems wholly irrelevant. We understood topics were to be within the list we included in the invitation to be a panelist. Why are we submitting to this discourse?", her voice demanded and then whined to a stop.

"Well . . .", the chair began and hesitated, . . . "the list was an assumed group of topics."

The man who had begun to speak when Gertrude had started, spoke now, "This is most uncustomary. For the last three years I have sat on this panel and all the topics for prospective publication have been along the lines of postmodern thinking. How do you expect to get your thesis published?", he demanded of David in a rhetorical question. "This is making me wonder what is going on at Edinbridge. I think I can speak for all of us here", and his hand swept over the rest of the table where some of the faces smirked knowingly and others nodded, comfortable in their little clique. He continued, "We had counted Edinbridge amongst our circle. Certainly all learned intellectuals have progressed beyond the impractical and unpragmatic thinking of the early aged philosophers. Bringing up God is . . . something else all together", he ended in a raised voice and tone of incomprehension and disgust.

"Mr. Solomon . . . I'm sorry but your time is up now and we must move on to the next graduate student", the chair said and called out, "Melanie Meddle."

David left the building. Walking outdoors amongst the trees he was struck by a contrast. Unlike the Great Lawn these trees were thinner and shorter and the air was cold. His flight out of Washington was in a few hours, he was thankful to have been able to change the time of his flight. As he walked along the water the atmosphere from that room felt reflected here. The sky was overcast and everything felt heavy. The buildings in the distance seemed cold and gloomy, even the people passing walked with their heads down and with a leded foot. The experience had been a disappointment. He had felt hurt yet only briefly.

In seeing that he had little if anything in common with those professors he recognized that he was not meant to be among them. There were others to whom he owed responsibility and others with whom he would find relationship. Realizing that with the time he now had prior to his flight he could be present for his class via video conferencing he texted Sam to ask him to set it up on his end. He hailed a cab for the airport.

"What are you doing here", Will asked Nadine as he almost bumped into her in the sport pavilion.

"Swimming, and you've been . . . playing hockey", she replied seeing his skates sticking out of his bag.

" . . . passing the puck mostly . . . I've been thinking about Rong . . . what is her plan?", Will asked himself as he said this to Nadine.

"What are the whole group of them up to?", she asked in return. Then in a moment Nadine said with determination, "Let's find out." She pulled Will's arm in the direction of the exit.

"Where are we going?", he asked as they hurried from the sport pavilion.

"I have a feeling Rong is in Chartwell Tower hanging around the top floor."

"You mean Paslan's study?", Will asked.

"Remember the day Paslan sent us a letter to meet him in his office?" Will nodded. She continued, "As I was arriving that evening I saw Rong snooping around in the corridor. We know that Paslan's study is a special place. Maybe Rong thinks so too."

" . . . Yes . . .", Will said.

"Maybe it is imbued with something related to Paslan. The door opens for us, the books that can help us show up, and the light plays about to clue us to the fact that Paslan travels by light. If Rong could get in there maybe she could learn about getting to the Other World."

"Travels by light?!", Will shouted, astounded. "Travels by light . . . . where did you get that idea?", he demanded of her.

"Well it makes sense doesn't it?", she replied matter of factly.

" . . . Well . . . yes I think that it does . . .", Will's mind was churning, connecting dots.

They had reached Chartwell Tower and were climbing the stairs two at a time to the top floor. All the staff had gone home. As the top floor had only a couple of admin offices and Paslan's chambers it was quiet. Just as they reached the third floor landing Will took Nadine's arm to hold her back.

"Look", he whispered.

They had stopped dead. The end of the hallway was filled with light. Paslan's door was open and light was streaming into the hallway. As they walked towards the door they could hear a sound.

"What is it?", she asked Will.

Nadine pulled Will's arm and began walking as quickly as possible toward Paslan's study without breaking into a run. She didn't care who was in there. If it was Rong or one of her group, they were going to find out and get them out! It was hard not to run but both of them instinctively sought to be noiseless and if possible catch whoever it was in the act of doing whatever they were doing. They stealthily moved side by side through Paslan's door into the entryway. There was a sound like someone moving papers. They glanced at one another and moved in unison to their left to face the alcove and Paslan's desk. There sitting in Paslan's chair at his desk engrossed in reading some papers was Su Su Rong.

"What are you doing here?", Will's and Nadine's raised voices chimed in anger. Rong swirled around dropping something as she did so.

"What are you doing here?", she batted back, her voice rose in cold indignation and for a moment there was fear there too. She had gained the moment she had needed to take the offensive, "Professor Paslan is not in residence -

as I'm sure you know", she was standing now. The last words she twisted to intimate a guilty design on their part. "You are in violation of school conduct coming in here", she rushed on, "As such I will inform Principal Bale. You will be severely reprimanded." As she said all this she had moved away from Paslan's desk and was standing in the center of the room as though in command of her territory. "How did you get in here?", Rong demanded. Then she saw the door - it stood wide open.

She looked puzzled, uncomprehending. Both Will and Nadine could see it on her face, she could not understand how she had not heard the door open. She looked back at them, jealousy in her eyes. For a moment Will felt sorry for her. If she'd only just laughed at herself, been honest, asked for help. But that time was long gone. Her devious choices showed unmistakably in her face. She killed his compassion.

"What are you doing here?", Will repeated their question but this time his voice was low and deep and strong. It rang, not with anger, rather with the relentless light that uncovers darkness.

"You have no right to ask me anything. Come with me we are going immediately to the Principal's office," Rong almost shouted.

"He isn't there", Nadine said firmly and as fact.

"What do you know, yes he is", she sounded fretful and a note of uncertainty came back into her voice.

"Andrew McLellan is not in residence", Will and Nadine spoke in unison and this time their voices rang within the room as music strengthening the backdrop to a greater purpose, as a fine marching band announces the introduction to the nobles. Rong seemed to sway on the spot as though she sought to find her footing as well as her voice. Music filled the room and Will and Nadine looked up to the ceiling as it seemed to come from there. Rong felt dizzy, and not hearing the music, she followed their gaze. Now, both Will and Nadine, knowing she could not hear the music, felt sorry for her. Rong sensed it and could not bear the resulting feeling of punctured pride. The music sailed above them, violins and horns sang as birds in spring.

Rong was stumbling, making her way to the door, as though the music was an invisible barrier for her. Will extended his hand as she stumbled. She retracted like a cobra's head before striking. She got hold of herself and as quickly as she could got through the doorway, not looking back. As Will and Nadine looked after Rong she was lost in the light that poured into the hallway from Paslan's study.

David listened as Donna Druep spoke to her thesis. She was telling the class about the relationship of Machiavelli's thinking to postmodernist thinkers.

"Ironically there really is a 'good' in the art of the possible. Machiavelli moved thinking from the past premise of virtue as the goal of political life to the development of the art of the possible. He espoused the philosophy that we must look to what is useful, to what men and societies actually do. His thinking has proven classic, as Kant, Kierkegaard, and Nietzsche have employed it too. He conformed the ideal to the real. He is the father of pragmatism."

Sam Parker spoke up, "As pragmatism would bring us down to the level of animals why espouse such philosophy?"

With disdain Donna looked down upon Sam, who

was in physical height shorter than herself. The disdain in her voice matched her expression as she said, "In case you haven't read your biology 101 we *are* animals", dismissing Sam in an instant with her tone. She looked away as quickly as she had responded.

"As I was saying Kierkegaard for example picked up Machiavelli's train with his understanding of 'truth', that one can not find truth separate from one's own experience."

"Does this mean", Sam Parker, undaunted, returned, "that some are destined to not find truth?"

"Why would that be a corollary of Kierkegaard's thinking?", Donna replied.

"I don't know if technically it is a corollary or not. If however one can only learn truth through one's own lens then finding truth must be dependent upon the lens one possesses", said Sam.

The left side of Donna's mouth curled up in a snide little twist as she spoke, "You're back to the same old thinking that there is an absolute truth, why can you not learn that truth is moving like the times?", and she turned her head away from Sam in a triumphant toss and smiled at her cohort, Dahlia Domine.

"Thank you for the compliment that my thinking has foundation in classical tradition", Sam retorted directly to Donna. "As I assume you point to, if unconsciously, that classical thinking has lasted the ages for good reason."

Donna's hand tightened over her smart phone and she might have thrown it at him but for the fact that it was new. Before she could reply, David who was smiling at this interaction, pressed a key on his laptop and an image appeared on the wall of the classroom.

"Speaking of the classic and of truth, this is Lemoyne's *Time Saving Truth from Falsehood and Envy*, 1737." The image of the painting appeared before them in a multiplicity of brown and red tones. "Time spears Falsehood and Envy with his left hand as Falsehood and Envy rolls on the ground beneath him. Time holds Truth in his right arm, away from Falsehood and Envy who reaches upward to her."

"Can we think of Time as Father Time?", asked Lourdes Razgoodman.

"What are you thinking?", David asked.

"Well in the Christian faith we have a relationship with God, the father. In this painting Time is taking care of Truth, protecting her from danger as a father would do."

"Could we get back to philosophy", Donna said forcefully, not as a question.

"What is Falsehood and Envy holding in his hand?", David asked the class.

"It looks like a mask", replied Lourdes.

'Yes, he has been uncovered by Time", said David.

"I'll take that as my point proven", said Sam with a smile.

"What do you mean?", Donna shouted.

"Simply that time proves all true courses of thinking and action", Sam said. "And that our thinking proves our finest action and our place in time."

The bell in the corridor rang and the students collected their materials into their bags. David saw Donna shoot Sam daggers with her eyes as she walked out of the room. Sam hadn't noticed.

"Sam you are more confident. It is showing up in what you have to say", David's smile could be sensed through his voice.

"Thanks, I'm doing more thinking and thanks to Donna", he laughed.

David nodded. Everyone had left Keenan study except Sam. David's thoughts moved to the pressing situation now unfolding. Paslan was in the Other World and may not be coming back. David was trying to see his responsibility clearly. He must reach Nadine and Will.

"Sam, will you walk over to the picture window and tell me what you see?", David asked.

"Sure", said Sam and he walked over to the beautiful window in Keenan study that gave a view out over the lake.

"The weather is . . . strange. The horizon is clear though the clouds over head tell me it is raining now", Sam related. "There are few people out of doors. Is that what you mean?", Sam inquired.

"Yes. Thanks Sam. Congratulations on the real confidence you have found. Have a good weekend", David said.

David's mind flashed forward. What was best to do? Was it time to move to the Other World too? Have I done all I can here? What about the students? Sam's accomplishment was heartening. He has uncovered his deep confidence, and was exercising in his own thinking today. Others in the class have fortified their confidence because of Sam's efforts to stand up to the accepted thinking and Donna's aggressive stance with it. Lourdes knows her beliefs and today was the first time she has said anything without being asked a specific question. Mary Haber has gained ground too. David contemplated this. Yes it may be time to move to the Other World. What about Nadine, Will, and all the other students? Perhaps the most valuable service is to fortify the right place. To create the world you really want rather than merely fix or patch one that is a mere shadow of its true self. The reason this world is unsafe for thinking minds is that too many of us have not been thinking. People will spend all amount of time and energy exercising their bodies and leave their minds behind. In being lax, lazy, and out of practice, we have forfeited our freedom. We have defaulted to be governed by those who know no better and think that they do, and most perniciously, because their ends are far too often the ends of power. The ends of power is power over other people. The sad thing is that in this world, Edinbridge, has been one of the few fine examples of beauty, of grace of spirit, and freedom to create our lives as we would most like to live them. At Edinbridge history and time have carved a place on the landscape that example mind and spirit well exercised for the living. Most important is that this poisonous group Bale has assembled cannot reach the hard earned Other World where the key to entrance is a heart clarified in love, the source of creation. This Bale does not understand. David boarded the plane.

The next day David found himself walking amongst the trees of the Great Lawn. The atmosphere was much different than that in Washington, more alive, as University campuses are wont to be. For how long? What change would be wrought by the creeping rot of cobwebbed thinking and for the lack of courage that forfeits one's freedom to voice one's true thoughts and practice ones beliefs? It had begun to rain. He suddenly noticed that he was getting wet. I must find Nadine and Will he said to himself.

David entered the Great Hall to see the tables filling with hungry students. Some professors scattered among the different tables were also there for dinner. As David looked around he noticed that none of Bale's bunch were in sight. Moving past the main door heading for the center table he saw Sam approaching him.

"Professor Solomon? Oh excuse me I know that you are not a professor yet", Sam said and asked his question, "What if the test of Truth is beyond the rational?"

"Faith knows well to engage reason and reason knows

when the test of truth transcends mere rationality and remains within the parameters of that which can be sustained. That's from Ravi Zacharias, he taught here sometimes in the summer term", David said and touched Sam's shoulder before he passed on.

Nadine was waving furiously at David from their seat at the middle table. Will sat across from her looking relieved to see David. A moment later in unison the three said, "I'm so glad to see you", and they all laughed.

As soon as David sat down Nadine breathed a sigh of relief. The dynamic at the table changed in a moment to a comfortable feeling of being whole.

"What are we going to do?", she said looking at both of them.

There was a pause, David looked at Nadine and then at Will and replied, "It looks like we're thinking the same thing. I've been wondering whether I should stay and continue teaching classes. If Paslan has left permanently for the Other World then the situation is not going to be helped by our remaining here. In fact I imagine Paslan has a plan and we can better help him there."

"That's kind of what I've been thinking", Nadine said slowly, "only it is sad to think of leaving Edinbridge to Bale and his horde", her voice underlined the drear.

Will was silent as he toyed with his soup spoon. They waited for him to speak.

"I . . . I'm really into work on the Opposites Magnet ... I hate the thought of just leaving it", he said in a deflated tone.

"Doesn't Su Su Rong oversee your lab?", David asked.

"Yes", said Will.

"She is part of Bale's bunch, and a major part", David said.

"Yes . . . I've been trying to stay away from her", Will replied.

"Trying?", David inquired.

"She comes to every lab and observes. She's subtly aggressive. Rong's got an agenda and a big one. What it is though . . . I don't know. We caught her in Paslan's study the other day."

"What? How could she get in there?", David sounded incredulous.

"We don't know", Will looked at Nadine.

"How do you think she could have got in?", Nadine asked David.

David paused and poured some water into his glass. "She was not invited in that we know. She must have gotten one of the old keys through the Principal's office. What was she doing there?", he asked.

"We've been asking ourselves that", Will replied. "She was reading something when we caught her."

"I imagine that Paslan would not leave anything really important positioned for her or any of Bale's people to find. Therefore her visit most likely amounted merely to a snooping expedition", David finished. Nadine looked worried.

"What are you thinking Rong wants with you and your lab work?", David asked Will.

"It's something to do with the Opposites Magnet", Will responded. "Earlier this month she actually offered me some of her own related research. I was surprised but I used it and it was a piece of the puzzle that we had not yet gotten. It advanced the project by a few months. She was pleased and of course wanted a conversation on it, which I had with her."

Nadine's brow furrowed as she listened.

"Sitting across from her in her office during that

conversation felt like a debrief of a secret mission. She listened and kept asking questions and I could feel that behind those eyes was a steel trap from which nothing escapes. The space between us felt as cold as ice. It was then I realized that Rong is like a machine, calculating, emotionless."

Nadine interrupted, "Yet when we caught her in Paslan's study for one moment there was a note of fear in her voice", she looked at Will to learn if he had noticed it.

Will paused reflecting back. "Yes, yes you are right.", he said and continued. "She has one purpose and she is steadily on its track. While I'm not sure what that track is I am sure she has only her own interest in mind. She is extraordinarily ambitious. Which translates to 'succumb to my way of doing things or you are fodder."

David said in a serious tone, "Yes. This all fits in."

Nadine leaned in towards David, "What do you mean?", she asked.

"Bale spent a month in China last year. After which Rong was slated to join Edinbridge as the new technology head. He was over there doing more than hiring. He's on a few international boards and commissions. Paslan must know a lot more than I do about what this international association is doing. There is something else. Paslan wouldn't be content to merely escape to the Other World. He would want to help bring as many willing people over as possible. In a simple way this will be a brain and heart drain on this world. You see Rong would resent you not being here Will.

"What does she care?", Will said contemptuously.

"Care, no. However she is extraordinarily focused upon her purpose, though you say you don't know what that is exactly. I think we can safely say it is in a way quite simple. She wants the most prestige, power, and highest position for herself possible. She thinks anyone a fool who doesn't play the same game. She is assuredly connected to her communist government and they will be chomping at the bit to get their hands on this new technology. Without you she is seriously slowed and in fact may not uncover the crux of what will create an Opposites Magnet. Additionally, the fact that Paslan and Fenfrew and others are in the Other World before her, gets under her skin. It is like a sharp knife in the side of her pride."

Will was listening intently.

"And the heart drain . . .?", Nadine asked.

"Did Paslan tell you why you could get into the Other World?", David asked her.

"Yes, he said you can only get there with a pure heart", Nadine answered.

"You mean that Rong could not get in then?", Will asked in revelation.

"Right", said David, "nor Bale nor any of his bunch."

"So that explains why she hasn't talked to Fenfrew - she can't. Because he's been living in the Other World which is closed to her", said Will. "Is Paslan's concern then for those here who, oblivious to the Rong's of this world, will be left with limited defense?", asked Will.

"That's one thing, yes", said David. "Importantly he wants to encourage a world where people can be their best and can create their own life as they best understand it is meant to be lived. Without the detractors like Bale this will be most possible and a happier place too."

"Old fashioned freedom", Nadine sang out.

"If Paslan would have me move to the Other World of course I will", Will said decisively.

David and Nadine looked at their friend. Then Nadine held up her glass. David took up his and then Will his. The three raised their sparking goblets together and silently drank their toast, "To living this life in truth, beauty, and goodness."

Following their toast Nadine asked, "Do we wait for Paslan to show up?"

"There is a way to communicate with him", . . . David was thinking aloud.

"In his study . . . there is where we will find the way", Will said responding to David and rose from the table ready to go. Nadine drained the content of her goblet and David left his plate of food unfinished.

Chapter Ten

Thinking Deeper

As they strode the corridor towards Paslan's study the halls seemed spookily quiet. They passed no one and while this was a relief it was also disquieting. Before they had even stopped in front of the old oak door it opened for them. They looked at one another feeling reassured that their mission to communicate with Paslan was starting in the right place. Instinctively they spread out. Will went to the book shelve he knew well, Nadine to the picture window that looked out over the lake, David to sit by the hearth. Will pulled *Life and The Mind* off the shelf and sat on the floor to read it. Nadine let her mind play in free thinking mode with the lake and the horizon as mirrors. David sat quietly in the chair across from Paslan's where he had sat innumerable times, thinking.

Nadine stood before the window taking in the whole natural scene. Everything, from the grounds immediately below to the hills beyond the lake, was still. While it was December the tree covered hills and the lake and their position to each other had always provided a moderating effect for temperature. Now it seemed that something was off kilter. The lake looked black and the trees were brown. The sky was one blanket of immutable dark grey, even at the horizon. Not a wisp of a breeze stirred the tips of the trees. They stood as stone. Nadine shivered. There was a loud bang and Nadine turned back to the room. A huge book had fallen from the top shelf of one of the book-shelves. And something felt changed. It was something about the light in the room. It was sunlit.

"I've looked at this book before . . . it's full of funny pictures and odd writing in the margins", Will said as he began to leaf through the huge tome that had fallen in front of him. Nadine came over and bent down to see. On the pages before them was a contrasting scene.

The left hand page was in half tones of grey. The right hand page was a colorful picture in all varieties of reds, browns and yellows. On the left page in the bottom left quadrant stood a woman. Her profile displayed a forlorn and frightened face as she looked before her to the bleak grey forest of withered and dead trees and upturned stone. Her hands were clasped together fretfully. On the opposite page stood a boy facing outward. His head was raised high to the sky and his mouth was open in wonder. His arms hung in a relaxed manner by his sides. He too stood in a forest, a forest of color where the trees grew upward to the heavens. Sunlight beamed in from above and shone down to the ground where he stood. Will got up and walked over to the window. Nadine returned to the window and they looked out to the horizon.

"It's bleak outside", Will said.

"Where is the sun today?", she replied.

A little noise made them turn. David had moved over to Paslan's chair and was now facing the hearth. He had his feet up on the stone edge and a fire was just getting going in the grate. A log had just toppled into the main fire.

"Come over to the fire", David said.

"Oh this side of the room feels so such warmer",

cried Nadine as she settled herself comfortably between David and Will.

"I was stirring the ashes absentmindedly and it started up", David said.

They sat watching the fire for a few minutes not speaking. Will wriggled in his seat and reaching between the arm and the cushion of his chair, pulled out a book.

"*Light and The Other World* by Hale Paslan", Will read the front cover. "This is what we need", he said simply.

He handed the book to Nadine so that the three of them could see the pages.

"There is something we all have to understand, something about light", Will said slowly.

"You understand the properties of light", said Nadine.

"I don't think it's the technical properties we're meant to understand", he said slowly as the realization came to him. "There is some relationship of light, warmth, and life . . . that we are supposed to get."

"What is it that gets one into the Other World?", Will asked Nadine.

"Well . . . it's not something technical . . . it's more a state of mind", she stopped. "We've gone over this before", she said.

"We need to go over it again", Will responded.

"It was like I wanted to be in another place. It was like my whole being knew something that I didn't know. Does that make sense?", she asked them.

David nodded and Will encouraged her, "Go on."

"Well . . . it was that I knew, when Robin landed there before me and I took the time to see him, I knew I could fly with him."

"Yes . . . you could see him . . . with light . . . you wanted to . . . . I don't know", said Will. He was silent quite a few minutes and the others did not disturb him. Then he said, "Let's look at it from the opposite way. Rong and Bale can not get to the Other World. They want something from us. They can't ask us openly and directly. They can't . . ." Suddenly Will turned to David, "Have you been to the Other World?"

"No", said David.

Will looked at Nadine asking with his eyes - why have you been there?

"I've been trying to see it clearly myself", she replied quietly to his silent query.

" . . . And you've met up with Paslan there?", Will's voice was full of inquiry.

"Yes, and with another person too to whom Paslan introduced me."

"Who?", Will almost whispered the word.

"Terhaven . . . a wonderful woman," and she stopped. They were silent.

Finally Will said, "It has to do with who we are. Rong can't get in and Nadine can. Okay. That's a given. Paslan knew you would get in by the sounds of it. We're presuming that we can get in", Will looked at David. David nodded.

"So you were first", Will spoke to Nadine. "Why? Is that important?" He was thinking aloud and answering his own questions. "Will it tell us something about the nature of the Other World? I have a feeling Paslan would have us see something. Paslan has invited us here, right here, we have sat together with him in these very chairs. What is the difference between being here and being in the Other World?", Will looked hard at Nadine. He was looking at her so intently that she shrank back into the depths of her chair.

David began to laugh, "Maybe it's something simple. You are taken up with technical details in your labs and I with fine points of philosophy. Nadine exercises much more freedom of thought. That free place where you play", he was looking at her endearingly, "fuels the imagination which fires the pathway to greater freedom. Inside that kind of freedom is magic. Time is affected. Light?", and he looked at Will.

Nadine spoke, "Something Paslan said . . . when we appreciate something, when we appreciate life we save it, and time. In saving time and life we are in a position to create time and life", Nadine was gazing into the fire as she spoke.

"Paslan said that?", David asked.

"Well actually he said less, more just came to me now . . .".

The fire was growing in breadth and warmth creating an ever more comfortable space for them. The three sat together silently for a few minutes.

"Light . . . yes . . . light travels in its path and because it travels so fast it is free to continue, nothing gets in its way, this relates as well to gravitational waves and why - in some way - you could fly with Robin", said Will.

"Perhaps in some way my state of mind and the state of light are related?", she laughed.

"Hmmm," Will mused. "What am I missing?", Will was toying with the poker and a log in the fire.

"I think the question is what are Bale, Rong, Ginbreste, Hil Gore, and the rest missing?", David added.

"They've spent their lives focusing on power and ambition", continued Nadine. "They've missed the boat. Somewhere inside themselves they feel a void and they've become desperate. They are hungry and they think we have the store of food."

"Nadine is right", said David. They don't understand that we can not *give* them what they need. They have to find it for themselves. Only they are looking in the wrong place."

Will responded, "Paslan invited us here together. I think we have to trust that when the time comes we will be transported in some way to the Other World."

"Will has it, the readiness is all", Nadine said.

That night at dinner David, Nadine, and Will sat close together at the end of the middle table. Tonight the conversation was not what any of them had anticipated. Instead of plans with regard to the Other World they were sharing stories with each other about their childhood, friends, family, life.

"How did we end up here together?, asked Will. They looked back and forth at each other.

They'd been talking a good long time and a lot of the tables had emptied. Some of the kitchen staff were coming amongst the tables to clean. A woman with a long white baker's apron came along side their table with a plate of scones and said with a lovely smile as she placed them in the center between the three, "These are for you", and she walked back to the kitchen. Each of them reached instinctively for one of the big fluffy scones.

"They're hot", exclaimed Nadine as she reached for the butter in the middle of the plate. David had taken a bite immediately and after he'd swallowed said,

"These are from Paslan."

"That must be Jane", Nadine said as she jumped up and headed for the kitchen. In a moment Nadine returned with Jane beside her.

"Jane this is David Solomon, and Will Hamlet. This

is Jane Fairfield", Nadine introduced them in a happy voice, as she and Jane sat down at the table. Jane is in touch with Paslan", Nadine said simply.

"Professor Paslan has been giving me orders for the meals and his study through Robin", Jane said simply. "He suggested the scones tonight I think as a means to introduce us", she smiled.

Jane Fairfield was about thirty, very fair, with big blue eyes, and a lovely smile.

"He's been giving you orders for his study you said?", Will asked.

"Yes. He has me dust and sometimes lay out books for him." She paused and then said, "I've wondered if he returns unbeknownst to anyone and reads there sometimes." The three friends looked at each other with a silent question between them. Jane said, "I really must get back to the kitchen." As she was leaving she added, "Come to think of it I wonder if he was there today?"

"Why?", asked Will.

"Robin said Paslan would take care of his study himself today", said Jane and she was gone.

They were very quiet. Then Will said, "Do you think he was there with us?"

"The fire", replied David.

"His books", said Will.

"The light in the room ...", finished Nadine.

There was a long pause.

"He's traveling by light", said Will confidently. "You were right", he looked at Nadine. "Being able to travel by light relates to one's state of mind and it is the key to entry to the Other World. That is why Bale and his followers can not get in. They can not travel by light because their state of mind is opposite."

"And their hearts", said David.

"So they've been trying to get in?", Nadine said in a hushed tone.

"It's almost a certainty that Bale has been trying to get in since Fenfrew established the Other World", David said. "It is almost certainly the reason that Bale brought Rong to Edinbridge, to figure out how to get to the Other World. Bale's raison d'etre is power. In other words power over others. With fewer of us around, his power dwindles, along with his identity. You heard Paslan tell us how angry Bale was when Paslan was present at the Board meetings. Paslan's presence blocks Bale's power. But Paslan's presence also reminds Bale of something Bale does not have. That is, Fenfrew's ability to create another world, and Paslan's ability to move back and forth between worlds. Power to disrupt Paslan and what he stands for would mean everything to Bale. If he could enter and establish himself in the Other World, the one Paslan now values, in his mind he will have won the big battle in his war for power. While we're still at Edinbridge we've got to carry on our lives", David said. Are you both here for Christmas?", he asked.

"I'm here", said Nadine, and Will chimed in, "Me too. I've decided to spend most of my time in Paslan's library. I'm headed there now", Will added as he stood up.

"See you tomorrow", David replied, as they all left the Great Hall which was now, empty.

Will had three books spread out on the floor in front of him. *Light and The Other World*, *Life and The Mind*, and the tome of pictures, which, he discovered, was entitled *See The Eternal With The Internal Eye* by Noah Yorelf. The publishers note to the book gave no particular date for first publication and attributed ancient Greek scribes along with Noah Yorelf for the content.

Will had been flipping through the tome for some time when he came to an adjoining two pages streaming with color. He had been arrested by the scene, the book now lay open to these pages. Tall verdant trees, sunlight streaming from a pink sky at sunrise, animals in and beneath the trees, birds in song, and the grand colors of nature all played in a harmony calming the eye and stirring the imagination.

Will had paused in his investigation and was letting himself day dream, something new to him. His back had slumped down gradually from his position on the floor, leaning against one of the big chairs so that he was almost level with the top of the big book. His eyes lingered over the pages of the tome. What was that? Music? He remained very still, listening. Yes it was music! As he listened quietly it was becoming clearer and clearer. From where was it coming? There - near the top of the largest tree on the page sat a little red and blue bird singing away.

"He is singing and I can hear him!", Will exclaimed aloud. As Will inched his face a little closer to the page the bird's song became a little louder. Then he heard something else. It was the music. The bird was singing in response to this music. Will was engrossed watching the bird whose little head was bobbing slightly to the rhythm of the music. What was this music? Where was it coming from? Was it coming from the forest of trees?

Will had an idea. He took a scrap of paper from his pocket to mark this place in the book. He hesitated as the music was very beautiful. But the inventor in him pulled him on. He closed the book. He could still hear the music! Was it here then, in the study? He opened the book to the page. The music played on but the bird was gone.

"What is happening?", he cried out.

Something Nadine had said came back to him. When

she paid a lot of attention she connected with Robin. When you look away . . .

"Hummph!, this is definitely not science it's something . . . else . . . something deeper . . . much deeper", said Will.

He looked closely at the pages again. They were still beautiful to look at yet nothing was alive there, at least not at this moment. How had it happened he asked himself. Think. I had been day dreaming. Hmmm, that's not easy for me . . . he took a few minutes to let this sit with him. This will not be approached by logic or analysis. There is something else which Nadine instinctively understands. These pages hold a secret which I am to understand. I see that much. Will sighed and slumped back to his position against Paslan's chair. The wonderful sunlight that seemed always present in Paslan's room was pouring in the window nearest Will. He looked up to the window. The sun's rays were warm on his cheek. Will found himself humming the tune of the music he'd heard. There it was again! The music was with him again in the room. It was very soft and he lowered his own voice to hear it better.

There was something new, the sound a violin can make when it is expertly played, the music that pulls at your heart strings. The violin's song soared upward, yet, still gentle, it touched the sunlight and broke into a rainbow mist of notes flowing together so harmoniously that it was as the brightest color in the rainbow a deep rich color, a deep purple and then a rich red.

"Ohh help me", cried Will aloud. He wanted to understand.

As the music had become the color the color became a rainbow bridge and lifted Will up. He had become very small and was floating just above the book inside the notes. It was all there before him to see and to feel. And Will could understand. He'd let himself be taken up, taken up with the beauty of the color, the majesty of the music, and the simple delight of enjoying the beckoning of something wonderfully unknown. This was surely a risk to his ego and intellect. Floating like a little bubble above the book what a sight if someone should come in and see him. Perhaps he was invisible to them. Would he be invisible to Paslan? No, Paslan seemed to see everything whether he was present or not. Come to think of it Paslan was present even if he was not. The music filled his ears with song as he rolled about in mid air. The notes are like little particles of light carrying me and if I'm right, they would carry me forward to wherever I wanted to be. I'm very happy to be right here right now present in the moment in the note.

Then he understood. He had had to let himself go. He had asked for help. He had let any vestige of pride in his own ability fly out the window that the real source had room to arrive and to play. It had happened with help. He arrived gently back down to the ground on his own two size 11 and a half feet. The books were closed and the door was open.

***

The lab was empty but for Will. He had gone immediately from Paslan's study to his own lab. Something in the travel in color, light, and music had twigged him to a new perspective for the Opposites Magnet. He flung up all the window blinds which were usually down. The natural light he decided would uncover any blindnesses. If the sunlight blinded him from seeing his lab equipment or his own notes perhaps he'd see something new. For that matter perhaps he'd hear something new, if not music, something new in his own thinking. On the way over Will had the idea of using laser light to simulate sunlight. Will put on the laser light glasses. Perhaps if he could separate the elements or notes as he was now calling them within the magnetic field, the light could then help bring them together in a new harmony.

He looked up from the microndeveloper and stretched. Then he saw her. Rong stood in the entrance of the doorway. She had been watching him and now as he saw her she smiled slowly, a small half smile.

"You are working hard", she said as she studied him.

"What do you want?", Will asked directly.

If Rong was caught off guard by this response she did not show it. She walked into the lab toward him, "I've suggested to Professor Haliburton that we work on the Opposites Magnet together, that we can use my lab and I will be your supervisor", all this she said in an even tone with the condescension of one conferring a great benefit.

"I'm perfectly happy the way things are", Will held her gaze as he steadied himself for an onslaught.

"You were very happy with the exchange of work we had a few weeks ago. This has moved the project along by a few months", is what she said, her eyes in contrast kept their bead upon him and held their own agenda.

"And now I'm happy to continue on my own. I see no need to move labs or supervisors", he emphasized his last word.

"It is already arranged", she said firmly.

"What do you mean?", he questioned, his ire rising.

"I mean that I have already arranged it. I have gained additional funding from the Board of the university for our project and Haliburton has filled your spot with a transferring student."

"Your arrangement has been made without my consent. You, Haliburton, and the Board have made a false assumption in imagining that I am in favor of such an arrangement. As you well know false assumptions in science are dangerous", in place of his natural friendliness and warmth Will's voice was cool and businesslike.

She must have felt this new strength in his voice as she hesitated for the first time. Rong regained herself and her bead upon him and said, "You really have no choice Mr. Hamlet. It is done", and her voice was cold now.

"Yes we are done. Please leave Professor Rong I have work to do", he said. He was a match for her and he could see in her eyes that she knew it.

There was a pause then she said, "We should be able to work smoothly together. I know you enjoy good collaboration. Let's talk at the beginning of next week", and she turned and left the lab. He heard her retreating footsteps. Will let out his breath. He had not ever disliked anyone so much. He could not finish his work now. He disconnected the microndeveloper and sat down. He knew now, he would have to find another place to continue his work. He would have to find Fenfrew.

CHAPTER ELEVEN

POWER

He was a man of average build and height with medium brown hair. He walked with determination in every step yet not at a pace that aroused any notice. He smiled every so often at people who acknowledged him as he passed but he kept his eyes straight ahead. He knew where he was going.

Avaricis Bale was about to open and chair the tenth annual meeting of the Triumvirate for World Peace. He was not only the chairman he was the key Western representative.

As he walked down First Avenue towards Forty Fourth Street he was thinking about Vladimir Pravdan the Eastern Representative. He had Raul Bogachez the southern representative in his pocket. Bale's group had gained from the rest of the world the free trade agreement with the southern hemisphere. The South American countries were ecstatic. After years of failure with the Doha rounds they now had an agreement in place that would assure a 9-12% increase in their GDP. They had no idea what they had given up to Europe for this agreement. Of course that didn't matter because for a few years they'd be happy and that is all the time Bale needed to get his ducks in line. Vladimir Pravdan he was not so sure about. Pravdan was almost as inscrutable as Bale himself when he wanted to be. Lately that was all the time. It was twelve years since they first crossed paths. Bale and partners had been buying into a Russian oil company and Pravdan had decided they'd had enough control. While Bale's investment was cut short the encounter had provided the opportunity of seeing Pravdan up close and in action.

Now he saw him face to face across the table at the United Nations. Avaricis laughed to himself, United, what a farce. If he had not done all his homework Pravadan would now have the power. But it was too late. Bale had been ready for some time and now he was calling in his chips. What fools people were. Negotiating with terrorists, appeasing tyrants, not knowing their own ground and therefore in no position to defend it. The world is an oyster for the taking, my oyster. And he laughed aloud.

He had arrived. The security people all knew him, smiled and waved him forward. One thing is certain about Pravadan if he can not have full power himself he will go along with me. Today he will understand that he will have to follow me. Yes today he will see.

The Secretary General greeted Bale as he entered the room converted for the meeting of the Triumvirate.

"Avaricis. Will this be suitable?", Krator Animolis bowed slightly when he said Bale's name and then gestured to the arrangement of the chairs at the large table.

"Yes, yes this will be fine", Bale replied in an even tone and with a slight smile.

With a quick and deft glance round the table Bale saw that Pravadan had placed himself on the right hand side of the head of the table. There was Ginbreste on the left, Hil Gore beside him. Good he thought as he moved to the head of the table. He smiled at each player as he passed them. Each had a ready smile for him. He had decided to be as inscrutable to Pravadan as Pravadan himself. He would not grant him a special acknowledgment, a particular verbal greeting nor a nod. He would wait for Pravadan's own acknowledgment that he, Bale, was king.

Into the silence his entry had created, he spoke. "We are here today to sign the Tripac which will bind The Triumvirate for World Peace, the New World Order Commission, and the Global Uniform Education Forum, formerly the Global University Forum, into one effective body governed by members of the here present group. Never before has such a body existed in the history of the world", in speaking these last words Avaricis's voice held a pride and self acknowledgment so steely that no one present could have had effect upon its direction, even if they had so wanted. As he had said to himself just minutes before, it was too late.

"The effect of this Tripac will be 1. The elimination of variance from our standards for educating the youth of the world. The impact of this will be eradication of ignorance of the more important things of the world as for example what is valued on entering into the field of politics, government, and of course education all geared to mould youth to our determination of the social ideal. 2. War will be eliminated once and for all." The pride in Bale's voice could not be missed now. It was as though he was saying no one could figure it out until Bale. "As the governments of the world are arranged into this one body individual national identities will be obviated and people will come to understand the enlightened truth that we are all alike and this is the way to coexist peacefully. 3. Those with the intelligence and skill to run government will naturally succeed to the key positions." At this last declaration Hil Gore and Ginbreste raised themselves up in their chairs. Bale raised his hand and the women at the doors approached the table and began handing out a thick document to each person at the table. Avaricis continued, "This is our triumph", and there was triumph in his voice. "Sign the first page, page ten and the last page."

You could hear people rifling through the pages. Ginbeste and Hil Gore were the first to finish, their faces triumphal. One small woman at the very end of the table said in a small voice as she looked all the way down the table to where Bale sat, "What is this about relinquishing all rights of our government's sovereignty?", she said in a small voice as she looked all the way down the table to where Bale sat.

In an instant the atmosphere changed. A coldness filled the room. Bale looked down the table at her and an invisible ball of arctic air rolled from where he sat to where she waited. "We have gone over all this before", he said slowly, and then most condescendingly he continued, "What trouble are you having understanding this now?"

Bale delivered the whole sentence as a knife meant to twist into her head to set it right. How could she be so stupid? How could anyone so honored as to be sitting here on this historic day be so small as to raise a doubt of their genius now? The knife seemed to do its trick as she was silenced.

After all the documents had been collected and checked for all the needed signatures Bale rose and deigned to linger to shake everyone's hand. All that is but that little woman's. Upon signing the final page her pen had dropped from her hand and looking very green she had hurried from the room.

Chapter Twelve

The Courageous Ones

"We must reach Paslan, we have to talk with him", said Nadine determinedly.

"Yes and where do we find him?", asked Will.

"Doesn't he teach a class?", she was thinking aloud.

"Yes, one - once a week", Will replied.

"What class, when and where?", Nadine said impatiently.

" . . . What class?", Will said thinking aloud, "I don't know - I think it's something to do with stars."

"Stars? Hmm, astronomy?", Nadine was asking herself and Will.

Will was going back in his mind to when he'd first met Paslan and Paslan had offered him time alone in his study. Paslan had been leaving for his class and he picked up a book . . . to take with him . . . and the title of the book was . . . *Where The Stars Meet Your Eyes*.

"Yes that was it", he said out loud. Simultaneously Nadine asked, "Does Edinbridge have an astronomy department?"

"No", said Will. "Paslan is famous for his creation of an area of study, History of the Known Universe. Paslan has written a book entitled *Where The Stars Meet Your Eyes*.

I bet his class has something to do with this." Will was at his laptop searching the university website. "Here it is - History of the Known Universe - Stars Space and Time."

"I wonder if I can get into his class - after all I'm in History", said Nadine.

"I wonder if I can get in next year." Then Will said - "Maybe it won't be available next year", Will's voice trailed off. Then he said, "Let's go to the admin office and find out when and where the class is."

"Professor Paslan's class is closed." The little dark haired woman behind the desk looked at them with agitation.

"We aren't trying to sign up for the class", explained Nadine, "We just want to - sit in on it one time."

"Professor Paslan doesn't like visitors in his class", she said shortly.

That didn't sound like Paslan but Nadine didn't say so. Instead she said, "When did you say the class was - Mrs. Brown?", for that was the name on the wood plate sitting on her desk. Mrs. Brown had not said but Nadine was hoping that she would.

"Three O'clock Fridays", she had automatically responded to hearing her name. They thanked her and left.

"We've got two days to wait - if something else doesn't show us how to reach him in the meantime", said Will.

"If he's in the Other World . . .?", Nadine was seeking confirmation of her thought. "We could go there and find him", she said.

"How do I get there?", Will sounded incredulous and frustrated at the same time.

"Well", Nadine started, looking at Will. "Do you want

to go?", she asked simply.

Without pause Will said, "Yes."

"Good, that's the start. I've got to get to my History and Literature class. I'll see you at dinner?", she said as she went out the door.

" . . . right . . . see you at dinner", Will sounded bewildered.

Nadine and George Hand had tacitly decided to continue sitting together in the second row after their mutual experience with Herd back in September. And they had been sitting together ever since. Today Herd was late and they chatted back and forth about their essays for a few minutes. Then Nadine asked, "You said to me that 'time with Paslan is the best thing you can do'. What do you know of Paslan?"

"He is a great man", said George simply. Nadine nodded. "I've been to his study and had the privilege of conversation with him there. It was by chance, I think." ... George looked off into the distance recalling the memory, "I'd been talking with Jane in the dining room." He looked back at Nadine asking silently if she knew Jane. Nadine nodded and he returned his gaze to the distance as he recalled their meeting. "Paslan was there and he asked Jane something. Jane introduced us. I knew who he was of course", he looked back at Nadine. "His open manner makes him so approachable. We got into conversation about my classes and before we left Paslan invited me up to his study. I haven't forgotten that conversation. It was the beginning of last year. It was the most valuable and enjoyable conversation I've had", he paused and finished, "with anyone here. It was the most enjoyable conversation I've ever had," George said. They were silent for a moment.

Nadine nodded slowly and then said,

"Yes I know what you mean. He has a special quality that makes you feel at home in his presence. He understands you."

George looked directly at her, "Yes - that's it. I felt at home when I sat there with him by his fire. Do you know - that's saying something because even growing up - when my dad died it changed. We couldn't even be at home for any time at all, we were always out working, all of us." There was a long pause then George said haltingly, ". . . It was. . . precious . . . those moments with Paslan. Do you know? I think he knew - somehow, he knew . . . about me. Everything he said and the . . . kindly way he spoke . . . he knew what it was like to be me", he stopped.

Nadine didn't speak for some time. She just sat there with George. They'd been talking very quietly in their corner of the room. The rest of the room now had a loud buzz as students had begun talking in their impatience for Herd to arrive. The door at the bottom of the round opened. A young woman walked to the center spot, stopped and then said to the room,

"Alison Herd will not be in class today. She is on extended leave and another lecturer will be taking her place. The new lecturer will be here next class. You are to continue with the current study laid out and your essays. Thank you." And perfunctorily left. Almost in one movement the class got up and the buzz broke out again at a louder pitch.

"They could have told us. I would have continued playing hockey", said their nearest neighbor in an irritated tone.

"I could have gone home earlier for the weekend", said another, as in chorus.

George and Nadine were still sitting in their seats.

"What do you think it's about?", Nadine said, not so much in a question as in a preface to an idea.

George caught her meaning and said, "Do you know?"

"I think so", Nadine began. ". . . I think she has work to do for Bale. I think the extended leave is forever." George waited. "Paslan has been taking more time in the Other World", she looked at George to see what his reaction would be to this. He was not reacting he was listening. "We're not sure about all that he is doing. However we are sure that Paslan is living there now and only visiting here. What he did specifically tell us is that Bale and his group are taking over. Something else too. Bale and company, can not enter the Other World. Too many people were too late in understanding Bale and his group. And the result is what you see, our freedoms mitigated, and a direction of thinking and ideas aligned with this pre-emption of freedom. This is why Paslan and others have moved to the Other World. They have moved with like minded people who care enough to think and act according to their deepest beliefs."

Nadine had stopped and George was looking out into the distance again. "Do you know - in that conversation we had, Paslan was asking me about my classes and professors, about the people with whom I'd worked and was working in my full time and part time jobs. He was really inquiring into the temperature of the circles where I was living. I imagine he learns a lot in his conversations and through this gains the foresight required to make the move you are describing." he paused. "So he has gone, gone from this university?, George turned to Nadine.

"He has moved from this world", she said.

CHAPTER THIRTEEN

COLD

Snow had arrived. The trees were laden in a white blanket and all was quiet along the lawns and court-yards. Christmas was here but it didn't feel very Christmasy. Students weren't stopping in the corridors to laugh and talk. They were rushing away to family or friends. Nadine, Will, and David had decided to spend Christmas together at Edinbridge so they could figure out together what was best to be done. Or, though none of them had voiced it, until Paslan's timing. Also unspoken, to absorb and enjoy the last vestiges of a great university, and of a great heritage. Nadine's family had been disappointed when she told them she wouldn't be home for Christmas. Though they had always encouraged her to do what she really thought was best. They sent ahead her presents with lots of goodies her grandmother had baked. Will had not planned to go home to the States for Christmas. David, being Jewish, did not celebrate Christmas in the same way.

Nadine brushed off the snow from a spot on the bench with her mitten and sat down in the courtyard to wait for Will. His voice had sounded excited when he asked her to meet him here, after explaining he'd be in the

Lab early in the morning to work.

Whosh - thump! A big snowball landed right in the middle of the bench beside her and sprayed her with wet cold.

"Hey where are you!", Nadine called out. Will walked out from behind a column in the courtyard laughing.

"Good thing you're a good shot. That would have hurt. You did mean to miss didn't you?", she asked on second thought.

Will smiled and said, "Yes of course." He came over and brushed off the remains of the snowball to sit down.

"How'd it go in there?", she looked up at the windows of Zembley. "I thought you said you had to find a new place to work."

"Rong's away so I can be there until she returns. I think I've figured something out", his voice was animated.

"Tell me", she said, excited too.

"The principle of the Opposites Magnet is simple. Magnets have an invisible magnetic field around them that pulls on nearby magnetic materials and repels other magnets. Rong gave me an idea, though she doesn't know it."

"Go on", said Nadine.

"David and I are assuming, that like you, we can get to the Other World. Paslan has told us Rong cannot get there. Let's say that there is a force field around the Other World and that this field bars entry to some. What elements is it repelling? This field is not defined in the language of science because it's composition is in a realm science does not even define. Rather this field recognizes character within people and accepts or rejects them. While Rong knows that she and others are barred from the Other World I don't think she understands why and this is because she lives in a world that languages little other than the scientific and because she doesn't care about why."

"Do you mean that if she cared enough to learn why she is barred she could position herself for the change that would actually remove the bar?", asked Nadine.

"Yes - if she cared enough to learn why, she would in actuality move herself closer to entry. However, pragmatism is her world view and she is myopic to anything else. If it works do it. So now Rong is confronted with a world she can not understand because she will not face its reality."

"This sounds like David's area", Nadine laughed.

"Yes and it's all our area because it's life. Nature is just. When we face reality we can move forward into the future", Will responded.

"And the future . . . ?", she offered.

"Is the Other World," Will replied.

The tables in the Great Hall had only a few students at each one. David, Nadine, and Will sat together as always at the center one.

"The food is as good as ever", said David as he talked with his mouth full. "This steak and kidney pie is scrumptious."

Will laughed, "You sound - and look - like a kid."

"I feel like a kid after what you shared. If the field that exists around the Other World is one that detects our interest in learning the truths about life, I'm all for it!", he said with gusto. Everyone will be faced with facing life head on!", he was sounding like a nerdie kid now.

"This broccoli carrot and onion casserole is delicious", Nadine said as she helped herself to more.

"Jane must be here!", Nadine suddenly exclaimed as she sprang from the bench and headed for the kitchen. In two minutes Nadine returned with Jane in tow.

"Hi Jane", Will said with his great warm smile.

David stood up, "Happy Christmas Jane. This meal is delicious."

Jane smiled broadly, "Happy Christmas and Hanukkah."

"You are going to join us", said Nadine as she gave up her place beside Will to Jane and went to the other side of the table to sit by David.

They passed the steak and kidney pie, the roast beef, and Yorkshire pudding, bean salad, bread, and the vegetable casserole, all at once to her. And David poured her request of juice into a glass. Then Will said,

"Paslan told me that you've been carrying on a conversation together once a week for years."

"He's wonderful isn't he", she exclaimed.

"He's Great!", the trio said in unison. They all laughed.

"I didn't know one could have conversation like that", Jane said. "To be able to talk one to one and be so comfortable. To ask questions and to be asked about what one is really thinking and feeling. To be able to learn with someone so personally about anything one is truly interested in and at such a depth. It is an irreplaceable treasure."

The three were eating more slowly now listening to Jane. Then Nadine asked with concern,

"Are you going to the Other World?"

"I just moved there", she had lowered her voice.

"Oh!", Nadine responded with surprise and relief.

Will said, "Tell us about living in the Other World? Are you keeping your job here then? Do you live near Paslan there? . . .

"I'm going back tomorrow. Would you like to join me and learn for yourself?", she asked.

"Yes!", they cried in unison.

Jane had suggested that they all meet in Paslan's study at 9 O'clock in the morning. At about five minutes to nine Nadine and Will almost bumped into one another as they arrived at Chartwell Tower. They took the stairs two at a time and strode down the corridor. As they did, Paslan's door opened in anticipation of their arrival. There was Jane standing in the center of the room smiling at them. David had already arrived and stood beside her.

"As neither of you", Jane looked at Will and David, "have been to the Other World I thought we'd leave from here. You may have noticed that Paslan's study has some unusual characteristics. Have you heard the music?"

David and Will nodded and Nadine said "Oh - yes", remembering the experience with Rong in Paslan's study.

"Have you noticed the presence of sunlight here - at all times during the day?", Jane asked.

The three nodded.

"When Paslan is present - I should say when he is visiting with you here - one may notice other unusual things", she paused.

"Once I'm sure I noticed the fire spark up and blaze when Paslan became enthused in our conversation", said Will. Jane smiled knowingly.

"Because of the energy field here we will be protected in all ways. A great advantage at this time of year", Jane glanced outside where snow lay on the trees. "It will be easy for us all to leave together and fly to the Other World from here", Jane said.

"Fly!", Will gasped out. And David's mouth dropped open.

"Yes we fly", said Nadine happily.

"Alright then hold hands", and Jane took David's hand and reached for Will's. Will took Nadine's hand and David gave his other hand to her.

Then Jane said, "We are going to lift off together. However once we are airborne you will have to fly on your own."

"Use your arms like a bird would use wings and your body to veer left and right", added Nadine. You'll get the feel of it right away", she encouraged.

"What about landing?", Will shouted out.

"You'll see as we arrive", said Jane. Before they could get worried she said,

"Alright now - we're ready." Will felt this statement most presumptuous. "Think light, sunlight, and air and gentle breezes, and cotton floating, and ..." ... they were gone.

Nadine was laughing, gliding up and down on the air pockets that felt like waves in the ocean only they were high up in the clouds.

"David you're doing fine", said Jane.

Nadine looked at David and then at Will. Will was looking very serious, his face screwed up in concentration.

"Will - relax and stop thinking. Enjoy yourself", Nadine said firmly.

"How is this happening? I'm flying. . . ", Will kept saying.

"Are we going to Paslan's home?", Nadine asked.

"We're going to Terhaven's, Paslan will be there. Apparently Paslan feels she knows better how to welcome new arrivals", Jane explained.

Nadine looked below trying to recognize the landscape and thought she did. Ahead of them to the east was a scattered group of houses amongst the trees. A large forest lay to the north of the houses and a meandering lake further east. To the west of the community were open fields and meadows. She was a better flyer now and feeling much more relaxed she could take in everything around her.

"We're about to land", called Jane.

Nadine sensed Will tensing up. "Will, I'll go ahead of you just glide in behind me. You just kind of pull your legs down beneath you and land running on the ground", Nadine told him.

David had followed Jane in and managed to land stumbling to a stop. Nadine was about to land when Will cried out, "I'm going to run into the house!"

She pulled up with him and circled around. "Will", she said firmly, "relax. "This is not a physics lab. You have it in you to fly and you've just never recognized it. Now let go of yourself and follow me", she commanded.

She slowed up and lowered herself gently and slowly downward to the ground clearly showing Will, who was now directly behind her, the right arm movements to help with speed and descending.

"Whoa!", Will shouted as he came to a running halt and fell into a bush. Nadine offered her hand. Laughing she said, "You did fine once you let go of the calculations you were making in that brain of yours!"

"How did you know?", he asked sheepishly brushing off some earth from his jeans.

"Oh come on, I know you. If it doesn't make scientific sense your brain is diving in all directions to make some kind of logic of things."

He was looking at her, "Okay, okay you got me. As I

had no choice I listened to you. You were right apparently", Will said grudgingly. Nadine laughed.

"Just a few scratches?", asked the deep rich warm voice they recognized and loved.

"Paslan!", Nadine cried out.

"You are all here safe and sound", Paslan said with a little catch in his voice. He looked very happy to see them.

"Welcome", came another voice which wafted to them from a greater distance. It was a voice that could never be mistaken for any other. Terhaven came down the steps of her front porch and seemed to glide toward them along the lawn.

Chapter Fourteen

Terhaven

" **S** top staring", Nadine remonstrated David and Will who had suddenly stopped preening themselves after the flight to gawk at their hostess. They had landed at the edge of her property and the lawn was long. They had ample time to take in the grace, elegance, and beauty, of their hostess as Terhaven approached. Her long thick auburn hair streamed back from her face as she seemed to sail toward them. Nadine suddenly realized that Paslan had appeared amongst them in an instant when he must have been in the house with Terhaven a moment before.

"May I introduce Terahaven, David Solomon, and Will Hamlet", Paslan said simply as Terhaven glided to a stop before them.

"It is a great pleasure to meet you both", she said as she extended her hand.

For a moment Nadine thought David was about to bow and kiss it. However he simply shook it. Will managed to politely extend his hand though his mouth was agape. Neither seemed able to speak.

"It is lovely to see you again Nadine", said Terhaven as she took both Nadine's hands in her own. "We have arranged a little party in your honor", she smiled and led them back toward the house.

"The community has been expecting you for some time. There is someone here whom you know well Will." Her smile and Will's name spoken in that rich resonate voice seemed to melt Will. He was still silent though he managed to raise a brow in inquiry.

"Bartholomew Fenfrew is looking forward to seeing you again and to meeting your friends", Terhaven said as she ushered them into her home.

The rooms seemed transformed from what Nadine remembered. They found before them perhaps a hundred people talking and laughing in a beautiful open sunlit room. The smell of sweet peas she did remember. A young man with a tray of goblets offered her a drink of golden hue and of a light mildly sweet fragrance. She sipped a bit and finding it scrumptious drank deeply. A tall thin man with a prominent streak of white hair, an energized manner, and clear green eyes who seemed to suddenly appear at her side said, "You look to be enjoying that drink. Do you know what it is?"

Nadine's eyes were riveted to this man whose presence had a magnetizing effect. When she did not speak in response he said, "It is called Chuva-de-Ouro which means Rain of Gold. The drink is named after the flowering tree that grows in Brazil." His smile lit up his eyes and face. Nadine felt that a warm sunshine had suddenly filled the room.

"Professor Fenfrew", Will cried out. Hearing Fenfrew's voice, Will had come over to them.

The man who had just spoken to Nadine turned to Will. In a moment the two friends embraced. David and Nadine stood smiling as they watched their happy friend.

Then Will, turning a beaming face upon them said, "Let me introduce you to my friends, Nadine Redwood and David Solomon, Professor Fenfrew."

"I'm happy to meet you", Bartholomew Fenfrew said in a voice so real and strong that it made one want to get to know him.

David said, "We're very happy to meet you."

Fenfrew began to ask them about themselves. He had a rare ease and real interest. A young woman came by and offered a tray of enormous prawns. Nadine was about to decline when Fenfrew said, "Try them, you have never tasted anything like them", as he took two at once and smiled at her with a nod.

Nadine had barely touched the prawn to her tongue when she stopped the woman to ask for another. Rather than merely something to eat this was a succulent delicacy to be experienced.

As it was obvious Will would be engaged for some-time with Fenfrew and as David was engrossed in listening to them, Nadine decided to wander again in Terhaven's home. Where was that painting she had visited last time? She wondered if she could leave the party for a few minutes and join the two young boys fishing. Where was that alcove with the circular table and the painting? Nadine went over to the window which she thought she remembered being near the painting. And there it was. That lovely stream with the hills and trees in the distance. Where were the boys?

"What!", she exclaimed aloud. The boys weren't there.

"Did you think that they would wait?", Paslan appeared by her side. "That was a pretty good fish you helped catch. The boys went home to cook it."

"What!", she repeated. She looked again at the painting. It was the same lovely little stream amongst the trees but no one was there. She looked hard at the big tree for the robin. He wasn't there either. What did this mean?

"I have often admired that painting", Paslan said looking at her with a mischievous grin. "That particular painting - is special to me, interesting that you were drawn to it", he continued.

"I noticed it when I was here last time", she replied.

"Yes" . . . , he said slowly, "you were drawn to it then." She was now listening carefully. "That meadow is particularly beautiful. It's in Suffolk and in an area of great natural beauty, Dedham Vale, near where I grew up", he said.

Nadine was listening hard. There was a pause. Then she said, "That was you - in the boat when you were a boy..."

A slow smile broadened his mouth. Then she said, "... and Fenfrew when he was a boy. . .", she stopped.

"Yes, you are right my dear", and he gave a truly deep warm smile of acknowledgement. "Bartholomew and I have known each other a very long time." They were silent a moment. Then Paslan said,

"You were a big help. That was an energetic fish and pretty big too for that stream. I think we might have lost him if you hadn't - popped - by."

Nadine dropped down and sagged into a nearby chair. Looking up at Paslan she sighed, "I don't think I understand all this. Would you help me out?"

Paslan said, "Let's go for a walk."

He led her out the french doors through Terhaven's garden and onto a grassy pathway. The surrounding grass was newly mown and Nadine breathed in deeply to enjoy one of her favorite smells. The pathway led to a field with a loose forest of trees. The sun beamed down upon them and Nadine felt it's warmth on her skin. She could hear birds calling each other and she felt, calling her. And then Paslan began to share some of his life story.

"Fenfrew and I grew up in a wonderful part of England many years ago. It was a different world then. We walked to school and home each day. Our backs were not burdened with backpacks full of books nor our time after school with homework. We laughed and talked with each other and that was far more important than listening to noise through headphones. Our experience of music was live in one's drawing room or parlor or on special occasions in the Great Room. On weekends and all summer long we played outside in fresh air and as you briefly experienced, in clean streams. It was a beautiful time to be able to play in the English countryside", he said dreamily, reminiscing nostalgically. "The industrial revolution changed all that. Railways and factories were the main reasons."

"Do you mean to say that you were a boy prior to the Industrial Revolution?", Nadine broke in, her mouth hanging open.

Paslan threw his head back and laughed a full deep rich laugh that came from the bottom of his stomach. Nadine began to laugh with him. She knew it was ridiculous and she knew at the same time that it was true.

They had been walking for some time. Nadine noticed that the sun was in the west. They came to something of a clearing and Paslan led the way up a small hill. At the top a great variety of trees stretched out before them with rolling hills on either side of the valley. Just off in the distance to the right was a meandering stream with lovely large trees scattered along the bank.

"That's the stream we were fishing in together!", she exclaimed.

"It is the remembrance of the Suffolk stream in Dedham Vale from my youth", he said simply, . . . "brought back to life so to speak."

"It is beautiful - so beautiful" . . . and Nadine began to run towards the stream down the side of the hill.

"It will be nightfall soon", Paslan called after her. "It's further than you think. Why not fly there?"

"Ohh . . . I can fly", she cried aloud, "I can fly!", and with her running start she simply spread out her arms, jumped, and lifted from the ground.

The perspective was heavenly. She was sailing above the meadow towards the trees and stream with the sun about to set on the horizon. Nadine now found it easy to fly and she angled in and out between the trees. The air was soft, fresh, and fragrant, with the smell of grasses and flowers, pine and cedar, and the clear running stream. The fresh flowing water of that bright little stream where fish lived and birds played nearby glinted in the light of the sun that sat on the horizon. The glow of the setting sun colored the horizon in warm dusky pinks and reds. She came down near the far bank. Her first desire was to take off her shoes, wiggle her toes in the grass, and cool her feet in the stream. She stood silently on the bank barefoot in the cool grass for many minutes listening to the quiet of the stream, the birds and the air. She eased her feet into the water and was pleasantly surprised at the fresh coolness without shock of cold. A whippoorwill began to sing. She sat quietly listening and looking for him in the trees. What was that bird that had just joined in?

"That's a blackbird", said Paslan, answering Nadine's unspoken question. He had just appeared nearby and was taking off his shoes to join her on the bank. "I'm afraid I can not resist", he said as he sat down by her on the bank, his trousers rolled up to the knee, and sank his feet into the cool stream. "This is one of my favorite places of all time", his eyes twinkled at her.

They listened to the whippoorwill and the blackbird and a chorus of song began and even Paslan could not name all the birdsongs.

They had been sitting a while when Nadine asked, "Can Rong learn how to get here with the Opposites Magnet?"

"The Opposites Magnet could help someone get here. As you know she will not learn from Will. This will be a great frustration for her."

"Is there someone else from whom she will learn?"

"No, there is no one else who can help her. She knows a lot about it herself. She may figure enough out in time. She is an impatient woman though and I think will look to any means she can to get here."

"Why do they want to get here? They are not a fit", said Nadine.

"There is much wisdom in what you say. They are not a fit here. People like Bale can not be happy. Unfortunately it is not in their character to change. They believe that they have figured out the best way of going through life and that is what they do - they go through life, rather than live it."

"Are they a threat to us?"

"They are a threat to our way of life, to our freedoms. That is why we are here. They are not a threat in the deep sense. They will die at the end of their lives. You see, even if they managed to get themselves here, because they are not a true fit, they can not remain. At some point in time they would have to leave - in one way or another."

Nadine sat quietly by Paslan, letting his words register within. They sat together and enjoyed the sound of the stream and the birds.

"Did you hear that bird?", asked Paslan. "That was the

Tawny Owl. It is almost dark." He got up. Nadine got up too and put her shoes back on.

"We will get back to Terhaven's a different way. Come here, stand face to face with me."

Nadine came over and faced him.

"Move closer, place the tips of your shoes touching the tips of mine", he placed his hands lightly on Nadine's shoulders. "I'm going to take us back through the painting in Terhaven's alcove. Are you ready?"

"Ready", she said. And they were gone.

Dinner was a festive occasion. Nadine, Will, and David were guests of honor and everyone wanted to be involved in their conversation. All the tables were circular which suited the occasion well. They sat at Paslan's, Fenfrew's, and Terhaven's table, the largest one. Terhaven rose raising her glittering goblet of deep red wine and said, "A toast to our new friends, Nadine Redwood, Will Hamlet, and David Solomon, may their new lives here be fruitful, fulfilling, and joyous."

The room erupted in a happy chorus "To Nadine, Will, David, - Joy!" and they all drank deeply.

The lady on Nadine's immediate right, for she was a lady, wore a deep green velvet floor length gown with white embroidered sleeves that reminded Nadine of what Maid Marion or Guenevere may have worn. Her blond plaited hair was pulled back from her face and fell to her waist. A circular braid lay as a crown on the top of her head.

"I've been here for many years, many many years", she was saying. "My husband was killed in King Arthur's war. He had prepared me. John, my husband, had been a very good friend of Merlin's and knew of another world. One night when my husband and Merlin were talking by the fireside he called me over. It was then that Merlin spoke to us about being in this world. John was killed not long after Merlin died, or - disappeared", she hesitated and then went on, "and so I left and came here."

Nadine saw Fenfrew looking at her from further along the table. He gave a nod of his head to confirm that this was not merely a story rather it was this lady's story.

"I understood that this world is years though not . . . centuries . . . old", replied Nadine inquiringly.

"Bartholomew could explain that. Merlin believed in the possibility of another world and helped prepare us. When Bartholomew helped create this one we could come here. Merlin and Fenfrew were friends you know."

Nadine took this in and set about digesting it along with the pheasant she was eating.

On Nadine's left sat a small quiet man. He seemed much occupied with his own thoughts yet she had the feeling that at the same time he was listening and connected to the general conversation at the table, about who lived here and why.

"Have you been here long?", Nadine ventured, turning to the man and smiling.

He looked up from his plate and from his thoughts too, his eyes were far away. In the next moment however those deep blue mirrors were as bright and shiny as the waters of the Dedham Vale stream.

"Not so long" . . . he said crisply.

Nadine wasn't sure if she should ask anything more as he had looked back down to his peas. However before she could consider any further he began in earnest, "It was the middle of the last century. I could see it coming. The television arrived and books went out the window. We were doomed. If we won't read, we won't exercise our minds, we won't be able to think. The advent and permeation into life of television, particularly in America, meant the beginning of deconstruction of language. All communication came to be expected in sound bites. It became no longer convenient to express oneself in a real conversation. And real conversations stopped taking place. Where did they think ideas would come from? Without their means of conveyance, conversation, ideas would die on the vine. Only trivialities became convenient to express and so the culture went. Then I left." Nadine thought he was about to resume with his peas when he looked right into her and said, "You are here now and we may have a real conversation", and this little man's words were infused with energy and his eyes were dancing with life.

"Yes please!", Nadine cried out. "There is little I love more than a real conversation."

His face suddenly lit like a sunbeam, he put down his fork, took her hand and said, "I am Reginald Battersea and I am very glad to make your acquaintance."

"How do you do. I am Nadine Redwood, I'm happy to meet you too", she smiled.

"Well of course you've come with Paslan." He looked over to where Paslan was sitting and an expression of deep respect came across his face. "You mustn't feel you've given up your education in being here for you will now have Paslan, Fenfrew, and other great professors to teach you."

"Ohh I didn't know . . . ."

"My dear girl you have come to a place where much will be given you and much will be asked of you. Creation requires the best within us as God would tell you if he were sitting here himself. What could be more fulfilling than helping with his creation? I ask you, what could have greater meaning than stretching yourself to be all he has given you to be?", he expostulated.

She was amazed at this little man. His words were on fire, alight with life. Did he expect an answer from her? She didn't think so. He had wanted to make his point and was now ready for anything she would say. He was enjoying his peas again for a moment, then he said, "There are very evil people indeed and that has put a stop to ordinary folk congregating, dreaming, and being free enough to create in the world we've left. Here", and he smiled, and waved his fork, where a pea was stuck to a prong, in a circle above his head, "there are people like you who care about life and want to put there whole being into life. If I were you I would create a table of contents and give it to Paslan as an idea on what you'd like to learn. . . . What would you like to learn?", the deep blue of his eyes beamed upon Nadine.

"Oh that sounds wonderful I must give it some thought. Though right off the bat I can say that I'd like to understand why people would waste their lives on power mongering, chasing after achievements, and what I imagine they think of as rewards for their abilities."

Reginald Battersea began to laugh so hard and so suddenly that a pea popped out of his mouth and shot into his wine goblet. A few table neighbors looked over to see what the commotion was and then went back to their conversations. After a full minute or more he was able to say,

"Oh my dear what fun you have given me. You hit the nail dead center. You can teach your own class. They just don't get it do they. They are chasing all the wrong things and first it's not a hunt and second it's not about things at all. Yes I feel so sorry for them, the Bales and Rongs of that world."

"Oh you know them do you?", Nadine asked, surprised.

Mr. Battersea paused, his goblet in mid air, and with

a raised eyebrow, his mouth in the frown position, from over his spectacles he bore his blue eyes into her hazel eyes and gave one nod saying, "They have existed in every Time. And there are only a few who will fight them. They must be fought if freedom is to exist."

He drank, Nadine pondered, and then she said, "The trouble is their desire for power. If they just went in the wrong direction themselves, well so be it. Pulling others onto the wrong track with them is another thing altogether. They are making a train wreck of the world we knew. What is really disturbing is that so few people could see far enough down the line to uncouple their car and get off the track. If more people had made thinking a regular activity then Bale would not have the power he has. His lot would have been cut off at the pass."

"The junction my dear - to continue with your analogy of the train", he said kindly.

"What concerns me is that they want to get to this world", said Nadine.

"They can not get here", he said matter of factly. "They do not have what it takes."

"No", she said slowly, "yet they will manipulate and connive to try and find a way."

The young man waiting the table was just clearing Mr. Battersea's plate away. He looked almost sad at the disappearance of the unfinished peas. When they were definitely gone he turned back to Nadine and asked, "Do you mean that you think that they may show up here one day?"

"Yes", said Nadine.

"I hope that you are wrong my dear", said Reginald as he picked up his dessert spoon and fork and prepared for chocolate mousse cake.

"So do I", said Nadine.

Will was motioning her to join him in the now empty

seat beside him. Mr. Battersea had become so engrossed in his mousse and his thoughts again, that Nadine's, "Excuse me", went unnoticed.

"Isn't this a great dinner?", Will enthused as Nadine joined him.

"Have you been talking with Fenfrew the whole time?", she asked bemusedly.

"Yes", Will said with his charming smile full upon her, "I've only looked up now as Fenfrew excused himself to meet with Paslan."

"I guessed, given your smily face", she replied.

Will laughed, "There probably isn't anyone else with whom I enjoy talking so much. Did you have a conversation with someone?", he asked her.

"Yes, that man across the table engrossed in his thoughts and dessert. He doesn't imagine that Bale and Rong and others like them will ever make it to this world", she looked at Will.

"And you do", Will said.

"Yes. What do you think it means that people, who left a world behind because what was most important to them had been destroyed by others, now fail to see that those same destroyers will stop at nothing in order to continue to feed their empty void by continual acquisition of power over others? In other words the same thing could happen here because of a lack of vision to see these destroyers for who they are," she finished.

"You know what they have said in different ways through the ages", said David, who had taken the other empty chair beside them, "Use it or lose it. In this case what we have been losing is our ability to think. Those who do not learn from history are doomed to repeat it, George Santayana. A republic if you can keep it, Benjamin Franklin, as in the best way of living requires the most responsibility.

It's up to a few, the majority go about their own business and that is plenty for them", said David.

"It gets my goat that people will not learn and can not be bothered to stop and think to save themselves", declared Nadine.

"David's right", said Will. "The reality is that it's up to us, we could wait until doomsday if we expect everyone to be on their toes and on guard, ready for the likes of Bale, who is - most certainly ready."

"What is our next step then?", Nadine asked simply.

CHAPTER FIFTEEN

REMAINS OF EDINBRIDGE

"I've got an idea", Nadine enthused, I can do it on my own." Nadine and Will sat together in Paslan's study where they now spent a lot of time when they weren't in the Other World.

"That's not a *good* idea", said Will firmly.

"Why not?", Nadine was determined. Basically I got to the Other World on my own the first time. You and David had to be taken. Besides Rong will be watching you and you're the one who knows about 'Traces'.

"Listen to yourself. You're sounding a tad arrogant Miss Redwood", Will said teasingly though with a meaningful look. "Rong has probably figured out about 'Traces' and she has seen us together. She knows we're friends. She could come after you."

"What would she do to me even if she could follow me into the Other World - which she can't?"

"I don't know what she'd do, that's just it. She is inscrutable. Anyway it's dangerous. We don't know much about traveling from one world to the other. There is a time gap where you could get stuck and not be able to come back. For all I know you could end up in another world all together."

"Another world?", Nadine asked rhetorically. "In my

145

mind I know the world I want to be in and it *is* the Other World." She continued, "Concoct some alteration to your findings on 'Traces' and leave it for Rong to find."

"What do you mean?", Will sounded bewildered.

"Haven't you thought of that?", Nadine asked impatiently. "If you alter the research findings she'll get stuck in the gap you're talking about and we won't have to worry about her bringing all her buddies to the Other World and destroying that world too."

Will was silent, thinking, then he said, "It's an idea. Bale is going to be pushing her. She may get desperate. Once we're gone he'll resent the loss to his power. He won't even understand why he needs us besides to know how to travel to the Other World. The thing is, should he get to the Other World he may not want to leave."

"Why? He isn't going to appreciate the beauty or anything else about it", Nadine said.

"No, he won't appreciate it", Will said slowly. "It's that the elements there are slightly different. They're in a purer state. This means that they are more powerful, more potent, depending on what you are looking at them for. He'll see a gold mine, a gold mine of opportunity for bringing the elements to market in this world. Speaking of gold, it is eight times more pure in the Other World. He could create his own markets. He'd be in control of the highest quality product available anywhere", Will finished with a serious frown.

David was standing in the entryway to Paslan's study listening. The door had opened for him. Nadine smiled at him and plopped herself into a big armchair by the fire. Will followed suit and David joined them and said,

"While going about our business we missed seeing that the foundations for our way of life were being hammered away under our feet. A restriction here, a regulation there, a new law, and over time the boundary line has been pushed so far into left field that we no longer recognize the game. A whole new team is up to bat and we're not going home anymore. We've been making hay too long. We forgot to mend the fences and now there is no need for the hay because all the horses and cattle are gone." David stopped, "Sorry I've interrupted you", he waited for one of them to speak.

"Nadine wants to drop the information that she is going to the Other World to Rong's and Bale's group. The thinking being that they'd try and trace or follow her track and be foiled."

"I wonder", said David.

"What do you mean?", said Nadine.

"Do you think that Bale or Rong would stop at our thwarting their entry? Do you think that they would stop at anything?", David's voice was very serious.

"If you are right why try?", Nadine retorted with some resentment.

David sat back in the big armchair putting his feet up on the stone edge of the hearth.

"While of course we have to try", he said as he put another log on the fire. "We have to find a way to spark people's imagination so that they can begin to conceive of people like Bale. If we can stir up their desire to think for themselves perhaps they will see that it's up to them to say no to the Bales' who would ensnare them with promises of position, entrap them in the false promise of power, and capture them with their own pride. So that they find themselves lost in a life they no longer value hating themselves or worse - not even recognizing themselves and what they've given up. If we won't use the mind we've been given, to what are we condemning ourselves and the world?"

"Slavery", said Will. "We will passively regress to a time before the American civil war and all who refuse to think will become slaves of the Bales' of this world."

"You're right", Nadine was looking into the fire that had rekindled in the hearth.

She said, "No wonder Bale could lasso the Herds' of education. If we were to study real history we'd have a chance to learn for ourselves what kind of debate is required to provide voice for real ideas. Real debate takes time and thought. In Lincoln's day he and Douglas debated for hours at a time over a period of days and people came prepared to be there, they ate their food there, they stayed to listen. They expected real thinking and were prepared to engage in public discourse. They were readers and understood the price of freedom is thinking for oneself."

"How did you know that about Lincoln?", Will asked admiringly.

"I read history", Nadine said with a little smile.

"All that is necessary for the triumph of evil is that good men do nothing, as Edmund Burke offered more than two hundred years ago", David said.

"Would taking people back to witness history get them to start thinking?", Nadine asked David.

"You'd think so", he replied.

". . . I wonder", Nadine's voice trailed off as the three of them watched the fire which was now ablaze.

CHAPTER SIXTEEN

HISTORY

"Sarabeth? Hi it's Nadine."

"Hi, it's nice to hear from you", came the welcoming voice of Nadine's classmate over the phone.

"How would you like to take a flying lesson with me?", she asked her friend.

"A . . .what?", came the voice over the line.

"A flying lesson. I figured that as we both feel we've lacked for any real history in our History and Literature class that we should join forces and do something about it. So I've asked Professor Paslan and an old friend of his to teach us. I've also asked George Hand from our class", she waited in anticipation.

"Paslan? . . . Sure I'll join in", she said no longer hesitating.

"Okay. The lesson starts tonight at 8 O'clock. Meet us on the Chartwell Quadrangle lawn", she said.

"Outside - 8' O'clock?", Sarabeth asked in surprise.

But Nadine had rung off.

That evening as it was just getting to be dusk six figures gathered on the lawn outside Chartwell Tower.

"Thank you for coming", said Paslan. He looked to Nadine to introduce them.

"This is Professor Paslan, Jane Fairfield, and Will Hamlet, this is Sarabeth Holt and George Hand.", said Nadine.

"Oh this is delightful", Paslan said and his eyes twinkled. "It is good to see you again George." The biggest smile Nadine had seen on George's face suddenly appeared. "Did Nadine tell you what we are about?", Paslan looked at George and Sarabeth, and tilted his head inquiringly.

They shook their heads silently waiting for they knew not what and yet trusting the man with the sparkling eyes.

"We are going to take a journey together into history. The idea is that we should be able to learn a lot quickly if we can see for ourselves cause and effect. Our journey today will be to France on the eve of the French Revolution. All you need do is stick close together, Bartholomew Fenfrew and I will be your guides. Bartholomew will join us there." As he said this a warm wonderful smile lit his entire face and his eyes twinkled like the stars.

He motioned the group into a circle and to stand close together. He asked them to stretch out their arms to the center of the circle. Then Paslan whistled.

They found themselves on a cobbled street in the middle of the afternoon. People were going in and coming out of shops and generally going about their business. Nadine spotted Fenfrew standing under a shop awning. He saw her, smiled and strode over to join them. Paslan introduced them all.

A man in farmers breeches was walking in the middle of the street coming towards them with several animals following behind. As Nadine stood watching she wondered why they were all in a tidy file. Then she noticed the dog. He was a border collie and was encircling the group to keep the goats and sheep together. The seven of them moved closer to the shops to be out of the way of the farmer and his animals. Then the farmer seemed to notice Paslan and spoke to him.

"Vous allez à la réunion d'administration locale? Les autorités de Paris seront là évidenment", a little sneer appeared on his face as he said the last part.

While speaking the farmer continued on his way and Paslan took up beside him responding, "Pouvons-nous vous rejoindre?"

The farmer looked up from the straight path he was making along the street for one moment to take in the others whom Paslan had indicated. The man nodded and said, "Oui arrivent."

They all joined the two men. Will and Fenfrew walked side by side and with the animals. Sarabeth and George were walking close to Paslan and both seemed amazed at how he'd immediately taken up with this man of the land. Jane and Nadine were in the middle taking in the whole scene, entranced with the shops, the people and this sudden situation.

The cobbled street ended and they were walking along a packed dirt road leading away from the little town and into a countryside that was much less green than the country they knew and with a flatter landscape. Paslan and the farmer were in conversation. And while Nadine knew some french she could not hear them above the baahing of the sheep and goats and the voices of her friends. And they were all friends now. Even though they were on a road to where they did not know she felt quite at home.

The farmer was pointing toward a steeple peaking out prominently from the landscape. People and animals could be seen mulling about and this is where they headed. The farmer gave an order to his dog and in a few moments the animals were herded together into a tighter group. They moved as a unit down the hill towards the church. In a few minutes they had all arrived amongst a small throng. Swiftly the farmer tethered the goats and sheep. The dog lay down on the ground nearby to guard his sheep.

The farmer motioned to Paslan and as they all walked together toward the entrance of the church Nadine noticed the clear weathered face of their new companion transform into an unhappy angry expression. At the entrance to the church were two men dressed in red and white uniform apparently guards of some kind. They stood not in the erect manner one expects of guards in uniform but in a disrespectful slouch, with sneering faces. One of them was chewing tobacco. As Jean, for that was our farmer's name, approached the door the guard who had been chewing spat out the tobacco at Jean's feet. Jean took a step to the side and continued through the doors.

The pews were full of farmers and towns people. It was a simple church with one cross at the front and a bare altar. A table had been placed where the communion would have been and there sat three authority figures. They were dressed in formal attire the brass buttons of their jackets polished and protruding from their fat forms. They wore high brimmed hats on their heads and haughty expressions on their faces. They could not have offered a more striking contrast to the people in the pews.

Paslan sat on one side of the farmer and Nadine sat down on his other side. At the table the man in the middle took up his gavel and let it drop three times on the sound block. The pews became silent. A torrent of formal french spewed forth from the man in the center position at the table. A small man sitting in the first pew with quill and paper was taking notes. Nadine began observing the faces of the people to learn their response to what the authorité was saying.

The farmers and town folk looked humbled in an unnatural way. Apart from their animals, separated from their work, and removed from the natural flow of their day, they were as pinioned to another's dictate. She looked at the face of their farmer. His brow was contorted in a knot and his mouth hung open as though wanting desperately to speak yet stopped as though by a power unnatural. He was restless in his seat, shifting his weight from one side to the other.

Suddenly the church was quiet, the authorité had stopped speaking. There was a pregnant pause as the man in the middle held himself stiffly and looked down his long nose towards his audience. Now Nadine understood those in the pews were waiting for permission to speak from those at the high table. And the man in the middle was withholding it until he could see them squirm. Nadine wanted to jump up and pummel him with words of derision. She leaned forward grasping tightly the wood of the back of the pew in front of her. She saw Paslan lean forward and raise his brow at her. Nadine released her grasp and let herself slip back into her seat. The authorité motioned to our farmer.

That was his cue. He stood and began to speak. The tithe was too great for him and his neighbors to pay. Every year it had been increasing and now it was required of them more frequently and without notice. He had had to sell some of his livestock to pay the tax. If this continued he would no longer be able to be a farmer and then . . . who would feed the townspeople. By this time he had worked himself up into a worried sweat. Nadine was eager to hear the authorité's reply but as soon as their farmer had stopped speaking before he was even in his seat the man in the middle had pointed to someone else who was now speaking. This regimen went on for some time and the three men at the front gave no response.

Nadine patted Jean on his sleeve and indicating the man taking notes whispered, "Prend-il vos inquiétudes à la plus haute autorité?" [Does he take your concerns to the higher authority?] Jean made an emphatic gesture and went to spit only at the last moment catching himself remembering that he was in a church.

"It is only a show, the notes. They do nothing", he said in disgust.

They had left their farmer and the farms of the countryside for the city. The city was noisy, steamy and filled with the smell of hops and they were enjoying being together with all the Toulousians in this typical town pub.

"Frenchman seem to enjoy their pint as much as the British", Jane said loud enough to be heard above the throng.

"Some of them are ordering by the quart", George replied pointing down the length of the table which was packed with boisterous drinkers, eaters, and talkers.

"Where are Will and Fenfrew going to sit?", asked Nadine, as she looked up and down their table.

"There they are", said Sarabeth who saw them enter the pub.

Paslan waved, letting them know where the group was sitting. The twosome, seeing their friends' table was full, surveyed the crowded room and found a place close to the door at a smaller table. Fenfrew pointed to it in response to Paslan's wave.

"They've found a table", said Paslan.

"Que faites-vous ici milady?", asked an admiring young man of Sarabeth.

Nadine heard him and seeing that George had too, said, "He's a handsome fellow."

George looked more closely at the fellow now talking with Sarabeth. "Yes, I suppose you're right", he said a bit grudgingly.

"I wonder what Sarabeth is telling him about what we're doing here", Nadine laughed.

George laughed too and held up his glass of beer to clink with Nadine's glass of syrup. Paslan was engaged with an older gentleman who sat at the table across from them. The two men were leaning close together and looked to be in deep conversation.

"If you remain tonight you will see a forced fete in which we are expected to participate, light bonfires, and rejoice. Now pray tell me what party can be enjoyed when you are pushed to give it, pulled to attend it, and taunted into paying for it?", the man said.

"What does the central authorité hope to gain by such commands?", Paslan asked.

"I do not think they have an objective", replied the man. "They are not thinking. It is a long time habit this regulation, the only expectation is one of obeisance. If you listen to the conversations around these tables", as he said this his brown eyes full of concern scanned the room, "all will carry the same two notes, exhaustion from this tutelage and growing anger against the system."

George and Jane were talking with a couple who had joined the table. They were newly married and had purchased a farm with monies their parents had given them as a wedding present.

"We had planned to raise chickens and pigs", the blond young woman was saying.

"But now the central authorité says as we did not consult them we will not be able to raise pigs and must plant crops instead", said the young man his brow creased with agitation and anger. "Crops require a lot of equipment which we neither have nor can afford to buy."

"And we know how to raise pigs, my father raised them", his wife continued. "En plus, we don't want to grow crops", and now her voice was rebellious.

"What can be done about this?", Jane replied with concern.

"Something must be done", the man said with finality.

That night Paslan moved them to Paris and they found themselves dressed and dining formally in a grand room of a palace. This time their neighbors, rather than farmers and local towns people, were nobles and government authorities. They stood together in a grand foyer that was entrance to the dining room. On either side was an enormous gold and filigreed mirror.

"Isn't this a marvellous dress", said Jane excitedly, looking in the mirror. She fingered the lace along the edge of the red cuff of her sleeve and smoothed the black velvet of her full length gown. Sarabeth admired her own deep green cotton and satin gown with a high neck that made her feel like a princess.

A butler bowed before Paslan, assuming him the head of their party, and led them through to their table. At their table sat a Viscount and Viscountess, a German Count and his son of about fifteen years years of age, and a young princess from Sweden. The room had a dozen chandeliers and enormous windows draped in heavy crewel. The floors were of pale colored wood adorned with many colored carpets of ornate design. But it was the clothing, the costume, of many around them that, rather than resplendent, was gaudy and grabbed the eye.

The Viscount and Viscountess de La Mere, as they had now been introduced, were similarly adorned in red dress with black trimmings and a smattering of yellow threaded throughout. The Viscountess wore a complicated mix of woven black and yellow material braided in her hair with a stiff cap of white and gold atop her head. The Viscount had a less obtrusive ornament for his head, a tightly fitted oval hat that sat almost flatly upon his reddish blond hair. The German Count and his son were more conservatively attired and the Count in particular looked stiff and stuffy with a soldierly posture and stern countenance. Princess Sophia Gertrude of Sweden looked pretty and bored in her white and rose empire waist gown.

The soothing tones of the harp wafted from four corners of the room. This seemed to be the cue that one could commence eating the feast that had now been placed before them. The clatter of forks, knives, and tongues, suddenly gave the room a less formal air.

George and Will with full mouths and full focus on their plates were obviously delighted with the fare. Paslan and Fenfrew had happily engaged the Viscount and Viscountess in conversation. While the lady delicately dabbled with a medley of vegetables she laughed and tossed her head at almost every word Fenfrew spoke.

"I had no idea how charming Fenfrew could be", Nadine said to Will.

Will laughed, "Oh boy can he ever be!" Nadine shot Will an inquiring glance with raised eyebrows. Will smiled and holding the bread basket for her was noticing how perfectly Nadine's burgundy gown fit her. He said, "Your dress seems to fit you like a glove - that's lucky."

"It is not luck", she said pointedly and smiled mischievously as she took a piece of bread.

Will continued to admire her gown, in particular, her bare-necked bodice, and remained holding the basket in mid air.

Nadine said, "Thank you Will I have my piece of bread now."

Will cleared his throat in embarrassment and hastily took a piece for himself.

Both Sarabeth and Jane were endeavoring to stir the Count or his son into conversation. Jane would say something and then as the immovable face of German royalty remained fixed upon their plates Sarabeth would take a turn.

"I understand that your countrymen are great horsemen", said Jane to the Count. A slight jerk upward of the royal head indicated assent.

"I have travelled to your fine cities; Munich, Hamburg, Berlin, and the lovely countryside along the way", Sarabeth offered.

"Yah", this time a sound was made by the Count. Apparently until the father spoke the son would be silent.

After two more dual forays Jane twisted her mouth into a facial shrug and Sarabeth rolled her eyes, saying silently let's give them a rest. And they began talking together.

George was sitting next to Princess Sophia. They had been exchanging polite pleasantries. After twenty minutes or so and the first course had been removed and replaced with a lovely little sorbet, the Princess seemed to have shaken off her boredom and was more fully alive to her dinner partner. Nadine caught her tapping George's sleeve with her fan as she leaned in to make a conversational point. George was most gentlemanly giving her full attention.

Nadine's smile and roguish expression directed to George went unnoticed, though not by Paslan. Taking in the activity in George's corner, in one instant, Paslan squinted his twinkling eyes and smiled at Nadine indicating with a slight tilt of his head George's direction. In the next instant his complete attention was back with the Viscountess who with feigned shyness had been focusing her eyes downward and missed the momentary exchange between Paslan and Nadine. Looking up again she found Hale Paslan in full attention.

Sarabeth and Jane were enjoying themselves laughing and talking and finding they had a lot in common. Suddenly beside them the chubby German Count broke out in laughter.

"Yah yah, the dachshund is wunderbar! It is my favorite dog. I have thirty dachshunds, they hunt mit mir."

Sarabeth was pulled up short with this sudden stirring from their neighbor. Jane had stopped in the act of eating a delicious soufflé.

"You have only one dachshund?", the Count carefully inquired of Jane.

Jane taken aback, that their dinner companion had suddenly come to life and realizing that the Count had overheard their conversation said, "Oh . . . I had one . . , as a child. . . she was my friend", Jane was unsure of how to talk with this man. She had almost forgotten he was there.

"Oh dear, you have gone without the great dachshund since you war eine little kinder?", he asked with sorrow in his voice.

"Well yes, you see I work all day and no longer live at home and . . .", Jane finished off realizing it was not a good idea to explain. The Count was looking at her uncomprehendingly.

"I must give you one of mine." He said this with so much energy and conviction that Jane knew not how she would be able to refuse him.

Just then the music stopped. There was a bit of commotion at the head table. A regal voice spoke in beautiful french, then italian, german, and finally english.

"My dear guests I do hope that you are enjoying yourselves."

There were some hearty affirmations from the tables near the regal voice.

"We are so very proud to be your hosts. We, France, being the . . . a . . . great power and with the finest musicians, painters, and talent generalement, and of course food and wine, offer all this to our great neighbors, from Italy, Germany" and the King gestured to our table, "America, Sweden" and he looked again towards us. . . .

After the King sat down the music began again and this time the notes were those of light and airy flutes.

"We have been traveling in the countryside. We learned that taxes have been increased without notice. What effect does this have on the local people?", Paslan asked the Viscount and the Viscountess.

A little furrow appeared on the brow of the Viscountess. She opened her fan and began fanning herself. The Viscount had slowed only slightly the rhythmic back and forth movement of his left hand to the goblet for drink and his right hand with fork and meat to his mouth. Paslan waited. The Viscount, looking to him now with slight irritation, took up his napkin to pat his pouting pudgy mouth and as one interrupted from a far more important occupation than the one he was about to address, said, "Oui, the Royal Council takes the trouble to vote on the amount of the taille and the people must pay that which is decided." The Viscount said this in a matter of fact tone, as a courtesy to his dinner partner. He replaced his napkin neatly in his lap and returned to the stationary dance he enjoyed so well.

"The people are not happy with the strict central control that holds them so tightly. What do you think will be the result?", Fenfrew enjoined.

The Viscountess fanned herself more vigorously. Her husband this time however did not interrupt his enjoyable endeavor and only when he had swallowed his mouthful of venison paused to reply, "I wonder at what you mean? The people must be thankful we take such interest in them - to vote, to send the Intendants, to be involved with what farmers and towns people are doing."

Paslan continued, "Do you believe that a man who works on the land all his life and manages to make a living through the sweat of his brow", the Viscountess dropped her fan inadvertently, "and the agility of his wits could welcome the intervention of authorities from Paris who know nothing of him, nothing of farming, and care even less?" Paslan had been watching the Viscount whom he could now see clearly had no room for digesting these words when he so much preferred the venison, and he added, - "And cares more for the food he eats at dinner than the just treatment of his fellow man?"

The rest of the table was now quiet but the Viscount did not notice. He hailed a maidservant for more wine. The princess was whispering to George who was nodding. The German Count was looking pensive his fingers fidgeting with his beard. His son was now wide eyed, leaning forward to hear every word Paslan spoke, seemingly quite enjoying himself.

The Viscountess was inwardly pulling away from the group toward her husband. She was feeling somehow quite uncomfortable, unexpectedly disconcerted, lost. A few moments before with the attentions of Paslan and Fenfrew she had been in her preferred role of having attention lavished upon her. She had not recognized that the attention she had been receiving was the gentlemanly behavior of two men of exceptional character who would have treated anyone the same. Now she was experiencing something unknown. She felt alone and this was why she pulled closer to her husband. What she did not understand was that she would be even more alone there. Her only comfort would have been herself if she had known. But she did not know herself for her only reflection had ever been in the mirror.

CHAPTER SEVENTEEN

WORK

Terhaven stood in the center of her arboretum. She looked most natural, appearing rooted in the earth along with the trees and shrubs, and unmoving, she sensed the state of her garden. If you had been there you would have seen birds alighting in the trees and bushes and heard them singing most sweetly near her. Terhaven began to turn, slowly turn, taking in all the shrubs and bushes nearby. At one moment she paused and leaned down into a particular bush and whispered to it. When she had completed a three hundred and sixty degree turn, she moved forward deeper into the arboretum and could no longer be seen from the porch.

Alabaster, Terhaven's gardener, had been asked to move the tea table to a particular place on the porch for David and from this position David was now writing. As the light moved across the gardens during the course of the day the sunlight was never in David's eyes, yet lit his books and his writing. The tea table was the right size for his papers and books, although today there were books underneath the table too. The three of them had shared a light lunch on the other side of the house near the kitchen. Terhaven had handed out the dishes from the kitchen window and they had sat quietly together listening to the birds, watching the squirrels on the lawn, and the clouds in the sky. As Alabaster had commented there were an unusually large group of cumulus clouds today.

Alabaster was a small quiet calm man with a happy manner. He seemed fully at home outdoors in the garden. His little cottage sat snugly in the elms at the end of the property by the stream. David would have liked to have learned more from him about the flora and fauna here. However Alabaster, being strictly considerate of David and his work, stayed away from that side of the house when David was working.

That evening it was just Terhaven and David together for dinner. They sat outdoors on the lawn at a small table. Having placed the table near a large oak and on a little prominence, they now had a beautiful view of the valley and the sunset.

David asked, "Is anyone married here?"

Terhaven tossed her head back and laughed. "Oh goodness yes. Those with families or who imagined families, wanted children, yes they are married. I had not the vision of children and to be honest never met the man to love deeply enough to marry."

"Do you know I can fully see that about you. You are particularly independent and perhaps more of the truth is that there are few to match you."

She looked at David and he held her gaze. Then she smiled, a slow simple smile. And a warmth came from her that spoke in silence to the truth David had voiced, an appreciation for his understanding.

"What of Alabaster?", he asked.

There was a pause and then she said, "I don't know. He lives alone." Then she continued, "He loves the garden and is very happy here. He says very little. His comment about the clouds today was a surprise, he rarely speaks. I think he doesn't need to. He understands the garden the way you understand the laws of nature."

"What do you mean?", David responded.

"You understand better than most the direct connection between liberty and personal responsibility. You value thinking and reflection and act upon your conviction, encouraging others to take up the gauntlet. You have an appreciation for life that allows you to enjoy it, and with others. Appreciation and understanding are inextricably linked."

She looked across the table at him her eyes aglow with love and life. David understood that love of life, it was a deep well within her that she shared unstintingly with her fellow man. It was the love that sources beyond oneself. And this is why it was a font that held a perpetual spring.

"It is wonderful of you to let me be here at this time", David thanked her as they took the dishes back into the kitchen.

"You are most welcome. Paslan thinks so highly of you and knows that the work you are writing must be published - if not at Edinbridge - then here. And - you need a place to think. This is a very good place for that." Then she asked, "Do you miss your friends?"

"Yes and no. Your home, the gardens, and the weather, create a special environment, an atmosphere that draws one out, allows one to see more clearly, see anew. It is like drapes not merely drawn back but removed so that all the light can arrive. After a bit of time this great simplicity comes to mean something." He continued, "Nadine and Will have come to be as family. I do miss them. I don't think that they will be away for long."

After their return from the Time trip to France Paslan went away directly. Nadine was completing another essay for what had been Herd's class. Will was working madly on his Opposite's Magnet and madly was a good description. He had cleared the big table by the window in Paslan's study of all books and papers and set up his equipment there. Bent over a green box with numerous apertures, a torch like stylus in hand, and a welders mask covering his face, Will looked the mad scientist.

"Hay Ho", Paslan greeted them enthusiastically as he appeared by the hearth.

"Oh Professor Paslan", cried Nadine in surprise as she looked up from her books.

"Will!", Nadine called loudly to Will who was maneuvering his torch and stylus.

Will started, looked up, and as he flipped up the mask said, "Professor Paslan . . . hello . . . we . . ."

Paslan broke in, "What fine examples we have here of hard working Edinbridge students. I'm happy to see you found a quiet place with good light." The sunlight as always was streaming in the windows. "And lots of room for your books . . . and equipment."

"You see Professor", Will felt he had to explain and as he took off his mask and put down his stylus he said,

"I can no longer work in the Zembley Labs because Professor Rong changed my schedule. Where I had been assigned to Professor Haliburton she reassigned me to work with her."

Before Will could continue Paslan said, "Bartholomew told me. Do not be concerned. I am glad that you can use the study to work. Do you have everything you need here?", Paslan was looking at the pieces of equipment lined up on the floor and against the wall.

"Oh Professor this is just the place to work. I'm very

comfortable here and I know Rong can not . . .", he stopped.

" . . . get at you here", Paslan finished his sentence. "No she can not."

Will let out a sigh. Then he said, "I'm sure you're wondering about the safety of the books with my torch and chemistry. I'm . . ."

"No Will I am not concerned. Nothing will happen to the books here", he said kindly and as fact. "In fact", Paslan continued, "I think that we should have all the equipment you need set up here. What else do you need?", he asked.

"Oh . . . . .", Will hesitated.

"Yes?", encouraged Paslan.

Will then said directly, "The microndeveloper in Haliburton's A Lab, the mini wind tunnel from the same lab, the Dynamic Processor from . . . Rong's lab", he hesitated only for a moment, "And a Mini Scalpon Dual Dialator from . . . well from where I don't know. Edinbridge doesn't have one. I haven't needed one yet. But I will," Will finished firmly. Paslan threw back his great mane of dark hair and gave a hearty laugh.

"We will get you all that, including your Mini Scalpon Dual Dilator, whatever that is", he said as he laughed again. Then he turned to the alcove and finished with, "Now I've got to do some work."

He pulled open the main drawer of his desk and took something out. His back was to both Nadine and Will and they could not see what it was. Then he pulled open another drawer, a tiny one in the center of the desk. Nadine looked at Will who was looking at her. They had been staring at Paslan and now both feeling a little guilty for all their curiosity, set back to their own work. After all, here they were in Paslan's study. They had never really asked him if they could use it. Of course Paslan hadn't been around much.

Since that meeting of all the professors backing Bale, a lot of people had been asking them a lot of questions. They didn't have too many friends these days. Students were keeping more to themselves. When they did pass other students in the halls or on the lawn Will and Nadine were more often the recipient of furtive glances and whispers than friendly greetings. Paslan's study had come to feel like home.

About an hour later Will's and Nadine's attention was caught by Paslan getting up from his desk. He seemed to be in another world. He moved over to the fireplace and sat down in his chair, all without noticing them. Again Nadine gave Will a quick glance as though to ask are we being impolite. Will gave a slight shrug. Both of them watched Paslan. He was in a deep brown study with his feet up upon the ottoman facing the hearth. As they watched he absently picked up the poker and moved a half burnt log in the grate. In a moment a fire was kindled.

"She will try you know", Paslan spoke. He hadn't looked up from where his gaze was fixed in the flames.

They both started and Will asked, "Rong you mean?"

"Yes. She will try again to get in here and not only to see you." He paused as though determining whether to go on. Then he turned so they could see each others' faces. There was something in Paslan's face they had not seen there before. Will and Nadine sat very still, all their attention focused on Paslan.

"Come and sit with me here", his voice was quiet, almost soft. They got up and came to sit by him.

"As I believe you know the tide has turned. The energy of Edinbridge is no longer from the same foundation that created this school and fortified it for more than five hundred years. The coming regime is of a different material all together and one that will rent the fabric we know in twain, not to be salvageable. This is why we are not fighting them on their grounds. Unfortunately too many people handed over this ground, Edinbridge and all it has stood for." Nadine thought she heard a catch in Paslan's voice. Paslan finished, "Pernicious passivity. They handed it over to Bale and what he stands for." If she had heard a catch in his voice a moment before it was gone and in its place was fire. "We decided several years ago, that night Avaricis joined the Board, that we would create a world where Bale and the like could not be. That is what we have done. And it is this that activates them now in anger, envy, or pride, and in Bale's case all three."

Paslan turned to Will and said, "You know it is Rong who understands this. Bale does not stop to imagine that there is anywhere he cannot be, or anywhere he cannot go, or anything he can not have, if he decides that we wants it. Rong has already tried to come to the Other World."

Will and Nadine gasped. "I don't think that Bale knows that. And she probably doesn't want him to know", Paslan continued.

"How?", Nadine asked.

"I'm not sure. She slipped into this study when Jane was here cleaning up one day last fall. She understands about opposite energies and how to use them. The energy here and that around her would create a significant energy gap. And in some way she had calculated how to harness it."

"Why didn't it work then?", Nadine asked again.

Paslan smiled, "It's more than a formula . . . as you know," and he looked at her pointedly.

They were quiet for a moment and then Paslan said, "I do not want to disrupt your studies nor your life here. I am wondering about the timing . . .

. . . "Of when we should leave for good", Will finished off the sentence for him.

"Yes", Paslan replied.

"Can we take the equipment with us to the Other World?"

"No and once there you won't need it", Paslan was looking at Will.

Will's face fell and he was quiet. Paslan waited.

"How can I give up the discovery . . . we're almost there . . . it's going to . . . ", he stopped.

"Perhaps it is better not to bring it into the Other World", Paslan said.

There was a long silence. Then Will asked,

"Do you mean . . . that if I continue the work. . .Rong would use it?" Will's voice was almost shaking with realization.

"Possibly", was all Paslan said. He put another log on the fire and maneuvered it into place. They sat there together quietly while many minutes passed.

Then Will spoke, "I imagine that Fenfrew may need some help . . . and we could work on something together."

A beautiful, warm, loving, smile came to Paslan's face and he shone it upon them, "Bartholomew is very much looking forward to your living in the Other World. I am sure that there are many discoveries to be made when the two of you put your heads together. In fact, if I am not telling tales out of school", Paslan's eyes twinkled at Will, "he has something planned for the two of you to begin as soon as you are ready."

Will smiled, and swallowed, and could say nothing at all.

Nadine spoke up, "I'm starved, I bet Jane has something good for dinner. Can we go down to the Great Hall together?", she asked.

"Yes", said Paslan with enthusiasm.

As they left the study together Paslan said to Will, "It is important that you continue your work until the day you leave. The right timing will become known to us."

"Everything looks so nummy", said Nadine as she spooned a french pan roasted hen onto her plate. "Jane must know that you are here," Nadine looked up at Paslan. "It's all extra good tonight", and she stuck her finger into the Bearnaise sauce again. "Do you know what Bourride is?", she said as she looked at the menu on the table.

"Fish soup, I've already tried it, it's really good", Will smiled at her. "I wouldn't be surprised if Jane was given receipes while we were over in France", Will suggested.

"One of my old favorites", Paslan said delightedly as he spotted a large dish in the center of the table, "Goat Cheese and Herb Souffle."

" Oh . . . so you've been to France before . . . well of course", Nadine almost sounded hurt.

"Yes I have been to France a number of times. However", he said with sincerity, "Our adventure was not only unique it was particularly special as it was shared with my closest friends." Paslan's eyes beamed into Nadine and she could barely keep back a tear.

Just then Jane came over to the table. "How is everything?", she asked.

"Everything is delicious", Will said with enthusiasm. "Did you get these receipes over there?", he winked at her and smiled.

"I did", she grinned. "The chef at the pub was keen to give me a handful of his receipes. Then when the Count gave me one of his dachshunds the palace chef came by. I think the chef thought that if the Count could give away one of his dogs that he could give me one or two of his receipes." They all laughed.

"How is Luger working out?", Paslan asked Jane.

"He is lovely and really quite smart. I should have gotten a dog ages ago", she enthused.

"Luger?", Will asked.

"That was the name the Count gave him. It means gun in german", Jane told him.

Nadine suddenly felt someone watching them. Scanning the Great Hall she could see over on the far wall at the center table Su Su Rong sitting with Professors Yarnick and Devolve, and Mally Framer. Though it was quite a distance Nadine felt Su Su's and her own eyes meet. Her blood ran cold. She was surprised that Rong held her gaze. They were out in the open now, Bale's bunch, a team of sorts, a destructive team. Nadine looked over to Will, he was busy enjoying his meal and talking with Jane. Paslan caught Nadine's eye and slowly nodded his head letting her know that he was aware of her thoughts, and agreed.

It was three in the morning when Nadine was awakened by a strange sound. It was a harsh grating sound that came from somewhere outside. She looked out the window. No one could be seen. The noise had stopped but it had awoken her. It was a disconcerting and unfamiliar noise. Then it came again. She got up. Where was it coming from? Nadine threw on her coat, slipped into the shoes at her door and went out. By the time she was outside the sound had stopped. She was walking toward Chartwell Tower and to Paslan's study before she even realized it. There it was again and it was more distinct this time. It was a harsh, grating, unnatural sound. She was nervous as she knew that Paslan was not at Edinbridge and that who she would find in his study was Rong. Yet every step that brought her closer she became less nervous and more angry. The light of the old lamps that lit her way was soft to the eye, not harsh like the sound that she had just heard. There ahead of her was Chartwell Tower. While there was no moon tonight the stars were unusually bright.

As she mounted the stairs she realized that the sound had not come a fourth time. The building was silent and as she came to the top floor she saw what she had known she would see, the door of Paslan's study opening for her. Nadine took a deep breath and almost marched towards it.

This time Rong was not surprised to see her but interested to see Nadine alone.

"Where is Will?", she asked in a sly even tone.

"Asleep I imagine", replied Nadine watching her very closely. "Why are you here?"

"You know very well why I'm here", this time her voice was cold with malignant pride. "Why would we, the best, remain here when there is another world to explore", she replied rhetorically.

"Exploit, you mean", said Nadine.

Rong opened her mouth wide and let out a sound which might have been her laugh. But it was not a laugh for it was devoid of mirth. It was a cackle. Then she said, "You and your friends are such fools. You seem to think that life is a gift to be enjoyed. But you are wrong. If you understood that the game is won by those who seek and gain power you could use those brains of yours to some better end. Instead you waste your time and let others gain power. That is what I do not understand." She stopped and looked with - was it sadness - at Nadine.

"No you don't understand do you?", Nadine replied. "You think that life is a race for power and victory but you don't stop to think victory over what. The pursuit of power, or power itself over other people cannot lead you to anything good in the long run."

"Haven't you heard - in the long run we're all dead", and Rong let out another cackle.

"Yes I have heard that and I have not subscribed. It is the truth only for those who will not conquer their own pride and learn that there is a power far beyond what we can understand, God. In believing, we are given deep understanding and to use your word, power beyond any that one can take for oneself."

For a moment Rong seemed to be captured by Nadine's words. There was a pause. Then the open look in her eyes vanished and was replaced by the old mask.

"Listen to this Miss Redwood", becoming belligerent, Rong continued, "I intend to get to the other world and you are going to help me." As she said this she strode to Nadine and taking her arm pulled her over to Paslan's desk. Nadine's anger welled up from deep within her igniting a firepower beyond what any would expect from this slender young woman. But she waited. Just as a lioness waits for the right moment, still and quiet, she waited for Rong's mistake. Rong shoved her down into Paslan's chair.

"Now sit there." It was a command, cold and threatening. "The strongest power here is where Paslan is most often, where you are sitting", she stated with triumph.

She's got that wrong Nadine said to herself. She is thinking only physically. Besides Paslan is over at the fireplace most often. Rong moved over to the table where Will's equipment was lined up.

"Too bad for you that Will is not here. At this time he knows more that I do. I might make a mistake", she said with a smirk and bent her head to the equipment. Nadine stood up and faced her.

"I will not sit here and wait for you", she said. "I am not like you. You and Ginbreste and Hil Gore may choose to follow - Bale. But I would never follow you and your kind." Nadine stood straight, strong in all of herself, and her words came as arrows of fire to her meaning. "You will never have me help you get to our world." As she spoke her energy rose and she felt herself becoming stronger and stronger. She was completely focused on Rong.

Rong stood looking at her, overtaken in surprise. Then she said coldly and resentfully, "Sit down."

"I will not", said Nadine simply.

"You will do as I say or I will make you", Rong's expression was menacing.

As Rong made a move from the table towards Nadine Nadine's energy became focused and magnified to the singular intention of willing Rong immovable. Rong stopped stuck to the spot.

"What's happening? Why can't I move?", Rong shouted.

Nadine's eyes bore into her adversary. "Turn off the Mini Scalpon Dual Dilator", she instructed.

"I will not", Rong hissed.

"Then neither will you be able to move", replied Nadine.

Something else was happening. Nadine could sense a change in the room. From Paslan's desk she could see the lake. Why could she see the lake? There was no moon. Then she noticed the stars again. They were glistening. She noticed three stars straight in front of her over the center of the lake twinkling so brightly that she blinked in the light. As she opened her eyes again they all twinkled at the same time as though blinking back at her. Okay get a grip she told herself. But as she held her gaze upon the night sky there was no denying that those three stars were most unusual. Then she saw it. A rain of light from each star simultaneously began to flow. Rather than just falling towards the ground or streaking across the sky as with shooting stars this light traveled towards her in beams.

Nadine glanced at Rong. She stood stiffly, unmoving. Nadine looked back to the window. The beams of light were much closer now. Nadine relaxed. She felt as though in summoning her courage another energy had been called forth.

A scrambling sound made her turn. Rong was suddenly upon her. Two cold hands grasped Nadine's shoulders and shoved her down into the chair. A chill ran through her. She felt Rong's malevolent intent. Nadine looked to the light which was almost at the window. Suddenly the beams poured through the window onto the desk and filled the room. Rong's hands went limp and she fell back. The light was dancing about touching everything. The books glinted as with golden drops of sun. The hearth was ablaze with a beautiful fire of gold. Light drops glistened in every corner of the ceiling and seemed to play and jump above them. Nadine moved from the chair to see Rong. She lay on the floor in a heap, her mouth partially open. Nadine stooped to take a better look. Rong was out cold. She was alive but her coloring was odd. Instead of the usual tan of her skin her face was pale, her expression stunned disbelief.

Nadine went to the table and turned off the Mini Scalpon Dual Dilator. As she unplugged it and looked up there stood Paslan in the center of his study with Rong at his feet. He looked very serious and said,

"I'll take care of this. You go back to your room. I fear you may not get back to sleep but try and rest."

"What was the noise I heard?", Nadine asked simply.

"It was Rong trying to get into the Other World. And she almost did", replied Paslan.

Chapter Eighteen

The Other World

"It is time. If your hearts are for it we must all move to the Other World," Paslan addressed Will and Nadine as they sat together once again at his fire.

"Rong will recover in a day or two and will be all the closer to figuring out on her own how to get into the Other World. With all of us there together she can not use one of you either to help her or as hostage. And we can be ready for her and her band on the other side. You may invite George and Sarabeth if you believe that they truly want to be in the Other World", he spoke to Nadine.

"Is there anyone you would invite Will?"

"No I don't think so," Will's voice held sadness.

"How are you?", Paslan asked him.

"It is the right thing to do", Will said simply. "It is sad that so many have let this happen through pernicious passivity as you call it." Paslan nodded. "I am ready. And I am now looking forward to working full time with Fenfrew", Will said and a deep confidence rang through his words.

"When do we go?", asked Nadine.

"Will you invite George and Sarabeth?", asked Paslan.

"Yes", she replied.

"We will give them a day to decide and then we will go." As he said this he stood up and his fit slender form silhouetted by the fire seemed to emanate light. His eyes met theirs in turn. Nadine and Will were warmed deep inside. Something was happening, something was now within them to be uncovered over time.

"We will leave from this very spot Thursday evening at 8 O'Clock."

Without another word Paslan crossed the room to his desk. The great study door opened and Will and Nadine left the study in this way, perhaps for the last time.

Will and Nadine walked silently out into Chartwell Common and toward the lake. When they reached the lake Will turned to look back at Chartwell Tower and the Great Lawn and said,

"So we are done here."

Nadine was taking in the great steeples and towers of Edinbridge University and after many moments nodded her head.

"You've at least had almost two years", he said.

"I'm sorry Will, I know you love it here", she said.

"Paslan is right. I don't want to leave any discoveries in Rong's hands. It is better, far better, that we move on and be with others whom we can trust and who have a similar sense of personal responsibility to life," said Will Hamlet.

They walked in silence until they were half way around the lake. The buds were out on the trees and birds were singing, making ready for their nests.

"Oh you are free of worry you little birds. Life goes on the same for you without the Rong's and Bale's of this world to corrupt it", said Nadine to the birds nearby. Nadine stopped to watch a pair of robins making a nest in an old oak tree. After they flew off to gather more twine and twig she remained still, her eyes roaming the part of the forest that was in sight. There just a little distance into the forest was a deer family. The stag is watching me, Nadine thought. The doe, waiting by his side, was with two fauns who were close by nibbling the little buds on the bushes.

He's moving toward me! The doe followed with the fauns on either side of her. Within a moment they were face to face. He is present with me here and I am entirely present in this precious moment, and she felt her tears come to her eyes. The stag's nose was within inches of her own. The fauns had both come forward and one brushed her leg as he reached round her to a particularly appealing bush. Remaining very still her eyes met those of the stag's. He looked into her, reaching she knew to that something that Paslan had given them. I can feel his strength, the natural care and responsibility he has for his family. Moving her eyes to those of the doe she met a gentle being, warm, attentive, and very aware. The doe moved closer and bent her nose to Nadine's cheek. It was moist, like Jane's dachshund's but broader. Then she gently rubbed her fur covered cheek to the skin of Nadine's cheek.

Tears flowed down Nadine's face. The doe took one step back and stood with her mate for a moment then turned her head slightly towards him. He extended his head and neck to Nadine and with his tongue licked a tear from her chin. The great wonder of the moment was strangely over taken by the tickle she felt at the sensation of his rough tongue on her skin. She smiled, happy. The stag moved back one step. For one more moment the three looked directly at one another and then in another he turned and leapt back into the forest his family close behind him.

Nadine watched until they were gone. Then she

turned to where Will had been. He must have moved on while she was scanning the forest for he stood fifty feet off looking at her.

"What was that?!", he cried incredulous.

Nadine beamed and ran towards him. "Did you see that?!", she exclaimed.

"See it? I'll never forget it! What did her nose feel like? And his tongue?!"

"Oh Will", she cried aloud as she threw her arms around his neck and hugged him with all her energy. They continued walking the circuit of the lake Will questioning her and the two of them laughing and talking.

"I have a feeling that even I may have such an experience in the Other World", Will said with wonder and anticipation.

Their circuit of the lake brought them back to the Great Lawn where the huge oaks towered above them.

"Do you know, the day I arrived at Edinbridge and was on the way to meet Paslan, walking under these trees . . . I think it was just over here . . ." He led her to a particularly large oak whose branches, spreading out over the lawn, were a street in width. "I thought that I heard music . . . music from the trees."

Nadine laughed, "I'm not surprised."

They stood together beneath the tree. Then, as from an unseen conductor standing on his podium having readied his orchestra, a symphony began. Violins and cello's, french horns and bassoons, and then a trumpet. The melody was enchanting and perfectly fitting for this beautiful spring day. It was as new beginnings and as they were lifted up above this grandfather of trees, they moved beyond the body boundaries to meadows of purple heather and yellow daffodil that led to green rolling sunlit hills at the horizon. There they were met by an arch of sunbeams leading beyond the horizon to new days while all the while the music moved within them pulsing through their veins and coursing through the arteries of the heart. In a moment they were back on the grass beneath the oak. Feeling the wonder they saw in each other's eyes, the wonder of life, without a word they walked on.

"What were you doing in Paslan's study if not to succeed in getting to the Other World?", Bale's words came like bullets.

"It was necessary to take the risk. With each failure there is learning", Rong said with confidence.

"Failure! I know no failure", he spoke as a dictator might dictate a lesson to his generals. "How could you have failed? Once you discovered the 'Traces' you said that that was the last step. You've been monitoring the 'Traces' from Paslan's study for months now," Bale sounded disgusted.

"It will happen . . . I will . . ."

Bale interrupted with, "There will be no more of this. I will find a way."

"You are not familiar with the technology and it would take a long time . . ."

He cut her off, "There are other scientists where I found you. A number of whom have been beating down my door to get here and be involved in the Other World."

She was thinking fast now. There was no way she was going to give up anything she knew to another scientist who would take her place. There was something that Bale did not understand. Something she had never spoken of with him, with anyone. He did not understand that entrance to the Other World was not strictly a technical matter. In fact if it had been she would have succeeded before now. If she told him would he believe her, would he dispense with getting someone else to help him? She watched him as he suggested names, associates of hers in Bejing. How humiliating that he would think that there was someone better than her, that he could replace her with another scientist. Has he forgotten why he chose to hire me? She had realized that Bale was getting restless, impatient. That was the problem with Westerners they have so short a time horizon. They did not bother to apply the discipline to look at history and think further out. She was making up her mind. But she would not jump to a decision like Bale was doing. No she would wait.

Little Su Su had always had to wait, wait until her older brother went to school and got a good job in the bank. Wait until he climbed the ladder and made enough money to send her to university. Well she had all the brains and while she had started late she had taken little time to catch up. No. Little Su Su was not so little anymore and no, no one not even Avaricis Bale, was going to get in her way. She would get to the Other World and if he didn't treat her well she would leave them all behind.

"I can see that you are not going to recommend any of your colleagues over yourself so I will choose for you. When he arrives I suggest you be prepared to work closely with him that we waste no more time in extending our purpose to this new world", Bale concluded.

By the time he gets here I'll be gone and you will be further behind rather than ahead, she said to herself. When Bale excused her she got up immediately. She took one glance back at the man who cared nothing for her. But it wasn't that which angered her. It was his lack of appreciation for her abilities. She walked out the door and whispered under her breath, "This is the last time you will treat Su Su Rong this way."

Will had gone to meet four classmates to let them know that he would not be back next term. He had decided to tell them that he was taking some time for an independent study project with an old professor friend and that he could not pass up the opportunity.

"But Will what about your buddies, hockey, and soccer?", said Tim Brand showing his dismay.

"Of course I will miss you guys", Will looked at the four first years who sat together at the dinner table in the Great Hall. Tim was his hockey buddy, Enlai his lab partner, Ravi his sparring partner in philosophy, and Beau his roommate.

"It is so beautiful here. And there are all the others you can study with - you may get bored with just one old professor buried away in the lab", Enlai was trying to convince him. They were excellent lab partners. Will diving in with all the ideas and Enlai thinking through all the detail and tailoring the experiments to maximize their efficiency.

"There will be an empty space without you Will and I don't just mean here at the table", Ravi looked at Will with his huge dark brown eyes which showed how much he cared for his friend. Will looked at Beau who could not even speak. They had had their conversation back in the dorm.

"I'll be in touch," Will said as he wondered how.

"Well you'd better be", broke in Tim. You'll want to know how we're doing in our games - which without you . . .", Tim broke off with a frown.

As they said their goodbyes and slowly pushed back their chairs they got up as a group. "I've got to have a conversation with a classmate", Ravi indicated another table, and moved off.

Tim took his hand and shook it, "See you Will."

Beau nodded and joined Tim.

As Enlai and Will left the Great Hall together Enlai said, "We've got to be in touch Will. You know we have gotten so far with 'Traces' that the work we've done on the Opposites Magnet . . . I don't know how you could stand it if we just gave it up.", Enlai's voice was quiet and serious.

"I know. I think we will continue. It's just that I don't know when", he looked at his friend. They were outside now walking on the Great Lawn. All the trees were in bloom. They stopped. Enlai looked at his friend and there was a tear in his eye. Will had never seen emotion from his friend other than the odd half smile. Will waited. Enlai readied himself to say something. It was one or two minutes, a long time when you know that another must gather himself in order to speak. Then it came.

"This is a special world here at Edinbridge. I hope that my country will have such a place. You help make this place what it is", Enlai looked up to the trees overhead and over to the roof tops then his eyes rested back upon Will. "There is something in you . . . something that is so alive, alight with fire and a particular energy. It is as though that energy is a gift to you because you will take the proper care of it . . . see it out to what it is supposed to be. And place that energy in all that is supposed to come alive. Don't ever let it die Will. Fight to keep it alive . . . no matter what."

He stood still his black eyes seeing into Will. This time the tear was in Will's eye. He embraced his friend and said, his voice strong and deep, "Yes Enlai yes."

It was almost 8 O'Clock and they, Paslan, Nadine, Will, George, and Sarabeth were assembled in Paslan's study. There was not a cloud in the sky. The stars were out and as bright as Sarabeth had ever seen them. She was standing at the big window closest to the hearth.

"I've never seen anything like it. They are so bright tonight." She looked back over her shoulder and to Will she said, "Is it a special time of year or confluence of planet positions or something? It's extraordinary."

Will replied, "Not that I know of", looking to Paslan with raised brows and a smile.

"There is something Sarabeth", Paslan offered. "Did you know that your interest in the stars may actually make them brighter?", Paslan winked at Nadine.

"What . . . excuse me... what was that?," Sarabeth left the window and joined them by the fire.

"Where the stars meet your eyes something happens. It is an ancient wisdom that tells us that when we look beyond ourselves, look up and outward to the heavens, having done our own homework here", and he patted his heart, " just as we extend our vision we can stretch our very understanding and deepen the meaning for life", said Paslan. The room was very quiet but for the crackling of the fire.

Nadine registered again that the fire was always alight whatever the season. She looked up to the windows and the twinkling stars seemed to wink at them from on high. Their light shone in through the windows. On the carpet in front of Paslan's desk starbeams created their own little dance, a warm golden ball in motion with star like points of light sparkling out along the rim of a golden globe like a crown glistening in the sunlight. Sunlight and starlight came together here.

"Are you ready?", Paslan looked at each of his companions in turn and seeing their faces laughed.

George shrugged his shoulders, Sarabeth had a slightly frightened look, Nadine was excited, and Will's brows were still raised.

"I suppose it is really a rhetorical question for I suppose we are never really ready for a whole change ... something quite wholly different than what we have known. I suppose in a way it would be like being single all your life and then at forty waking up to a spouse and five children", he seemed to be imagining this for himself and quite vividly by the look on his face. They all laughed. And Paslan broke out laughing with them.

"I think that we are ready", and he stood up. There won't be any flying. That delight is reserved for you for another time", he looked at George and Sarabeth who looked relieved, though bewildered.

"Just stand close together", they all moved forward and inward toward each other. "Join hands and take a deep breath." As they all breathed in the warm air by the fire... the study vanished before their eyes and it felt like the sides of their bodies were being slightly compressed. At the same time they felt lighter than air, feathery, as they moved through space. The air around them was warm and comfortable it was as they were on their own soft cloud that moved them along. Perhaps it was a minute and then they all stood together in a field with a big white house on the crest of a hill ahead of them.

CHAPTER NINETEEN

TERHAVEN'S HOME

"How are you all?", Paslan's warm voice asked as he looked to the four faces in front of him. George and Sarabeth were rooted to the spot looking all around and did not speak.

Nadine asked, "When did you let go of my hand?"

"At the last moment", said Paslan.

Will said, "It was like you stood with us and then were behind us too, supporting us sort of . . ."

Paslan smiled and at the same time beckoned them toward the house saying,

"Come, Terhaven is expecting us."

They headed toward the white house trimmed in green. Terhaven stood on the porch waving to them. As they arrived the front door opened. It was David. Nadine rushed up and hugged him.

"It's so good to see you again", she said as she continued to squeeze him. He gave her a great hug in return.

"It is very good to see you", and he kissed her cheek.

"Will how are you?", David gave Will a hug, which was a little unexpected by both of them.

Terhaven welcomed each of them as she ushered them into her home.

"Are you tired?", Terhaven asked. They shook their heads.

"Good because I expected instead that you'd be hungry", and she gestured to a large table with a white linen cloth and all variety of dishes. "Please sit down and help yourself."

"Will sit at this end", she suggested a seat for Will. "Bartholomew will join us momentarily and wants to be able to talk with you." Will's face lit up. Jane came out of the kitchen with a plate full of roast beef.

"Jane!" they chorused.

"I'm happy to see you here", she said as she set the plate on the table and sat next to Terhaven.

Jane and Terhaven had begun a friendship when Jane first moved from Edinbridge. Terhavaen was taking cooking lessons and Jane was learning to garden. Their combined expertise made for the fine little feast now offered their friends. Paslan talked with Sarabeth and George while David and Nadine caught up with all that had been happening.

That night when it was finally time to get to sleep Will and Fenfrew, who were still deep in conversation, went off to Fenfrew's home. Jane had found Terahaven's home to be as her own, David had settled there too for the time being and Nadine, Sarabeth and George remained with them. Terhaven, having anticipated years before that she would have many guests, had many rooms to offer. Nadine's room was on the very top of the house.

The ceiling, about twelve feet high, was peaked in the center at about eighteen feet. The walls were a very pale yellow and the wainscoting a third of the way up was a lovely medium green with the base boards a paler green. The room was simply furnished with a small double bed with a beautiful mauve and white duvet. A very large old armoire sat against the wall to the left of the bed. Beside it hung a large mirror in a beautiful wood frame. Along the opposite wall to the right of the bed was one long low dresser with three long and deep drawers painted pale green to match the base boards. Two rectangular windows sat together in the corner, one on the wall adjacent to that with the bed almost touching the other window on the wall opposite the bed. These had white wood louvers which were now closed. The other window, directly opposite the bed, was enormous with airy white and green cotton curtains of two layers. Although Nadine did not know it yet, this window faced east and in the morning her room would be flooded with light and she would awake to see a distant rolling green hill awash with purple heather and pink daphne.

When she was ready for bed Nadine drew the curtains all the way back to look at the night sky. There in a perfectly black sky above their heads were the stars. Wonderful bright twinkling stars, beams of white light shone in the great distance. She climbed into bed and onto a very thick and very firm mattress and propped her head up on two enormous pillows to watch the stars. She was thankful to be here. What a warm welcoming they received. What wonderful people Terhaven and Paslan are. Fenfrew must be too she thought. She hoped to get to know him better. It made her happy to see how much he meant to Will. She said her prayers in gratitude and asked as she had since a child, to be the best she could be, to live up to her responsibility for who she was given to be. And then she fell asleep.

She was flying over the meadow when she saw it. It was a hole in the ground. It wasn't that broad but it must be deep for it was black. The hole was at the edge of the forest and some of the nearby trees were down. It looked like something had landed at high speed and wiped out the trees because they were not just broken or bent but blackened as if burned. Then she heard something, it was the same harsh grating noise she had heard that early morning in her dorm when she'd gone to Paslan's study to find Rong. When she opened her eyes it was morning, she had been dreaming, and any remnant of the dream was gone.

Before her the distant green hill carpeted in purple and pink was as a Monet painting framed by the enormous picture window. As she lay there a smile broadened across her face. "How beautiful", she sighed aloud. The side windows were open and birds were singing and chorusing each other. Somewhere in the middle of the song she heard the gentle chirp of a bird she and Paslan had heard together by the stream, the whippoorwill. A refreshing breeze wafted into the room. Nadine closed her eyes and breathed in, she was thankful.

She got up and dressed and felt that all was right with the world. Looking in the large square mirror, she decided that her hair sat just right and a brushing would only disarrange the slightly wild wind swept look she liked. A delicious smell greeted her in the hallway. Someone was making a breakfast for which she was very hungry.

"Good morning my dear", Paslan said cheerfully.

"You are cooking us breakfast", Nadine said with surprise as she entered the kitchen.

"This is my favorite breakfast. Jane wanted to help however I sent her off for a walk. We have fresh fruit." An enormous wooden bowl sat on the counter behind him filled with apples, oranges, ataulfo mangoes, small sweet apricots, and medium red plums. "There is bison sausage, bacon, and hash brown potatoes." One very large pan was filled with this mix of meat and potatoe and the smell of onions and garlic.

"Homemade bread," Nadine enthused. Three loaves sat steaming on the island counter. This is what had smelled so appetizing from the hallway above.

"And my secret omelette."

Paslan was tending the omelette at that moment. He had three enormous pans full but the ingredients could not be deciphered. "Would you pour out nine glasses from the pitcher?", Paslan asked.

"Mmm this juice smells wonderful, so fresh, what is it?", Nadine looked to Paslan.

"That is another secret. I call it Four Flowers juice."

"What are the four flowers?", she asked directly.

Paslan laughed and looked sideways at her, his smiling eyes lighting upon her, he said, "It would no longer be a secret if I told you." Then Nadine laughed too.

"Okay but if I guess . . ."

Just then Terhaven came into the kitchen.

"Good morning Nadine." Terhaven took an appreciative breath. "It all smells ready."

She began to take the food out to the porch. Nadine picked up the jam pots and followed.

"Did you sleep well in your room?", Terhaven asked.

"Oh yes, so well. It's a lovely room, simple, spacious, and cozy and so full of light. The picture window brings the outdoors inside", Nadine said.

Terhaven nodded and smiled, "I'm glad you like it." As Terhaven laid the bowl of fruit in the middle of the linen covered table Fenfrew and Will arrived along the path to the house. As usual they were engrossed in conversation. Seeing Terhaven and Nadine in the same moment they rang out in unison, "Good morning."

Terhaven and Nadine laughed. "Come and sit down and continue your conversation at least until we are all here together", Terhaven patted Fenfrew on the shoulder.

Nadine smiled at them both and raised a quizzical brow to Will.

"Bartholomew lives just down the windy road about half a mile. You should see his study it's a lot like Paslan's though with more equipment than books", Will beamed back at her. Nadine went back in to find a tray for all the juice glasses. She returned with the glasses and pitcher and began to pour. Jane and David came up to the porch from the direction of the forest, "I wanted to help but Paslan wanted to make breakfast for us", Jane said. "The forest is extraordinary have you been yet?", she asked Nadine.

"Not this part of the forest", Nadine replied.

"I entered right over there", she pointed to a place about half way down the lawn. "There are a surprising variety of trees and forest bed flowers. About ten minutes into the forest you come to a stream. I waded across and found a path that wound up a hill where the trees cleared. That's where David and I met up."

"I was up early writing and later decided to go for a walk before everyone was up. I found the hill and sat there for a while. From the top there is a lovely vista of the surrounding area", David said.

Paslan and Terahaven emerged together through the open French doors, Paslan with the omelettes and Terahaven with the bread. Terahaven had set the table with silver and large squares of soft elegant white linen napkins.

"Did anyone call Sarabeth and George", Paslan asked.

Will and David looking at one another, called up in unison to the windows above, "Sarabeth, George."

In a moment a window opened out above them and Sarabeth leaned out.

"I'm coming, it smells wonderful", she smiled and closed the window.

In another moment another window opened further

along the house and George stuck out his head. "Good morning everyone, I'm on my way down."

It was a warm sunny spring morning and the birds were singing from high atop the trees along the house, from the bushes, and from the forest.

"I'm going to take a guess", Nadine held her glass and looking at Paslan said,

"Grapefruit, orange, pomegranate and … what is that fourth ingredient?"

Paslan smiled and said nothing.

"It's very good isn't it", Will said as he poured himself another glass.

Nadine looked to Jane who looked to Paslan.

"Go ahead take a guess", Paslan said to Jane.

"Is it mango?", Jane asked.

"No", Paslan shook his head.

"You are not going to tell us are you?", Nadine was bemused.

"It would not be a secret if I told you and secrets can be a good thing," finished Paslan.

They talked and laughed and talked some more. Finally David said, "What are we thinking? I mean about ensuring our way of life here."

In a moment Fenfrew spoke, "Paslan and I are thankful and happy that you are here. As you know we wanted to establish a life free of dealings with evil. The evil that exists where we were living had become pervasive. It appears that those who live with evil seek to be here too." He stopped.

Paslan pushed his chair back from the table and looking out over the forest, his eyes seemed to rest at a great distance. The table was quiet. Then Terhaven spoke, "A significant reason that life got so far off track was not because evil existed, it has always existed. It was because we did not stand our guard against it. While it was organic for some of us to refuse to engage with Bale many did not take a definitive stand against what he was espousing. If we had stopped to think about what was going on, asked others to stop with us, and formulated a plan, fewer people would have followed Bale."

Paslan, looking at David, and responded to his question, "We are waiting to learn the right time."

CHAPTER TWENTY

DAWNING

After breakfast a few days later Nadine nabbed Will, "What have you and Fenfrew been working on? You've been holed up since we got here. At meals the two of you are in deep conversation and we feel we shouldn't disturb you", Nadine said chastizingly. And then added, "I miss you."

Will looked like a dog hanging his head after digging up the garden.

"Well . . . we didn't imagine that any one would be interested."

"Oh come on! Between the two of you you have enough brains to run the universe if brains without sensitivity were the ticket", she added impatiently.

Will was hurt. And said, "Well I guess I have been spending a lot of time in Fenfrew's study and lab. Maybe we've been working too hard. Even Fenfrew is tired lately." After a pause he said, "Come on let's go for a walk. The forest from this point should be explored."

He led the way out to the back porch and down onto the lawn to the gap in the bushes which led into the forest. He noticed the spring in Nadine's step and not being as insensitive as accused, he could see that Nadine had missed him.

The tall trees were in full bloom reaching and spreading their leafy fingers toward the sky. The rich green of every branch was as welcoming arms inviting them forward. As they walked along the dirt path leading into the forest the young trees and bushes were wearing the lighter spring green of being newly touched by the sun unlike their older or more aggressive taller neighbors. This tableau of greens offered the perfect backdrop for the little yellow, purple, and red, flowers that made the forest bed their home.

"We've been working on so many things, I don't know where to begin", Will offered.

"I was sure that you'd be working on only one thing, the Opposites Magnet, to keep Bale and his bunch out", said Nadine.

"No. We are not working on the Opposites Magnet rather we are working for a better life here."

"What? I don't understand", she asked bewildered.

"Fenfrew and I talked about it when I arrived. Fenfrew and Paslan had spoken about it before we came. Rather than spend energy trying to keep people out we are investing our time in a better life here. Let's take this path", Will pointed to a little path that led up a hill.

"Rong and Bale are going to get in here then", said Nadine with passionate exasperation and anger.

"They might", Will replied.

There was a long silence and then Will continued, "Let me tell you what we are doing. One of the ideas Fenfrew has had for a long time is the idea of Time, Time and The Mind he calls it. It is related to how we got here in fact. You know something about this", he smiled at Nadine.

"Go on", she said, still impatient.

"It has to do with where we place ourselves." They were winding upward along the side of the hill toward the top.

" . . . where we place our thinking. Bale and Rong are a simple example in contrast to Paslan and Fenfrew. Bale and Rong are placed diametrically opposite to Paslan and Fenfrew. When Rong tries to enter the Other World the harsh grating sound that results heralds her entry because to enter she must take what is not hers. She is pulling then on the 'chord' of the diametrical plane that runs parallel across the circle of life and as in harmonic music the chords can only be played by those who understand the music. Dissonance results when one plays the wrong note. Because she can not play the right note Rong pulls on Fenfrew the creator of the harmony, the co-creator of the Other World, and in so doing weakens the harmony and in this case Fenfrew," Will finished.

"What?!", exclaimed Nadine. "And what do you mean co-creator?"

"Well... there is creation beyond all of us. Let's stick with what we know here", Will replied.

"Okay . . . this is what we are working on. Fenfrew has invented a set of binoculars that help people see clearly", Will said triumphantly.

"What! What do you mean? Binoculars were invented in the 1800's," spluttered Nadine sounding very impatient indeed.

"That's right Fenfrew was friends with Lemiere," Will continued.

"What are you playing at Will?", Nadine demanded, sounding angry.

"Think about it Nadine. Why do you think Paslan looks so young and yet has been a senior professor for over thirty years? Have you noticed Fenfrew's books I've been reading? Some of them date back to the 1800's. Now listen", his voice was firm.

He led them up the last bit of the path that crested at

the top of the hill. He could now see clearly all the way to the horizon. Will turned to see where Nadine was looking. She too was looking out to the horizon.

"Our friends are people who have learned about Time." He kept looking at her to see what was registering. She had a far away look like she may be seeing something beyond the horizon. He smiled.

"Fenfrew is quite upset with himself. If he had invented these binoculars before this, more people would have looked out further, seen deeper down, and figured out who Bale is. We might be back at Edinbridge and just visiting the Other World."

"Will I'm confused. You're jumping around from time to binoculars. Can you stay in one place?"

"You're listening now", he laughed. "Okay . . . it's kind of like this. Why do we come back home? When children grow up and move away why do they come back home and some stay home?"

"Well because their families are there, they have memories of growing up with people, and of places," Nadine said.

"Yes, they have memories there. Those memories are like fine binder twine that forever tug at their heart and pull them back. The memory is something that was and in a way still is a part of them. They have to reconnect for the sake of the whole. So it is with time. It is as Time is the center or core thread in the binder twine and we are connected in Time through the memories we hold. For someone like Paslan and Fenfrew, people with excellent memories, a deep interest in history and time, they hold within them very strong twine that twins them to Time."

"Is it the same thing to say that it twins them with the past?", Nadine asked.

"Rather than being attached to the past it is that they

are connected in Time with the past and then of course the future, though it is a different relationship. The better connection one has with the past the better one is connected with the present. The more present and engaged we are with the present the better too we can be connected with the future. In a simple way when we lose 'interest' in the present we lose connection with the future," Will said.

" . . . like old people who lose family members and then lose interest in life?", Nadine said this with a question in her voice.

"Yes very much like that", Will said.

"What is the relationship one who is twined with Time has to the future?", she asked.

"Ah now that is interesting. He helps create it", said Will.

They were sitting on a large flat rock on the top of the hill with the horizon stretched out before them. The rock was a perfect seat and it crossed both their minds in that moment that others had stopped and sat here before them. The sun was warming them, the trees below were still and the horizon invited them forward to contemplate the beyond.

"The future unlike the past is not to be seen exactly. It beckons us forward with a degree of anticipation directly proportional to our interest in it. Its mystery too, interests us, almost separate from ourselves. This is our interest in life beyond ourselves."

Will paused and pulled at some grass with his long elegant fingers. He showed Nadine the white roots which he then proceeded to munch and offered some to her which she declined, wrinkling her nose. She sat quietly waiting.

"Fenfrew and Paslan see outlines of the future which I think they both would say is given to anyone who really cares and pays attention to life in the present. And there is an important nuance here, anyone who cares about life itself not just their own. I've been thinking that this is a big advantage Paslan and Fenfrew have over Bale and Rong. Bale's ambition to control so much is, in his eyes, his ticket to help write the future. Rong seems to understand more, though I'm not sure what exactly her understanding is."

Nadine had been listening and gazing out over the trees and valley. For the last few minutes her eyes had rested on a spot a few miles off to their right. She had just realized that something had caught her attention there.

"Will look over there past the taller trees on the right before the first hill in the distance. What do you see?"

"I'm not sure I see where you are pointing", Will said as he squinted out over the landscape.

Nadine shimmied over to Will and taking his arm and grasping his hand she stretched it out along the length of her own. "There now look along the line your arm and forefinger make and tell me what you see", she demanded.

"What is that?", he suddenly exclaimed and stood up.

They stood together side by side looking at the spot.

"It looks like the land has been disturbed there", Will said slowly and hesitantly.

Nadine's voice was slow and deeper than normal, "I was waiting to see if you would say that." Then she said, "I had a dream the first night we were here. There was a horrible grating sound. It was the same sound that I had heard once before at Edinbridge. And in the dream when I went to look from where the sound came the earth had been disturbed. There were trees downed and partially burnt."

He took her hand and said, "Let's go."

They started to run down the hill towards the spot. They ran for a few minutes and then slowed up to a fast walk.

"What do you think it is?", Will asked.

"I'm sure that it is Rong, that this time she has arrived", Nadine said with the courage of one facing reality. Then she asked Will, "What do you think she really wants here?"

"I don't know. That's something I've been asking myself for a while. In a way I think that she is a very brave person. I think she has courage to learn and understand. She is very different than Bale in that way. I imagine they are both as smart as each other in the typical form of intelligence but she has another intelligence, a curious and inquiring mind. And if she truly wants to know what is, if she is not side tracked by a driving ambition or a blinding lust for power then she . . . well it makes her very interesting."

They were within a quarter of a mile of the spot. All their senses were on the alert.

"Do you smell that - a burnt grass smell?", Will asked.

"Scorched earth I'd say", she replied.

"I've got an idea", Nadine said suddenly. "We could fly over the site and see more."

"You can fly over if you like", Will said in a 'I'm not flying and that's final' manner.

"Okay then I'll take a look", and with a run and leap she was in the air and over the trees.

As soon as she was off the ground the joy of flying flooded back to her. Even the anxious uncertainty of what she might learn left her as she flew. The ability to dip and dive with confidence, the freedom of effortless movement was utterly exhilarating and dispelled the anxious anticipation of meeting up with Rong. She circled around and lowered herself to see what she could see. There was a circle of earth gouged out of the landscape. Below Will was walking to the west part of the gouge. The darkened spot was about twenty feet in diameter. There was an oblong line of tore up ground extending out about a third way round from where Will now stood. Trees had been broken off at their tops and branches bent and scorched.

"What . . . . . . see from. . . ?", Will shouted up. The breeze brought her bits and blew other words away.

She circled around the gapping hole and torn earth a few more times asking herself what it meant. While there was no indication of how this patch of earth came to be like this she could tell by the green of the newly tore branches and the burnt smell that it was very recent. And she knew inside her that Rong had arrived. The dream had told her so too for that harsh grating sound she had heard was the same one she had heard before when she had found Rong in Paslan's study. There were so many questions. How had she been able to get here, through what means and conveyance? Why, was she here, what did she intend? Most importantly, what did it mean for the Other World?

She flew low and landed very neatly beside Will. Will, stumbling backwards to get out of the way, looked impressed at her neat landing.

She laughed, "You are so funny about flying."

He frowned and exclaimed, "Funny!"

"It *is* funny. With all your science knowledge you'd think you'd be aerodynamic up there and ready to try all sorts of stunts."

"We have two legs and in case you hadn't noticed these are arms", raising his voice as he motioned with his arms, "Not wings. But if you keep up this flying business maybe you will grow some", his voice was now almost a shout.

"You're jealous Will", she said softly.

"I'm not", Will sounded angry. "And besides why are we arguing. What did you learn up there?", he asked changing the subject.

"It's just happened. I can't tell what has done it. Could she have come in a vehicle of some kind?"

Will was shaking his head, "I don't see that. What did you say about a harsh grating sound?"

"The same sound that awakened me at Edinbridge was the sound in my dream. I'm pretty sure this", she pointed to the downed trees and scorched earth, "is directly related to the sound."

Will stood silent looking at the scorched area and said. "Could this be a reaction of her arrival? I don't understand it yet I don't see what else it could be. She has got to have arrived by something of the same way we all did, by light. Yet something else is very different."

"Let's head back, I don't think we can learn anymore here and this is not a pleasant place", Nadine said as she tugged on Will's arm to get them out of there.

They started their walk back the way they had come. As they were leaving the area they heard a rustling above them in the trees and looked up to see a family of squirrels scurrying along from tree to tree. Two larger squirrels were leading the way and three little ones were following. They were scurrying in the same direction Will and Nadine were walking. As they watched the squirrels got far ahead of them and then were out of sight.

"It wasn't organic", Will repeated his thought aloud.

"We've got to talk with Paslan and Fenfrew. Do you think they will know what has happened?", Nadine asked.

"When Paslan showed up that night you found Rong in his study what did he say?", Will asked.

"He said he'd take care of it. That's when Rong was

out cold lying on the floor. He told me to go back to my dorm and get some rest," Nadine replied.

"Did he say anything to you about it later?", asked Will.

"No and I didn't ask. I could see that he was very disturbed and I guess I didn't want to remind him," she said.

The light had changed. There were few clouds yet the sun didn't seem as bright. It must have been about ten o'clock when they left after breakfast and they'd been gone maybe an hour and a half. If anything the sun should be brighter now. They were walking faster and she sensed that they both wanted to get out of the forest. Above a flock of birds circled and then flew on away from the forest.

"Let's find Paslan right away and tell him", Nadine said as they came out by the gap in the bushes beside Terhaven's side lawn.

"You find Paslan and I'm going to talk with Fenfrew", Will said.

Just then Paslan arrived at the French doors of the house as though he had been waiting for them.

"You have been to the forest", he said and motioned them to the chairs on the porch. "Tell me everything", he said. "I know about the scorched earth."

Will nodded to Nadine to tell what they had seen.

"Paslan I'm sure that Rong has arrived", Nadine blurted out.

"Yes she is here", Paslan said simply.

There was a big intake of breath from Will and Nadine as their thoughts were confirmed.

"So you know", Nadine said. And in a low voice, "What does it mean?"

"Not just now", he replied. Then he said, "Please tell me everything you saw in the forest." Nadine related everything she remembered and the way she saw it from the air. Will gave his additions.

"And on the way back, did you notice anything?", Paslan asked.

"We noticed a family of squirrels scurrying along beside us hopping from tree to tree leaving the forest", she said.

"And just now a flock of birds flew out of the forest", Will added. Paslan nodded.

"We've got to tell Fenfrew", said Will. "He will have some ideas."

"I'm afraid Bartholomew is not feeling well and is resting", Paslan's face was expressionless.

"Will, I wonder if you would join me in my study? Would you share with me some of your thinking and discovery on the Opposites Magnet?", Paslan said simply.

Will did not hesitate, "Yes Professor Paslan. At what time?"

"Let's say half past three shall we and there will be some of those scones you like so well for tea. So plan to have your tea with me. I must go now. I wanted to see you as you returned from the forest", Paslan said as he stood to leave. He turned back for a moment and looking them both in the eyes said, "Be extra aware, and be careful", and he was gone.

Paslan sat on a chair next to the bed facing his old friend. "I feel ridiculous propped up in bed with pillows at this time of day", Fenfrew said.

"Well I don't know why. We can have the same conversation here as we'd have in the library downstairs", replied Paslan.

It was about 10 O'Clock in the morning and the two professors had been in conversation for two hours.

"I feel fine", Bartholomew said as he impatiently threw off the duvet and sought to get out of bed.

"Good I'm glad to hear it", Paslan replied. "And resting has a lot to do with it", curbing any ideas in his friend's mind about getting out of bed. "You did not feel fine last night."

Slowly the old inventor replied, 'No, I did not." There was a pause then he said, "We really hadn't anticipated anyone being able to get in . . . anyone who is not supposed to be here", he added.

"If we had we might have had the Opposites Magnet in place and she would have been repelled", Paslan replied.

"Would that have been the right thing to do?", his friend asked. "Our decision was that it was not."

"For one thing you would not be lying there right now", Paslan said firmly. Hale Paslan looking very serious said, "How do you think she got in?", he started with a question.

"I think it is what you think. There is an element within her which would naturally permit her entry, an element that has been corrupted. While corrupted by her associations and choices that element still exists and with a lot of figuring and calculations she managed to use it as a springboard to get here", Fenfrew said.

"And I think she understands why she had such difficulty", Paslan added.

"What is she going to do is the question", Fenfrew said.

"Yes . . . what is motivating her?", Paslan asked another question.

"We know that she is very ambitious. You have met her. What would you say about her?", Fenfrew asked.

"I'd say that she hides who she is. When I invited her for tea after she first arrived at Edinbridge I don't think she said more than two dozen words. She was watching, watching me, watching as though we were in a scene and she wanted to keep the upper hand or at least not lose any ground. I'd say that she is proud."

"Alright. If she is proud she will be both somewhat humiliated facing us in having had to arrive as she did, and proud that she figured it out and got here first over any of her association", Fenfrew said.

"Yes, I agree", said Paslan.

"Do you think that she is hurt?", Fenfrew asked.

"I do not think that she is badly hurt. I think you took the brunt of her arrival", said Paslan.

"What we don't know is her relationship with Bale. Do you think that she is independent from him?", Fenfrew asked.

"I think that she is likely the most independent of the entire group. I think that she is very proud and would not kowtow to anyone. Over time sublimating one's own pref- erence to Bale's would be a certain necessity to maintain association with him. The question is has anything arisen which would have caused a confrontation between them? Because if so then she may now be a free agent. If not she is likely to be preparing to bring them all here."

"I think that you are right Hale. How do we find out which is the case?", said Fenfrew.

"We ask her", his friend replied simply. Fenfrew smiled at the simple sagacity of his old friend. "She is in the forest and I will go in and find her," Paslan said. Fenfrew moved his hand in dissent but his friend continued, "She can not harm me Bartholomew. We need to learn what she is thinking. The others can not arrive here at least until the Opposites Magnet is complete. We can't have you dying old fellow, not before your time."

As their eyes met you would have seen, if you had been there, the twinkling of stars lighting many many years of history. You might have seen times and places created between them, past passed into present, that which was newly created, and a glimmer of what was to be.

CHAPTER TWENTY ONE

THE WHITE STAG

At twelve noon a tall strong slender man with an unusual presence appeared on the bank of the remembrance of the Dedham Vale stream in Suffolk county England. This spot along the stream was on the far westerly part of the forest. He stood still and tall listening.

In the moment of his arrival no sound from the birds could be heard. As he stood on the bank a young whip-poorwill flew into a nearby tree and began to sing. A few moments later a young robin stopped on a nearby branch, peered at him, seemed to smile, and then set about looking for worms. A few more minutes passed and if one listened closely the natural sounds of the forest returned. Squirrels began to forage and further up the hills the deer moved about again. One particular deer, a large strong white stag, came to the crest of a hill and looked out over the valley toward the most westerly part of the stream at the edge of the forest. The man walked into the forest following an unseen path to his purpose.

Rong had barely managed to climb out of the pit and in the dark she had scraped herself several times in doing so. Once out she had collapsed in a heap and slept until morning. Now having washed in the stream she tried to collect herself. She had been shaken by the arrival. However in learning that she was, other than the scrapes, physically unhurt, she was regaining her composure. Yet this is not how she would have liked to have arrived. She had calculated arriving at the center of where the Traces had indicated people were living. Paslan and Fenfrew were likely located there. And she would have liked very much to have announced herself more elegantly.

But now I'm here, she said to herself. Wouldn't Bale be surprised, and she laughed aloud. He had no idea. He was still pursuing Ho Liu, thinking that he would get them to the Other World. What was Avaricis thinking? Avaricis Bale snubbed me. He had tried to roll right over me. He had decided that I was not the one for the project of projects. He was wrong. Bale was not as smart as everyone thought. Su Su Rong knows better. She could do it without Bale. If Bale thought he could take over here . . . . I can not get Bale out of my mind. I should be planning my next steps. I'm here and that is worth celebrating. But I cannot celebrate with Bale. Even if he had let me be to get them here, Avaricis was not one for pausing to celebrate - always on to the next thing, gaining ground, seeking more and more power.

She sat on a tree stump near the stream where she had washed. It was the first time she had sat down to take in her surroundings, perhaps ever. The sun was warm and she was almost dry. Yesterday she had fallen asleep so quickly as though suffering jet lag. This morning it had taken some time to scrub herself clean. She stood and stretched her limbs.

The grass around the stump was flat and soft and she sat down on the earth and leaned her back up against the stump. As she let her mind relax she began to think about her parents and how they were doing back home. She hadn't been in touch with them since the first few weeks after arriving at Edinbridge. She'd been too busy. There had been people to meet, classes to teach, and lots of work to do on figuring out the Opposites Magnet. As she thought about it, the work would have gone much faster if Will would have worked with me. But of course why would he work with me? He wanted to do it on his own. Get the credit for himself. Well perhaps that wasn't so. He would have worked on it most likely with Fenfrew if he could have. But Fenfrew wasn't around. But I was around. Her temperature rose as she thought about it. Why wouldn't Will work with me? He doesn't like me. And why not? He knew I was working with Bale. And she was beginning to see why people did not like Bale. What if I hadn't been working with Bale? Would the brilliant Will Hamlet have worked with Su Su Rong then? She thought about this for a few minutes. She wasn't sure.

She wondered how her parents were. Would they be proud of her accomplishment? She wasn't sure about that either. She knew that they missed her and that they would be interested in what she was doing. She felt alone. She missed them too. She missed her mother and the dinners she would make for her, especially her favorite meal, war wonton soup and greens with fried shrimp. She was hungry and would like very much to sit down at her mother's table and eat and talk with her mother and father. What am I going to do now that I'm here? The plan had been Bale's. Now there is no plan. What do I really know of Paslan and Fenfrew? I know that I would have liked very much to have shared notes with Fenfrew when I was working on the Opposites Magnet. It would have been less frustrating, more stimulating. It could have been fun. She smiled. She got up from the ground and looked around. How far was she now from the community? It was walking distance she knew. Then it struck her. While she could walk there she was not a part of where she was headed.

She had never thought of being welcomed but suddenly she understood that she was in no way part of the community. She had left her community in China. Her ambitions had come between herself and her community. She felt disturbed by this recognition.

She paused to note which direction she was facing. Then she began to walk west leaving behind the downed trees and pit. It was quiet along the path she took. Perhaps she had expected to see little animals, squirrels, chipmunks, or a rabbit. Only the trees, quite still, accompanied her travel. Ahead of her rose a broad steep hill. She mopped her brow of perspiration as she began the ascent. She realized that she was quite out of shape having spent little time out of doors. Half way up she paused for breath. What was she doing?

Did she think that she could dominate these people? If anything Su Su Rong was realistic, practical. Should she go back? Could she go back? She was not very good at imagining yet she could certainly see that going back now was impossible. She would prefer to never set eyes upon Avaricis Bale again. So she set her eyes to the top of the hill and made her way upward.

For another hour she scrambled and plodded and paused and rested and scrambled upward some more. She came to the top of the hill out of the trees and into warm sunlight. The vista of the valley spread before her. And there in the center of the plateau stood the white stag.

"Ohh", she said aloud, surprised and frightened. She took a step back and then stood very still looking at him. He was looking at her. It struck her that this was the first animal she'd seen. He was unusual she thought. He was so white and very tall. He stood looking at her and this disconcerted her. Somehow as she collected her thoughts she would have expected him to have run away. She was wondering now if she could run away. But for some reason she remained, rooted to the spot.

"Hello Su Su", came a deep rich resonant voice.

She jumped. There a few yards to the left of the stag stood Hale Paslan.

Rong stared. What had she expected? Not this. She thought she'd surprise them where they lived. But Paslan had found her, surprised her.

"Hello", was all she could get out.

"You don't appear to be hurt", he said.

". . . no, no I'm not hurt", she replied.

He smiled, looking at her. She had never noticed his smile, she'd never really noticed his face before. He was so young looking. This was different for a westerner. He must be fifty something, older than her. But he looked younger.

"Why have you come?", he asked.

His question was so simple and it came so easily. She was caught for words. Then she said,

"I . . . I've been working on coming . . . working on the Opposites Magnet . . . for some time . . .", she stopped, surprised at herself for saying this.

"Yes", he waited for her.

"I had to get here. . .", she stopped again.

She realized that the stag had not moved, he was watching her. She was getting more and more uncomfortable.

"And now that you are here . . . ?", Paslan spoke.

She had been watching the stag and now she looked at Paslan. She paused and took a few deep breaths. It struck her that the air was clean, very clean. She registered that quite a few things had been striking her this morning.

After a full minute she said, "I don't know."

The atmosphere on the plateau changed. The stag moved a step forward, just one step.

A light breeze came wafting across the area where they stood. Su Su Rong was able to remove her watchful gaze from the stag and look beyond to the vista spread before her.

"What is your relationship with Bale?", Paslan asked.

This time she was able to answer without hesitation, "I no longer have a relationship with Bale."

Paslan had not removed his gaze from her eyes.

"Bale does not know I am here. Although it must be that he will know soon," she found herself continuing and then adding, "He went to replace me on the Opposites Magnet", her voice was fiery.

Paslan nodded his head. "And now. . . why are you here?"

"I don't know", she said again. "I only know that I can not go back."

They were all standing, but for Fenfrew, on Terhaven's porch at the back of the house facing the forest. The three of them walked out of the forest together. The tall man with the unusual presence stopped. And the woman and the stag stopped in the next moment.

The three looked to the porch and their eyes went immediately to the tall woman and then to the others. Terhaven stepped forward. Then Paslan continued up to the porch. The stag stopped short of the house and so did the woman. She looked to the stag for she could not hold the eyes of the tall woman. The stag gave her a slight nod and this gave her what she needed to walk forward. Then Terhaven stepped down off the porch onto the lawn with them.

"Welcome to my home", she said and smiled at Su Su Rong.

It was a long uncomfortable silence that even Paslan was not in a position to help. Su Su Rong stood facing the house unable to face Terhaven. Terhaven waited patiently. A breeze seemed to come up from the depths of the forest, almost as a huge sigh. The leaves of a book David had left open on the porch rustled and the french doors leading into the house swung gently back against the sides of the house to be completely open. Rong seemed to notice this, and perhaps taking it as a sign, took a step toward the house. In the next moment Terhaven was beside her taking her arm and the two of them walked up the porch steps together and into the house.

Nadine, Will, David, Jane, George, and Sarabeth stood still, silent, looking at Paslan and the stag. Paslan's face was calm and serious and for a moment he looked at them and said nothing. The stag stood unmoving. Then Paslan moved toward them up the porch steps. Nadine came round to be beside him and David moved over to him. The others gathered around, standing close in beside him.

"Are you . . . alright?", Nadine asked with a catch in her voice.

"Yes my dear I am fine", he replied warmly and put his arm around her shoulders.

She couldn't help herself, for a moment she lay her head upon his shoulder, actually just beneath it as Nadine is not too tall and Paslan is rather tall. "I'm so glad, we were terribly worried", she said softly. The white stag turned and moved silently back into the forest.

"Professor how is Professor Fenfrew?", Will's voice came unsteadily.

"I was quite concerned about our old friend", he said. "However", and Paslan looked to the direction Terhaven and Rong had gone, "I have a feeling he is feeling better already.

CHAPTER TWENTY TWO

A STRANGER

Terhaven was in the kitchen with her new guest. "Shall we help with lunch?", Jane asked Paslan.

"Yes, I'm sure that would be very nice", he replied.

Jane went to the kitchen and the others took seats at the table. No one said anything. In a few moments Jane stuck her head in the doorway, "Sarabeth would you prepare the juice with the juicer?"

Sarabeth jumped up and joined Jane. Then Paslan got up and said, "You all seemed to like my omelettes the other day - I think I'll make them now", he said with alacrity and was in the kitchen.

"Well I'm going to make some toast", Nadine burst out. "I feel like toast don't you?", she looked at Will. "Besides I like the butter all melted in and for that you've just got to get it straight out of the toaster, butter ready", she said all this in one mouthful and was in the kitchen before she'd finished speaking.

George said to Will, "Well I don't want to be left out, I'm dying to learn what is going on in there, there must be something I can do", and he got up and went to the kitchen.

Just as David said, "I think that it must be getting crowded in there", Fenfrew appeared off the end of the porch.

"Professor", Will exclaimed and stood up.

"Hello, is there room for me?", he asked the two. "I'm very hungry", he said and smiled at Will.

Will's happy voice said, "There's plenty of room", and he pulled out the chair beside him for his old friend.

Just then Terhaven and Rong appeared together from the kitchen. Terhaven had a huge plate full of bacon and ham and placed it in the center of the table. Su Su held an enormous pitcher of juice with both hands. Seeing Fenfrew, she stopped. Will had a deja vous moment, for just as she had stopped in front of the house unable to move forward, now too it was as though she had nowhere to go. Then Will saw a lovely smile come to Fenfrew's face. Rong came over to Fenfrew's side of the table and stopped. She looked directly at Fenfrew and said,

"Sarabeth has made juice", she hesitated. Will thought, she is not going to finish what she was about to say.

" . . . would you . . . may I pour some for you?", Su Su finished.

Fenfrew looking at her took up his glass and beaming those wonderful dark brown eyes upon her said, "Thank you I feel just like having some right now."

She poured a full glass for him. He held up the glass to her and said, "A toast to all present. May we know each other well and long, and may this be a home to all of us always", and he drank it down.

Suddenly everyone broke out talking. And if you'd been there you'd have heard such a clatter of tongues, laughter, and happy raised voices you'd have wanted to join in. They shared a very good lunch. The food seemed to be extra tasty. Perhaps it was the special interest each had in their part of the preparation. Perhaps it was the warm and fragrant breeze that continued to come out of the forest and through the open windows that set everyone in a particularly receptive

mood. Perhaps it was the people themselves who, appreciating the food, the fine atmosphere of Terhaven's home,
and the company, let their spirit rise to the occasion. Most
were curious, bewildered, and all were interested and
managed to welcome the new and unexpected guest, a
stranger really.

Chapter Twenty Three

Summer

The summer had begun and the days were long and luxurious, with whole days spent out of doors. Even the evenings, warm and filled with light until close to 10:30, were enjoyed by the edge of the forest on the lawn or the porch.

Rong was an excellent card player and taught them all Mahjong, all but Fenfrew. Fenfrew had traveled to the orient years before, he was telling no one how many years ago, and had been taught Mahjong by an old woman who cooked for the salt miners in Shanix China. Rong would play all night if she had three others to play with, betting and almost always winning except when Fenfrew played. Then it was an even battle. Many evenings though Paslan and Fenfrew would sit with Rong on one end of the porch deep in conversation, and then, the cards were left lying.

One evening in late summer Will was about to walk back to Fenfrew's when Fenfrew came round the corner of the porch. "I'll join you Will", he said, and sat himself down.

After Fenfrew was comfortably seated Will said, "We've all been wanting to ask you and Paslan about your conversations with Rong. We're assuming they are about Bale and his group."

Fenfrew smiled, "Yes you are right."

There was a pause. "We all would like to know. What is Rong telling you? What have you learned?", Will asked.

"Rong has not been in touch with Bale since she arrived. But she must be and soon. If she is to steer the situation she must have a plausible explanation for her absence. Of late we've been organizing that. Paslan wants to have a conversation with everyone . . .",

Fenfrew did not finish the sentence and began another.

"Let's walk back", Fenfrew said as he rose from the porch chair and Will stood with him. "I've got an idea for the ionization around the magnetic field." And the two walked home in close conversation as they were wont to be together.

The next morning all were assembled on Terhaven's back porch with breakfast laid on. A lovely little fresh breeze greeted each as they arrived at table and the clear blue sky promised another warm luxurious summer day. Paslan appeared after all were seated and had begun to eat.

"You won't mind if I don't join you in eating, other than some toast", he said this with the utmost decorum. "I had breakfast early with Rong." Fenfrew looked up from his eggs and sausage with one inquiring arch in his brow. And for response Paslan gave a slight nod of his head. Nadine did not miss this exchange and Paslan noticing, smiled at her.

"Rong has gone back", there was a slight pause, "for the time being", Paslan said. Everyone looked up and even Will stopped eating.

"Why?", Will and David asked simultaneously.

Paslan had seated himself next to Jane and looking initially at Fenfrew said, "We decided that Rong has to be in communication with Bale. It's a significant risk on her part. Bale is very powerful now and may use any means to remove anyone he thinks is in his way. We think that she can convince him that she tested the travel here and laid the groundwork and now it's ready for Bale. There is no question that Bale intends to come here and take control of what he believes is a new frontier for him. We do not intend to stop his entry."

Paslan stopped to butter his toast. All eyes were on the jam pots as he paused to choose. When BlueBlackberry had won out a sigh went round. He continued.

"Rather we intend to fight", said Hale Paslan.

The general agreement was that Bale would waste no time in getting to the Other World. The question became in what manner would they fight. Fenfrew and Will had initially felt that they would repel the entrance with a reverse effect using the Opposites Magnet which Su Su had helped them complete. However after much conversation they came to the conclusion that Bale, while deterred, would continue his machinations on the outside world and it was better to stop him once and for all.

"He is bringing Ginbreste and Hil Gore with him. He will take a look for himself and then I think go back and collect a retinue for the longer term infiltration", said Rong.

She sat by the fire in Paslan's study. Paslan sat across from her.

"What is Bale's thinking?", he asked her.

"He is very heady with all his conquests. He can not think that anyone can stop him."

"My initial concern is Fenfrew", Paslan said. "As co-creator of the Other World he is most susceptible to intrusive entry."

"Fenfrew and Will and I have been working on demagnetizing the envelope around the Other World. It makes intrusive entry easier which sounds an odd objective yet I know you can understand that if Intrusives are coming, better that their entry cause less damage", she said.

"There is something else", Paslan said. "There is an unseen fortification that is an essence within the Other World, an energy that began with the creation of the Other World. It has grown as each new member of our community has arrived. Like the tradition at Edinbridge that kept Bale at bay for some time, this essence can not be touched by Bale. He is unaware of it and therefore does not have the opportunity to begin to understand it. This energy serves those who would serve the foundational principles of the Other World."

As Rong sat across from Paslan looking at him and listening, a feeling she had never experienced arose in her. She felt lighter, healthier. In place of a driving anxious forceful ambition which she had always felt there was a calmer and surprisingly stronger feeling. Then it dawned on her, she was enjoying the moment. While she might not have been able to put it in these words, she had gained an appreciation for life. Two small tears came to her eyes. Embarrassed she looked away, out the window. Had Paslan noticed? She hoped not.

"What do you think is the best way to fight Bale?", Paslan asked her.

She was looking at Hale Paslan in a completely different light. A deep respect for this man welled up within her. This too was a new sense. Here she was, now received in Paslan's study, invited to be with him here and welcomed in conversation with him. And as this recognition came to her so did another. There had never been respect for Bale. Rather it had always been a competition, a frantic, anxiety ridden race to prove something, to achieve, and with no vision in sight. She realized too, that there had never been fulfillment in all these years. She had never felt any happiness.

"I don't know", she replied. And then added, "Yet."

Tilting his head a little to one side a small smile arrived on Paslan's face. Then he nodded. And left unsaid was the reflected word . . . Yet.

The four sat at the conference table in the Principal's study. Bale sat slightly slouched in the new chair he had had placed for himself there. McLellan's tall noble looking old chair sat by itself in the corner of the room. Hil Gore and Ginbreste huddled close to Bale on opposite sides of the table looking excited and ready to tackle any challenge he might toss their way. It reminded Rong of dogs waiting for their bone. She sat one down from Hil Gore watching and listening.

"You can take us safely into the Other World then is that correct?", Bale inquired curtly of Rong.

"Yes", she answered simply.

"Are they expecting us?", Bale's voice was cynical and his mouth moved into a sneer.

"Yes. I imagine they think we can all talk it out", she replied.

"You imagine?", he mocked her. "Talk it out?", he guffawed. Then he laughed at the mere idea.

Rong checked herself. She had never used the word 'imagine' before. Bale had picked that up but he had lost it as the ridiculousness of the idea of talking things out had struck him.

Hil Gore spoke up, "Tiny, Mally, and Snatch are chomping at the bit to be in on this. Are we going to let them join us?"

"I will not let them join us, not at this time.", said Bale. Hil Gore stifled a rebuttal and a frown.

"I'd like to keep a low profile and begin immediately on establishing the laws and our order of things for the Other World. I see myself quite in the background while I dig the foundation for the future we see", said Ginbreste with confidence.

Bale looked cross and piqued at Ginbreste as though Ginbreste should only speak in reply and not initiate. As he contorted his mouth into another sneer about to retort Bale stopped himself seeming to change his mind and said, "Fine."

"We leave tonight", Bale said decisively.

Rong sat waiting she knew not for what. Something had told her to go to Paslan's study. Somehow the door had opened for her. She had come prepared to break in again. Though as soon as the door opened she knew stealing in was the wrong thing to do. She was going through so many changes now. It was as when she was a little girl and her grandfather had taught her her numbers and had taken her on long walks in the country.

"Su Su", she could hear his calm kind voice, "why do the little white flowers grow so happily here?" He was always asking her questions, funny questions, the kind no one else asked. Perhaps she had been happy then, on those walks with her grandfather.

She was startled from her reverie as she felt someone near. She turned and there was Paslan his tall straight figure standing in the center of the room. He smiled at her.

"You were right to come here", he said. Then he gestured for her to sit by him at the hearth. And as he did a small fire leapt alive in the space beside them.

"Bale intends to go to the Other World tonight with Hil Gore and Ginbreste", she said.

Paslan nodded. "Are you alright to bring them?", he asked her.

"Is that what you want me to do?", she replied.

"Yes, that is what we must do", he answered.

"Yes then I am ready", Su Su said.

"If Bale sees that you are now with us it will be most dangerous for you. Be aware." Paslan was watching her. She nodded.

"Bring them to my study when you are ready to go."

"What? Do you want me to bring them here?", she sounded incredulous.

"Yes. It will give you credence. And it will make for a smoother trip", he smiled at her and she was reminded of her grandfather.

"Thank you", she said in great appreciation, and a little smile came to her face. She suddenly felt calmer, she looked prettier.

Su Su Rong led them down the corridor of the top floor of Chartwell Tower.

"I've never been up here", said Ginbreste.

Bale had moved out in front of Rong ever quickening his pace. He stopped at the huge old wood door with the massive brass knocker.

"How will we get in?", his voice was gruff and demanding.

Rong arrived at the door and as she did it began to open. For one moment Bale stood still his mouth open, his eyes betraying surprise and disbelief. Then he moved forward and pushed the door in his impatience. The huge wooden door stopped and so did Bale. He pushed again but the door was immovable. He looked angrily at Rong.

"What is this?", he snarled.

Gently she moved in front of the door and in spite of himself Bale moved aside. The door opened completely making room for all of them to enter. Rong walked to the center of the study. Hil Gore and Ginbreste instinctively followed her. Bale seemed stuck in place at the entry to the room looking most uncomfortable. The three looked at him. Then he seemed to find his feet and joined them. Rong spread out her arms to join her hands with Ginbreste and Gore who took hers with a slight hesitation. As Ginbreste and Gore each offered their other hand to Bale there was a long awkward pause with their hands in the air as they waited for Bale. For a moment the three felt sorry for Avaricis Bale who looked so out of place not knowing what to do. Then Rong pulled Ginbreste and Gore together joining their hands. She moved across to Bale and took his right hand in hers and looked pointedly to Hil Gore to take Bale's left hand, while she took Ginbreste's. Then she pulled them all closer together. In another moment they were gone.

Chapter Twenty Five

Darkness

It was dark. The moon crept in and out of cloud cover. The tops of the trees swayed with the breeze, their leaves rustling. David and Nadine sat on the porch listening to the night. Will was with Fenfrew. They had demagnetized the envelope around entry and were together at Fenfrew's watching for the entry. Fenfrew was feeling better now. Paslan attributed this to Rong's transformation. The transformation of what had been a powerful negative energy into strong creative energy meant harmony again.

Terhaven and Jane had made a delicious meal for everyone and had gone directly to bed after dinner. Sarabeth and George were on standby should they be needed. While there was no certainty as to what tact Bale would take Paslan felt that either Avaricis would immediately confront them or hole up with his group and plan an attack. If the latter Rong could be compromised.

"David did you hear anything just now?", Nadine was leaning forward from the porch chair peering into the night.

"No. What did you hear?", he asked her.

"I don't know I thought I heard something from the forest. But if so it was nothing like what I had heard when Rong initially entered."

"It might be different this time", David said thoughtfully.

She turned to face her friend, "Why?"

"The change Fenfrew and Will have made to the envelope might make the difference. And then there is Rong, who is bringing them. She is in harmony now and so if they are joined with her - well - I'm just thinking", said David. Will appeared suddenly in front of them from the darkness.

"Oh! You gave me a start", Nadine said.

"What is it Will?", David said the next moment, as he registered concern on the face of his friend.

"It's Fenfrew. He is not well. They have arrived", Will fired the words out as three bullets.

The two stood up and Nadine spoke next. "Paslan must be prepared for this. We must tell". . ., she stopped.

"Paslan knows", David said. "They would have prepared together. What is Fenfrew doing?"

"He is alternately bathing and resting", said Will.

"Bathing?", Nadine and David asked simultaneously.

"Yes. While we were working on the magnetic field he was also concocting a solution. He invented a liquidized gel he calls Bartholomew's Brew."

"What is it?", Nadine asked.

Will looked at them and then said, "Dandelion extract and chewed lime rind."

"Is that why Alabaster has let the dandelions grow?", asked David.

David and Nadine laughed and then were suddenly quiet. David looked embarrassed at his own outburst and in the solemnity of the issue of Fenfrew's health and asked, "Is it working?"

"About thirty minutes ago he suddenly felt ill and the indicators told us that they had just arrived. He asked me to draw the bath pouring in the Brew and after one rotation from bed to bath he felt better. He's talking about looking like a prune but if he alternates from bed to bath every two hours he should be fine", Will told them. "The only thing is keeping this up over time", Will finished concernedly.

They all turned to the doorway of Terhaven's house. Paslan stood there in the flickering firelight from the great room.

"We will have to wait. When Bale makes his first move we will know something of his plan", Paslan's voice was calm, almost quiet. He sat down in a chair on the porch and they took seats beside him.

"Bale won't be long in making his move. My concern is Rong and Fenfrew and all of you."

He looked at each of them and his eyes were those of a father looking at his children seeking to provide for their care and protection.

"We will do our part", said Nadine simply.

David nodded slowly in complete confidence and certainty. Will's hands held the arms of his chair tightly, his face fixed in full determination. Paslan leaned back in his chair and they heard him sigh. I've never heard Paslan sigh Nadine thought.

Terhaven was standing in the doorway looking wonderfully calm.

"You all need some hot chocolate", she said and she was gone from the doorway into the kitchen. In a few moments she returned with a tray and five large tea cups of streaming brew. Will gulped deeply and when he came up for breath asked,

"What kind of chocolate is this? It is so good." And he quaffed it all off in his next gulp.

"Mmmm", Nadine was licking her lips. "What is this?"

"It is made from prize Brazilian cocoa beans and milk from Galago our prize goat", she smiled and sipped her drink. Paslan's eyes were twinkling at Terhaven and Nadine caught it. She said, "Wait a moment there is something else too."

"Tell us". . . , no response . . . "tell us . . . please?"

"Perhaps it is simply the way I make it for you", she said as she rose from her chair. In the next moment she wafted out with the empty tray and in another instant the light in the kitchen was out.

That night they all slept peacefully and dreamt of their favorite things. Will had just discovered a complete solution for all pollution and was happily distributing the product to the world. David was teaching students everywhere the thinking that awakens minds and hearts to live a good life. Nadine was flying to all the finest universities learning from the smartest and kindest professors around the world with Edinbridge as home base where her favorite professor Pasfrew, a funny cross of Paslan and Fenfrew, taught.

Paslan's dream is more difficult to describe. Imagine climbing to a verdant plateau and looking out upon a lush and colorful land of great beauty and then ascending up and off the plateau soaring to the horizon. Use this as an analogy to all the living of life that can be. This would begin to give you some idea of Paslan's dream. And Terhaven? Well remember she created that lovely hot chocolate drink.

CHAPTER TWENTY SIX

MACHINATIONS

"**P**aslan has to go", Ginbreste spoke matter of factly. He sat back in a casual posture with his legs outstretched before him and voiced his next thought.

"This is really all we need for the few days before we execute . . . our plan." He was looking around the small simply furnished house, a cottage really, which Rong had secured for them through Paslan. And now Rong, as she sat there with them, was listening and thinking quickly while keeping her face expressionless.

"I will take care of Paslan", said Bale with a note of both great irritation and delight. The irritation was for Ginbreste who should know better than to announce what Bale had intended all along, and the delight, for his own anticipation of the deed.

"What exactly is your relationship with Fenfrew?", Bale turned to Rong. "He will be the next to go." She waited an instant to see if they would just continue talking. But they waited for her reply.

"He works", an imperceptible pause, "on his own for the most part. He is beginning to include me", she added. Bale smiled slyly, repulsively.

"What of the rest of the community here?", Hil Gore

asked. "Will they go along with us once Paslan and Fenfrew are out of the way? They started their own community in order to live more closely with what they knew as best. I don't see them suddenly taking to us."

"Of course they will follow us. It is unimportant if they like it or not", this time Bale was matter of fact.

"It won't be as easy as that", Hil Gore replied.

Bale snapped his head around to her with a menacing look. "What do you mean", and this was not a question. Rong saw that this was the first time Hil Gore, perhaps anyone, other than herself, had pursued their own thinking with Bale. There was a pause then Hil Gore said, "It's wise to consider with whom we are dealing", she proceeded cautiously. "In our world people followed. The time was ripe for us because most people had stopped thinking for themselves." She stopped to let her point register. Then she continued, "Those who chose to come here are different", a sense of excitement and challenge could be heard in her voice. Rong watched Bale's face to see if he picked up on what Hil Gore was saying. She wasn't sure. She glanced at Ginbreste and he was oblivious. Suddenly she was reminded of Gradgrind in those books her grandmother had encouraged her to read. Like Dickens's Gradgrind Ginbreste was all about facts, nothing else moved him except facts, in Ginbreste's case, for the purpose of power. As a result he could not see who others really were and that was an interesting fact about Ginbreste. What was Hil Gore thinking?

"Enough", Bale said with absolute finality. Suddenly the room was silent.

"I will . . .", Bale stopped himself and continued . . . "we will move Paslan and Fenfrew aside and then we will be placed to deal with our new opportunity." Bale got up from where they were sitting together and went to the study, closing the door behind him. So he had recognized what Hil Gore was saying, at least he was aware that they were dealing with a different group of people here. And that he could use their help. If he could catch this, alter his perspective, would he catch that her own perspective had changed? Could he imagine that she, Rong, had shifted her sight lines completely - that she was no longer with him? She did not know.

Ginbreste got up the moment after Bale closed the door. He moved to the table by the window where he had set up his desk. He set instantly to work. Hil Gore had watched Bale until he closed the study door and then turned to look at Rong. She said nothing for two or three moments and then she said,

"What do you think of this group of people here? What will be their response to us?"

Rong took in a breath and said, "They are thinking people who care deeply about their way of life. They are involved in their own lives and care enough about their neighbors that they contribute to the community." She stopped, attentive to Hil Gore. Hil Gore nodded her head but said nothing. If she expected Rong would continue she was disappointed. Hil Gore looked at Rong again and this time she looked more deeply into the dark eyes that faced her. But Rong was inscrutable and for the first time Hil Gore saw that. Perhaps she realized in that moment that she had not paid very much attention to this woman. Just as Bale had not bothered to think about with whom he was about to deal in the Other World, Gore had been perhaps just a little too consumed with her own ambitions to learn more about those around her. Why then had she neglected this homework? As a result she had missed something she might not now be able to learn.

"Would you like to go outside for a walk?", she asked Rong.

The reply was instantaneous, "No thank you I will go for a walk on my own, which is what I do each morning", and she got up from the table and went out the door.

While it wasn't exactly true that she went for a walk each morning it was going to be true. This would be her time to breath and think and as she recognized this, this too would be how she would connect with Paslan. She moved instinctively to the forest. Its quiet beckoned her and there she would be free from watchful eyes. A narrow path opened up in front of her and she took it. She breathed deeply the fresh newly washed air from last evening's rain. A bird sang in a tree close by. What a good idea to take a walk each morning. She had wasted too many years in the laboratory from morning to night where each day passed unnoticed, unappreciated. As she rounded the curve in the path she came upon a little clearing and saw Paslan seated on a log by the edge of the stream.

"Good morning Su Su", he said and the warmth in his voice spread over her like sunshine.

"Good morning Paslan", she replied happily.

"How are you?", he asked and she heard his interest and care.

"I'm fine and glad to be out for a walk in this forest", she said.

"What a good idea. You had no trouble in getting out on your own?", he asked.

"No and I will do so each morning", she said firmly. And he nodded.

"Hil Gore has alerted Bale to the need to think about who they are dealing with here."

"Good thinking", Paslan laughed.

Su Su found herself laughing with him. Feeling a great

release she let herself continue laughing. She noticed that birds were singing in the trees above them. Paslan sat smiling and enjoying her laughter. A few minutes passed and Su Su enjoyed them very much.

"First they plan to move you and Fenfrew out of the way", she said simply.

"Yes we expected that. I imagine that Bale is figuring that out now. He will likely want to take me on himself. And Fenfrew . . ."

"He doesn't know that Fenfrew is weakened by their entry", she said.

"He will find out", Paslan replied.

"What can I do to be prepared to help you", her voice was softer.

"Watch out for yourself is the first and the main thing", he said.

He always looked right at her when he spoke with her and she had come to appreciate this very much. If she got into trouble they would come to help her and this she wanted to avoid. He rose. She got up and smiled at him, and Paslan smiled back. Then she went directly to the path to the cottage and walked out of the clearing. She turned to look over her shoulder. The clearing was empty.

The warm happy feeling of being in Paslan's presence surprisingly stayed with her even as she approached the cottage. She had expected the opposite, that as she came closer to her would be tormentors she would feel anxious and wary, and perhaps even fearful.

Hil Gore sat in the little living room and looked up from her laptop.

"How was your walk?", she inquired.

"It is lovely in the forest", she answered truthfully.

"You look refreshed", she said observing Rong closely. Rong smiled.

"Will you show me around? I'd like to meet some of our new neighbors", Hil Gore said.

Her request was so simple that Rong felt she could not refuse. "When would you like to go?

"No time like the present", said Hil Gore.

Rong took Hil Gore to the market, a practical trip where they could stock up on food they needed and where they would run into neighbors busily shopping. Perhaps too she thought it was a good idea that the neighbors get a glimpse of Hil Gore. While they were choosing vegetables she spotted a neighbor of Terhaven's Mrs. MacWilliams. Rong paused only a moment before deciding to engage her.

"Hello Mrs. MacWilliams you look like you know your vegetables", said Rong as she looked at the vast assortment the woman was carrying in her basket. Su Su avoided introducing Hil Gore and now waited to learn if she had diverted any necessity to make an introduction. Mrs. MacWilliams launched into her plan for making mulligatawny soup. And Hil Gore became another self. She was engaging, cheerful, and interested to listen to this elderly woman's plan for her dinner. Whether Mrs. MacWilliams was too delighted in the interest to bother to ask any questions of Hil Gore or whether it was politeness, Su Su did not know. Either way she was thankful that the encounter had gone smoothly. Hil Gore was on a roll. Once Mrs. MacWilliams had walked on she immediately addressed a man studying olive oil. After offering him advice she decided to change her tact.

"Would you introduce me to someone you know? You seem to fit in well here, you appear to be accepted, that is important", she said this firmly and paused for emphasis. "Bale may not appreciate this point. But he will come to see it." And the look on her face read that when he does I want to lead the way.

"I'll keep my eye open", Su Su replied succinctly. In fact she had been avoiding eye contact with a few gregarious types she'd spotted. Then over by the juices she saw Sarabeth. She decided to take a chance that Hil Gore had never seen Sarabeth at Edinbridge. And what if she had? It was likely important that Sarabeth gain an impression of Gore. And something told Rong that Sarabeth could handle herself.

'Sarabeth", she called to give her a moment before they arrived face to face.

"May I introduce Hil Gore", she tried not to make it sound too formal and she kept eye contact with Sarabeth. Sarabeth did not hesitate, the moment given when Su Su had alerted her by calling her name had been sufficient. Hil Gore had her hand out and was beaming saying,

"How do you do? What a fine market this is."

"Yes it is. I'm a great juice lover and the variety is exceptional", Sarabeth said happily surveying the juices.

"Buying them ready like this takes far less time than collecting all the ingredients and juicing", said Gore.

Sarabeth replied in a different vein asking, "How are you Su Su? Are you still working with Bartholomew Fenfrew?"

Su Su could have kissed her. Instead she said, "I'm well thanks. Yes we are working together."

Sarabeth smiled and responded, "I'm glad to see you." And then to Gore, "It was good meeting you", and set off down another aisle.

Chapter Twenty Seven

The Excelerator

Fenfrew had asked Nadine to come by his study. She was looking forward to seeing his home in the daylight. Once late at night Paslan had walked her over to deliver a dandelion bundle to his friend. All she could tell of the old professor's house was that it was small and cozy, filled with books, and had a lot of rather strange ornaments which Paslan told her were not originally ornaments. Rather they were bits of inventions which either had been advanced upon or were given him by other inventor friends over the years. Some were so old that the cobwebs were dusty and deserted, their owners having moved on.

Today Nadine had come by herself and she was secretly excited to get a chance to see the professor on his own. His little golden house sat amongst the trees, as all the houses here seemed to do. There was a well in the front section of the yard and Nadine stopped to look down it. The sparking waters seemed to shine up at her and this was surprising as she'd imagined a deep dark dank place. As she peered down she sneezed and then heard a voice say,

"Gesundheit und einen Topf voll Gelt."

She lifted her head up quickly in surprise wondering

at the well. There was Fenfrew waving cheerily at her from the open front window.

"Come in my dear", she heard him call.

"What did the well say to you?", he asked with a big grin. "It's been echoing through the ages", said Fenfrew.

"Oh . . . ", she replied. "Something like . . .Gesundtight gesuchfelt gelt"

"Oh you sneezed did you? The well wished you good health and a pot full of gold. Very good my dear", he nodded and laughed. "Now come over here I have something to show you", and he led the way to the back of the house.

"You seem very well professor", Nadine said and with an inquiring tone.

He smiled back at her, "Oh don't worry about me. I'm always happy coming up with a concoction or a brew."

The entire back half of the house was made over into a study and laboratory. It was an enormous open room with a desk at one end where all the books were. Starting in the middle of the room and extending to the other wall was a great assortment of equipment. He led her over to a large table on the lab side. Placed in the center of the table was a jumpsuit of sorts.

"Now do you think this will fit you my dear", he asked as he held it up to her.

"Fit me? Why ever for?", Nadine stood staring at the odd outfit. It was green, the color of trees and with odd sorts of shiny patches all over.

"Paslan feels that you should be able to fly as much as you would like and with our. . . new guests . . . you should be invisible", he said as he pulled at a loose thread on the sleeve.

"Oh I see!", she said, smiling now.

"Try it on", he suggested, handing it to her.

"It is so light, like a feather", she felt it sway gently in her hands, as though from a breeze you could feel but not see.

"Yes it is made of feathers", said the professor pleased that she had recognized the feathers, "and anti-visible creme", he added.

"Anti-visible creme?", she wondered aloud as she slipped off her shoes and began to climb into the suit.

"You've heard of anti-wrinkle creme? Well it is a little like that. How does it feel?", he asked what appeared to be the empty space in front of him.

"Oh my goodness!", Nadine's exclamation resounded within the room. "I feel light as air . . . And you can't see me can you?!", she said and her voice boomed forth and around the room.

"No I can not see you which is the plan. However I can hear you and did not anticipate the amplification nor the effect on the placement of your voice", Fenfrew was looking round the room with a perplexed furrow on his brow.

"I'm up at the ceiling now and doing a little loop de loop overhead", she laughed and her laughter boomed and bounced off the walls.

"Nadine I wonder if we should make a change. Would you like your voice to sound more natural?", he asked. There was no answer. "Are you here?", Fenfrew inquired of the space around him.

"I'm outside Professor", came a trumpet blast that shook the windows.

"Nadine", he called from the big window, "would you please come down here . . . now", he said firmly.

Something whooshed past him through the big window.

"Please take off your suit", he said as he turned to the

space in the center of the living room. In a moment Nadine appeared again before him, her hair somewhat disheveled from flight.

"Oh Professor . . . thank you so much", she said excitedly. "It is very comfortable and will keep me warm. It's funny, it makes the dips and dives easier. . . you'd think that the material would get in the way but it's the opposite . . . it seems to help lift me and make movements aerodynamic . . .". She would have gone on expostulating on the wonders of her new flying suit however Fenfrew cleared his throat and she stopped.

"Do you know the purpose of this suit?", he said slowly looking at her over the rim of his spectacles.

"No, Professor", she felt chastened.

"Paslan knows how you enjoy flying. With our new visitors perhaps it will become useful", and he held up the suit, "to be able to see and not be seen as you enjoy your flights."

"I see", she said.

"What do you think of the effect on your voice? Can you hear the change?", the Professor asked.

"I don't think I hear what you hear. I did though have a sense of greater power in my voice", Nadine replied.

"Hmm." Fenfrew had taken the suit over to the light and was turning it over in his hands. "This suit has a name", he said still holding it up to the light. Then he turned and walked back over to where Nadine now stood quietly. "The Excelerator. It is called the Excelerator for a reason my dear", he said looking directly at Nadine. "When you put this on you are expected to excel", he began. "Your best is asked of you. If we did not have the company of our visitors this suit would not be required. You could enjoy your flying without having to think about it. You are right this suit gives you extra powers and with them come extra responsibility." He was looking at her very seriously and she was listening.

"Yes Professor", she said looking down at her stocking feet.

Will sat beside Nadine on Terhaven's porch. They were alone. Terhaven was attending a Tree and Garden outdoor dialogue in Green World, a world established not long after The Other World and to which few visitors were invited, neither Paslan nor Fenfrew had ever been. Paslan had not said where he was going, no one had asked of course but they both thought he'd gone to Edinbridge. Fenfrew was resting. George and Sarabeth had wanted to visit their families and before leaving Paslan had arranged the journey for both of them. David had gone back as well to meet with a publishing house interested in his thesis Plato and God. Jane was having lunch with a neighbor.

"It's good to be seeing you around more Will", said Nadine.

"Fenfrew is changing his mind about how to fight them", he said simply. "So we're not investing as much time in the lab. The other day we went for a walk. And we didn't talk about anything we've been working on." Will turned to Nadine and he looked slightly forlorn.

She laughed. "Oh Will don't be upset by it. Did you enjoy your walk with Bartholomew?"

" . . . Yes . . . yes I did, it was different though. He started to tell me about his family."

"His family?", she chimed back.

"Yes . . . of course he has a family. I'd just never asked about them. He has two sisters and his brother died years ago. His parents aren't alive any more. He is American you know. I didn't even know that."

"Is he?" I thought he grew up in England with Paslan", Nadine sounded surprised.

"He came to England with his family when he was quite young. You could say that Paslan grew up with Fenfrew. Fenfrew is older, though . . ."

"Well he can't be that much older because I met them when they were young boys", she said.

"WHAT!", Will shouted.

Nadine laughed so hard at Will's reaction that she had to bend over and hold her stomach.

"What have you forgotten to tell me", Will shouted out again. ". . . Did you purposely leave this piece of information out? Was this one of your adventures in flying . . . in coming to The Other World before we all came?" Will was on a rampage and Nadine was still laughing.

"Stop your laughing", he demanded. "I would like to know about Fenfrew as a child."

Will's last sentence caught her and she stopped laughing.

"Of course you would. I'm sorry", she wiped her eyes of tears. "I'm going to get us some of Sarabeth's lemonade", and she sprang up and went to the kitchen. In a moment she was back and handed Will his glass. "Let's sit in the chairs", and she moved to one that looked out onto the crest of the hill where the view met the sky. Will joined her.

"The first day I came to The Other World Paslan took me here, to Terhaven's home. He and Terhaven were talking and I wandered around this house. In the parlor by the large oval table is a painting that caught my attention. As I was studying it I was drawn into the scene, literally. And the scene was of two boys fishing. I landed on the bank beside them and helped them reel in a big fish. Those two boys were Paslan and Fenfrew."

Will just looked at her for some moments. Then he said slowly, "What were they like?"

"Oh I don't know, I had never fished before and was engrossed in helping them reel in a big one. I was bigger than Paslan and Fenfrew", she laughed. "And we all just struggled to land the fish. Then I heard Paslan calling me and I landed back in Terhaven's room."

"Paslan called you . . . what do you mean?", Will asked.

"I mean he called me from the room where he and Terhaven were talking and I guess that called me back to … this time", she said. "So I didn't have much time with them. Yet it was the perfect time . . . as I think of it now. We were all equally engaged in the moment with that fish. Paslan was in the water, Fenfrew on the shore and I was half way between. We were all working to get that darn fish out of the water. We got wet. We had fun. So it is strange that you should say that Fenfrew is older", she was wondering aloud. "They seemed about the same age. But then I know what you mean because my experience with Fenfrew tells me he is older."

Will started in, "Up until recently we've been working on the Time Differentiator. Fenfrew had been working on this before I arrived. In fact he has been working on it for years and I mean years. When he and Paslan met in England Fenfrew was a man, not a boy. But just as you got to experience 'being a kid' with them at the fishing hole they decided way back that they should 'grow up together'. So they did", he stopped.

Nadine was taking this in, "So you mean that Fenfrew applied the Time Differentiator to . . . to . . . himself ?"

"Yes", Will replied.

"Whoa . . . so does that mean that he made himself a boy again for a time and then at some point resumed his true age?"

"You've got it", said Will. "And Fenfrew told me that he has never used it but that once to share the time with Paslan in the way that gave them what was needed to forge their friendship."

They looked out to the crest of the hill. The blue purple monkshood swayed amongst the tall grasses while the pure purple liatris stood tall against the sunlight. Scattered amongst all the purple was a stand of forsythia its delicate beauty showing in the yellows of its flower. The paler yellow of the petals and the deeper stronger yellow of the body made an exquisite contrast shining in the sunlight speaking out in stunning contrast to the greens and purples. This great beauty reflecting the heart of the friendship they now contemplated moved their own hearts. For it was the strength of this bond that had brought them here - to live free. And it would be the same strength which would find the way to move, or remove, their visitors. For if not ... this they could not contemplate.

The Excelerator seems to fit even better than it had when I first tried it Nadine thought after climbing into the suit Fenfrew had returned to her. She pulled up the zipper and the material closed in around her body concealing her from any and all eyes. Remembering her responsibility she added to her thoughts, this will be fun. And with that thought she was up and off.

She swooped and soared and dipped and dived for many minutes. The early evening was glorious. The breeze of the afternoon had gone and the air was still and warm and still summery. What a splendid way to enjoy life. After some fun her sense of responsibility kicked in and she decided to head into the forest and over to the visitors cottage to see what could be seen.

No one seemed to be about, at least outdoors. Nadine took three or four passes hoping to spot someone. It was all very quiet. She decided to land. Perhaps they were all inside and she could see through the windows. She landed on the path fifty feet from the door of the cottage. The windows looked empty but the daylight hid any view of the interior from this distance so she went up to the larger front window. She peered inside and no one could be seen.

Nadine walked to the smaller east side window to look in and there plain as day and three feet from her nose was Ginbreste working away at a large table by the window. She stepped back instinctively and a branch snapped under foot. Ginbreste looked up and out the window, staring right at her. She wanted to run but she held herself and remained standing in place. He went back to his work and she breathed a sigh of relief. I must be careful and remember that while they can not see me they will be able to hear me.

What is he working on she asked herself and moved closer to the window again. Many papers of charts and graphs lay in different piles on the table he was now using as a desk. One was entitled 'Gold', another 'Steel' and another 'Water'. He seemed to be working on what looked like an organizational chart with Bale's name at the top. Then she caught sight of her own name further down. 'Nadine Redwood' Disseminator of Propaganda for World Peace. Nadine almost struck the window pane with her clenched hand. She checked herself. Suddenly she heard voices behind her.

"Who were you speaking with in the forest this morning?", Bale's harsh strident voice asked.

Nadine turned slowly in place praying that another twig would not snap. There at the foot of the path to the cottage was Bale. He was walking with Rong toward the cottage. There was a pause which hung heavily in the air around them. What would Su Su say?

"Hale Paslan", she answered truthfully.

Bale stopped. He turned to her with a look of fury, "What were you doing talking with Paslan?", Bale's voice was low and steely.

"I know Paslan somewhat now and feel it essential that we learn what he is thinking and doing", she said and then added, "How else can we be prepared to deal with him?", her voice was self assured, convincing.

Now Bale paused. "What did you learn?", he asked. The fury had vanished and in its place was smooth and compelling inquiry. On the surface it sounded like the curiosity of a child if one was not listening too closely. But Nadine was listening closely and could see that Rong was too.

"He wants to talk with you", was all she said.

"So he wants to talk with me?", Bale's question was rhetorical for his pride was now in play.

Rong's bet had worked. She had set the trap and Bale's pride had led him to walk right in. Of course everyone wanted to be involved with Bale.

"And what does he want to talk about?", Bale hissed through his teeth. "Oh yes we will talk alright. I will talk", the conversation ended abruptly and Bale was monologuing now.

"Paslan can think that he will have a spot in this new regime if he likes. He can introduce me to everyone. He can talk as much as he likes about everyone and I will listen. I will learn who must go and who will follow my" ... he corrected himself, ... "our new regime."

Nadine could see a tiny smile arrive on Rong's face. Bale missed it. Bale was dancing with his pride and was oblivious to anyone else. But the false assumptions he was making about Paslan would not serve his end.

"Agree to a meeting. Arrange it for tonight", and he walked in front of her through the cottage door.

"It looks like you are right they are planning to take over the resources here, gold, steel, water", Nadine told Will.

"I wonder if Rong has reached Paslan about a meeting tonight?", Will asked aloud.

"Do you think Paslan will agree to meet?", Nadine asked in turn.

"I bet he's planned for this, yes he will be ready," Will replied.

Chapter Twenty Eight

Bale Offered Bail

At five o'clock Bale walked up the path to Terhaven's home. He would have preferred to have been picked up and driven over but learning that there were no cars in the Other World he walked. Fenfrew had invited everyone to his home to leave Terhaven's home free to facilitate the meeting Paslan wished to offer. The front door opened and Paslan stood on the threshold to greet his visitor.

"Hello Avaricis," Paslan said.

Avaricis nodded to Paslan, and made an attempt at a smile.

"I've set the table in the garden for our meal", Paslan said and gestured for Avarichis to follow the porch along to the back of the house.

"The weather is very good", said Bale as he walked along the porch and stepped down into the garden.

"Yes it is always quite lovely," Paslan replied guessing correctly that his guest was really inquiring into the general climate.

"Why are you here Avaricis?", Paslan said simply after they'd sat down and as he passed the meat dish to Bale.

"You have found a special place and I am interested," Bale replied as he took the plate of roast beef.

"Interested in what exactly?", Paslan asked as he dished vegetables onto his own plate.

"Let's not beat around the bush. I intend to take control of the exceptionally rich resources you have here for starters. I will bring them to our world and market them at very high prices. I think we can work out a percentage for you. Am I right in considering that you have no interest in bringing them yourself to our world?" This last bit Bale attempted as a gracious overture but his attempt failed.

"My interests do lie elsewhere. And I would like to apprize you of exactly what they are," said Paslan. And then he continued, "This world was created. The reason it can exist is the essence of why you can not take anything from it. You operate within a mechanical measurement system based in what you can get. Whereas the nature of things is based in what we give, namely ourselves."

Bale was disciplining himself to be polite. " . . . give ourselves . . . what do you give yourself?"

"It is what we give of ourselves. This world is created by and for one who knows oneself and takes personal responsibility to be themselves and thus act truly with all others. This world offers opportunity for those who would be their best and who seek to appreciate and understand life itself at a deep level. Rather than seeking comfort we seek to be the finest human beings we can be and in so being enjoy life most fully. Have you ever considered that you are taking the lazy man's way?"

"What do you mean?", Bale managed to reply evenly, evidently enjoying the roast beef and Yorkshire pudding.

"I mean that much more is required of us when we seek to uncover who we have been given to be. To thine own self be true, and it must follow, as the night the day, thou canst be false to any man", and Paslan smiled as he quoted Shakespeare.

Bale looked up confused for a moment and then reaching for another helping of roast beef said,

"Paslan you have always been a dreamer and I am a pragmatist. So we will work it out. I will be happy taking my resources and I will pay you a princely fee. And you will be happy too." This time his smile was real as he leaned back in Terhaven's comfortable chair and was really enjoying Jane's Yorkshire pudding and Paslan's choice of wine.

"Avaricis try and understand", Paslan's voice sounded sad. He spoke slowly, "You can not take the resources. They are not mine to give nor anyone else's to give. They exist here in the rich state you recognize because of the very nature of this world. They will not exist in the world to which you wish to take them and where you want to sell them."

"No I do not understand you", said Bale.

"If you persist in your thinking, in disallowing yourself to see that another way of being exists, you will cause inestimable damage to yourself and others", and Paslan sat back from the table.

The roast beef was finished. Bale had eaten three helpings. He became suddenly irritable.

"I will not be stopped and that is final", he said stridently and pushing back from the table he stood up to go.

"I am sorry", said Paslan. And he watched as Avaricis Bale strode away from Terhaven's home into the darkness.

CHAPTER TWENTY NINE

TERHAVEN ACTS

The day arrived grey and hazy. The individual fluffy white clouds usually seen were missing. Rather the sky was one grey mass, overcast with haze and gloom. The trees swayed indeterminately in a cold breeze that seemed to come from the center of the forest. Not a bird could be heard and even the stream seemed silent. Fenfrew was ill. The dandelion concoction had not been working the last few days and Paslan had decided to stay with his friend. They were working on a new brew but in the meantime Fenfrew needed to rest and Paslan was trying to keep him in bed. Will had moved to Terhaven's to be out of their way. Before Will left Paslan had assured him that he'd done his best. "We are prepared and now the only thing left to do is to be together", Paslan had said with the kindliest look in his deep brown eyes.

"Bale is planning to bring miners here to rip up the hills, mine the ore bodies, and bring it back to the old world", Will said this to the group now sitting on the porch after lunch.

"How is he going to get them all here?", asked George.

"He's got Su Su working on it", said Will slowly.

"What do you mean? How long can she fool Bale?", asked Sarabeth.

"Not long", replied Will. "Paslan is thinking of something, I imagine", he finished disconsolately.

Terhaven and Jane came round the corner of the house returning from Fenfrew's with empty dishes in hand. It was the first time any of them had seen Terhaven without a smile. Silently she moved up the porch stairs and into the house.

"She is worried about Fenfrew", Jane said as she stopped on the porch watching Terhaven's retreating figure. Will looked worried and shifted in his seat. Everyone looked concerned.

Jane said, "Terhaven's been coming up with new nourishing combinations of foods almost everyday and herbal remedies too of which I've never heard. I think she is creating them from all her knowledge of plant life. Fenfrew is very good about all these new dishes. He thanks her and says they help . . . but he isn't getting well", her voice trailed off.

Terhaven reappeared in the entrance to the french doors with Alabaster beside her. Her face was white.

"Alabaster has pulled these", she held up a handful of drooping dandelions, from the back garden. "They have been poisoned."

As she said these last words her voice became as a brewing storm unpredictable but most certainly about to rain down upon the malefactors. Everyone was silent. Terhaven's voice was as an entity onto itself, independent of all else but the woman who was its master.

For all their time together her voice had been a source of calm and had instilled a feeling that wisdom was with them and they were at home. Now this voice in its change was informing them that a great force had been stirred.

This force was rising to meet and fight those who would seek to harm the co-creator of this world. This was a force to quench evil with good. Those culpable for poisoning the earth and its inhabitants were about to suffer the consequences of their actions. Terhaven stood tall and still in the entrance to her home. Her energy, fired now with the force of nature, permeated the air. If you had been looking, the trees had stopped their indeterminate swaying and stood as still as the mistress of the forest, as if waiting for her command. The violet eye of the master of the brewing storm lit upon Will. Instinctively he stood. She did not speak withholding the power that was building within.

Will spoke instead, "I will go to tell Fenfrew and Paslan that the brew may yet work if fresh dandelions can be grown."

She nodded and he was off. Then she looked upon Nadine nodded to her and moved back into the house. Without a moment's hesitation Nadine followed her.

Twenty four hours later David was summoned to Terhaven's study. The door had been closed for some time. When the study door was opened, a smile had reappeared on Terhaven's face.

"Your herbal remedies must have helped counteract the poison. Thankfully Fenfrew took them conscientiously", David said as he sat with Terhaven in her study.

"I went to Su Su to ask her about old Chinese herbal remedies and her experience was enlightening," Terhaven said.

David nodded and then said, "Su Su is having a challenging time right now. She wants to be useful against Bale. If we can determine a way to engage her in having to defend them, Bale's focus on her will be dissipated. Perhaps in buying time we will also uncover a permanent remedy for Bale."

"Yes, ... the forest has been placed on standby", Terhaven said nodding.

David raised an inquiring brow, he could only imagine what this might mean.

Su Su Rong had been spending a lot of time behind the cottage planting and tending a garden. She had planned the garden in rows and sections and took great care to keep the sections separate. The herbs were doing very well, all that she had planted was growing happily in this earth. Only Terhaven knew that a special herb grown here was being given to Fenfrew to heal him of the poison.

Bale decided to send Rong back to Edinbridge to arrange for the miners. However rather than contacting the miners she met with Paslan in his study. The timing of Bale's dictate was fortunate because as she could no longer meet with Paslan, due to Bale's scrutiny of her, a new way of communicating had to be found.

"The only way Bale can get back and forth between worlds is through you", said Paslan. "Only you can bring Bale's cohorts or accomplices", he continued.

"I have no intention of bringing anyone else", she said firmly.

"You may have to", said Paslan.

She looked at him and waited.

"We are waiting for Bale to make a mistake. He can not kill us directly, not while we are in the Other World", he paused. "Fenfrew is in particular danger. Though I think we have the remedy again."

Su Su asked, "Do you think that bringing others will increase the likelihood of Bale making a mistake?"

"Yes", he said.

"And what will the effect be on Fenfrew when others enter the Other World?", she asked looking at this man whom she deeply respected and whom she knew loved his old friend.

Paslan paused a moment and then said, "It is hard to know as certainty. It will depend on the motivation of those you bring. I imagine that most will come for the job and will be neutral to Bale's ambition. In which case their effect would also be neutral. "I'm thinking", and his smile came lit from deep within, "that some will find a home in the Other World and then the effect will be beneficial."

Paslan rested back in his big chair and looked into the fire. Su Su waited. She was learning a lot about Paslan. And Paslan was teaching her about life. An awareness was awakening that she had not known existed. For all the credit she had taken for her intelligence and ability in science, she had wholly neglected that which she was now learning, she was gaining an understanding of herself and others which she now knew was the real key to life. As she watched Paslan gazing into the fire she wanted to know his thoughts. She looked into the fire. Many minutes passed. The fire was in full blaze and flames were leaping, dancing along the length of the logs. Amber, brown, light filled flames, shot straight up the chimney. She began to day dream about the miners and who she would bring. Ralph Portnoy was head of the mining department at Edinbridge, he would help her. Yes she was sure that he would find just the right people for the project.

"I will bring the miners. I will contact Ralph Portnoy and he will help", she said this out loud to Paslan surprising herself in having broken the silence. Paslan turning his gaze from the fire smiled upon her and nodded saying,

"He will be expecting you in his office."

She nodded and rose. The door opened. She left directly for the engineering building.

As she walked to Ralph Portnoy's office for a moment she checked herself. Why am I so sure he will help? I have not ever met him. But then she rested back in the knowledge that had come to her at the fireside, that Ralph Portnoy would help her.

Ralph Portnoy sat munching an apple, sipping his coffee, and smiling at the student paper he was reading. He was a short stocky jolly fellow with a grizzled chin of grey, white, and red beard. Actually it was almost, not quite, a beard. It wasn't that he was trying to grow a beard it was that he only managed to shave three times a week. He just couldn't get organized enough to get a shave in each morning. Su Su Rong knocked on his open door. Ralph looked up and seeing, as he peered over his glasses, another professor instead of a student, his smile faded. Su Su took in the scene of apple, coffee, student paper, and this jolly looking man and said,

"Hello Professor Portnoy I'm Su Su Rong. You were thinking I might be one of your students? Have I disappointed you?"

Ralph's smile returned in full measure. He put down the paper and rose to greet her extending his hand.

"How do you do? Won't you please come and sit down", he said in his Yorkshire accent, offering a warm welcome and gesturing her to sit in the other chair. The chair was heaped with books.

"Oh let me put these elsewhere", he said as he picked up the stack of books and looked about for a spot to put them. After a minute searching he said, "Well they will just have to go here on the floor." And he bent over and placed the stack underneath his chair.

"Now you are interested in recruiting some mining grad's for your project. Is that right?", he asked as he settled himself comfortably again.

"Yes", she said surprised, yet managing a lilt that said you've got it.

"Actually as I understand you want some experienced miners too. You know Edinbridge mining grad's are well placed and being so well trained", he paused and smiled at her with a little bit of pride, "get to know the good miners too."

"Yes indeed", she said encouragingly.

"Well I've called Andrew Macleod and Dick Wellman. They both are willing to help you. Now Andrew has to be available in about two months time. Do you think you'll be finished or at least well on your way and not in need of him after that time?" He didn't wait for her answer.

"Dick of course can help you out if you're not finished by then. I imagine you will need about thirty miners. Does that sound about right?"

This time he stopped and waited for her reply.

"Oh . . . yes . . . I should think that sounds just about right", she said, somehow knowing that this must be right.

"Good then. We're ready when you are", he sat back in his chair smiling.

"Do you think we could assemble everyone then. . .", she opened it up for him.

"When I spoke with Andrew and Dick early today they told me that the teams with whom they work had just finished a job, were rested and ready for the next one. So I'd say you can begin at the top of the week."

"That is just right Professor Portnoy and thank you very much", Su Su said with real appreciation.

"It is no trouble at all. Our boys like to keep busy and besides Hale Paslan is a wonderful man. It was a delight to hear from him. We really miss him here", he paused and corrected himself, "well I and the old fellows here do. It certainly has changed these last few months since he's been gone. Sometimes on the way home or the way in, I ask myself how did such a change come about and so quickly. Did you see it coming?", he asked.

Su Su suddenly burst into a fit of coughing and looked about for some water. She kept coughing and Ralph went over to the water cooler and poured her some water.

"Are you alright"?, he asked, handing her the glass of water.

Taking a few sips of water, and regaining herself, Rong was able to say, "Yes, yes. Thank you for the water." She looked up and smiled at him as he bent over her. He smiled back and having forgotten his question went back to his desk.

"I must be off", she said. "Thank you again. I will look forward to beginning with them as you say at the top of the week", she smiled broadly, very happy to have had all this help and to gain, she was sure, good miners.

The baskets Terhaven had given Nadine were now filled with dandelions and before returning through the painting she sat by the stream with her feet in the water. This was the loveliest spot she'd ever found. The quiet, the birds, the sunshine that beamed down warming her skin, not too hot, and the way the beams came through the trees lighting up the forest bed, created this haven divine. The leaves of the trees shone in the sunlight here, extra green, and the trees were tall and thick trunked.

Each morning now Nadine was here gathering the dandelions. Terhaven had given her a special powder the first day and she had sprinkled the powder along the edges of the bank and in the nearby field. It was like dusting powder and she had guessed that it was food for dandelions. Apparently it was ambrosia for dandelions as when she returned one week later the yellow flower was everywhere. The baskets were amazingly light, she could carry back eight full baskets. Terhaven was very happy with the crop.

"Hello", came a small voice just behind her.

Nadine turned fully around pulling her feet out of the water. There stood a young fawn, her spots still on her carmel colored coat.

"Hello", Nadine beamed back in a big smile.

"I'm Eloise", she said sweetly.

"I'm Nadine", said Nadine.

"I've noticed you coming each day now for the taraxacum", she said.

"Oh . . . yes. A friend needs it to be well."

"Well . . . is your friend a person?"

"Yes", Nadine smiled.

"Well then it will work", Eloise said as she placed the tip of her black nose in one of the baskets.

"This is special taraxacum", she said and looked up at Nadine inquiringly.

"Yes, you are right. A friend who knows a lot about plants gave me a special powder to dust the earth here so that these", she indicated the dandelions, "could grow very well."

Nadine could have sworn that Eloise raised the whiskers above her right eye as she tilted her head and opened her mouth as in a smile before she said, "I'd like to meet your friend."

"I'd be pleased to introduce you. I wonder how to manage that", Nadine said as she bent down to put on her shoes.

Eloise stepped back a few paces and said,

"It will happen if you will it so", looking at Nadine with that raised brow. "It was nice to meet you and I will look for you again", and then with two bounds she was gone into the woods.

"How do you like this cheese?", Terhaven asked everyone at the breakfast table.

David had cut a piece and was spreading it as it melted a little into his toast. Paslan cut a piece and popped it into his mouth.

"Mmmm. . . quite good", Paslan smiled up at her.

Terhaven looked around the table for reaction. Nadine and Sarabeth both realized in the same moment that they were expected to sample this new cheese and their knives clanged together over the square in the middle of the table.

"Yes, I like it", agreed David.

Nadine and Sarabeth still had a mouthful. Terhaven waited.

"It's really good. What is it?", responded Nadine.

Sarabeth nodded as she finished her piece, "I like it. It is a little stronger than the cheese you usually serve at breakfast."

"It is from Galago's milk. She is now eating ground thistle with grasses. Dandelions had been part of her diet."

They nodded.

"Tomorrow the miners arrive", Terhaven said matter of factly, not in her usual warm way. "What have you planned Hale? I am at a loss to see why you are letting them come to gouge and mar the landscape."

"That is what they think they will be doing", he replied with a smile.

She looked at him over her juice glass and then said, "Yes?"

"We must watch out for Su Su now. Bale must not realize that she is with us. And . . . I'm sure that Ralph has sent us some fine fellows some of whom will join us to help overcome Bale."

"And in the meantime?", Terhaven did not let up.

Nadine and Sarabeth looked at one another. Someone pressing Paslan was a first.

"In the meantime", Paslan quaffed the rest of his tea, "I must be off to Fenfrew's. Will was up very early working on. . . something", he smiled mischievously at Terhaven and got up from the table. At the bottom of the steps he turned to the table and said,

"By the way did you know that George has gone back to Edinbridge. He has gone to work for the Edinbridge Mirror," and with that mysterious missive walked off across the lawn.

Terhaven tossed her napkin onto the table and looked after the striding figure disappearing onto the path. Nadine burst out laughing. Terhaven stared at her, pushed back her chair and in one motion was off the porch and into the house.

"I'm sorry Terhaven, I . . . just couldn't help it", Nadine called to her through her laughter.

"Nadine", David's voice was reprimanding.

"I know. Terhaven is upset. She has been upset since she learned about the miners. But I know that Paslan has a wonderful plan. Don't you know the same?", Nadine asked David and Sarabeth.

There was a pause and then David said,

"What you and Paslan share is something we do not have. There is something inside you Nadine that as you say, knows. Of course we trust Paslan, as does Terhaven. Did you know that Jane left yesterday and is also back at Edinbridge?"

"No!", Nadine looked very surprised.

"Jane told me the other night that working in the Great Hall she gets to see and talk with a lot of students, hear their conversations and learn what is on their minds. She has been thinking that there she can be of greater service. She feels that she and George can compare notes, work together, help get more people thinking and help turn the tide from there. And that they would return when they have done all they can do."

"What is George doing exactly?", asked Sarabeth.

"He has gone to work for the old town newspaper", David replied. "The Mirror has been around for a hundred and seventy years. George feels that he can draw attention to the changes at Edinbridge and what they mean. Actually we worked on his first article together."

"May we read it?", Nadine asked excitedly.

"I think it comes out next week", David picked up his plate and got up from the table.

"Oh", she replied, a little crestfallen. And then in a moment realizing she should wait for the article, she said,

"Right," and smiled at David.

He turned back from the entrance to the house and gave her a warm smile in return.

CHAPTER THIRTY

EDINBRIDGE?

"It's very good to be able to still come here for my meals", George said as he graciously took the plate of chicken and vegetables Jane handed him.

"Well you'd paid your fees for the history and literature class that Herd casually neglected to complete. Paslan was right, you should receive equal value somewhere."

"I feel lucky to be able to eat the meals you prepare. You are a very good cook."

Jane blushed, "Thanks." "How is it going at work?", she asked George.

"It's not so bad. I was thinking that after time with everyone at Terhaven's it would be sad, and disappointingly dull. The editor is ancient and really smart. He's hired some good writers and staff over the years. I'm working with people who have a lot of experience. What I've yet to learn is their interest in the changes at Edinbridge."

Jane nodded thoughtfully. They looked around at the students who sat eating and talking at the tables. For a few minutes they took in the atmosphere in the Great Hall. Then George said, "Do you think Jane that this will ever again be, 'The Great Hall'?"

Jane looked at him hard. Then she turned back again to the students and looked up and down the tables. She looked to the faces of one and then another. She looked for first years and then for older students. She looked hard at some and then scanned the tables looking for she knew not what exactly. And then she came to rest on one young face at the far end of their own table. She looked to George and motioned to the young man who sat alone.

George saw a young man, perhaps eighteen years old, who sat erect. His face was bright, shining with curiosity and a great energy for life. In front of him sat an open book, *Atlas Shrugged*. Another larger black book quite old and well used sat beside it, *Holy Bible*.

Suddenly the young man turned towards them. His eyes taking in George and Jane's attention. His dark brown eyes cut the distance between them to nothing, his energy enveloping the space where Jane and George sat. He met George's eyes and rested there a moment giving an almost imperceptible nod then he turned to Jane and for an instant his eyes became a little more kindly. Then a broad confident grin came to his face. It was the happy expression of a man, not a boy, who knows himself and has found like minded friends. He laughed, throwing back his head oblivious to all around him, enjoying the moment. He turned to them, nodded nobly to Jane and then to George, then in another moment went back to his dinner and his books.

CHAPTER THIRTY ONE

MIND OF A MINER

"It's a wee bit strange don't you think? The way we got here and this Av . . . Bale fellow? What do you think?", the stocky Scot miner asked his mate.

"What d' I think? I don think. I do as am told to do," he replied disgruntled to be disturbed over his lunch.

"Well something's fishy I say", the Scot had stopped eating and was looking up the hill where they were working.

"We've been digging a week now and nothing is . . . well getting dug . . .," he turned to his mate for his response.

"Whad ya mean?", he said through his sandwich.

"Look at the hill", the Scot replied.

The dozers, mining trucks, and crushers, were scattered along the hill but the hill itself was unscathed. The haul trucks were empty. The mate looked and not registering what he saw went back to his sandwich. The Scot shook his head and not so much at his mate. He got up from the rock where they were sitting having decided to take a walk around.

Andrew Macleod had taken a walk about when they had first arrived and now he wanted to see, after seven days of working ten hours a day, what they had accomplished.

He stood for a while at the far westerly point of the hill surveying the landscape. He was taken in by the beauty. The trees reminded him of home, tall and thick trunked. He remembered the forests in the Western Highlands where he had hiked with his grandfather as a lad. Pappy had explained why some of the hill sides were shorn of trees or why the trees were small and scrubby. They had clear cut in years prior and the hillsides had trouble reestablishing themselves. As he looked around him Andrew saw huge healthy trees with lush undergrowth. He felt as though nature here was respected, in harmony with man as though they had a conversation going. He stopped, his eyes rested on a thick stand of evergreens along the bottom of the hill. He could have sworn that when he had stood here a week ago that stand of trees was further back at the edge of the forest. He blinked letting his mind go back to when he first looked at the landscape from this perspective.

He opened his eyes, he was sure that that stand had been ten no twenty feet back from where it now stood at the edge of the hill. He made a three hundred and sixty degree survey of his surroundings, breathing in the air and listening to the birds. This was a special place. What was he doing here - mining? Something told him that they were merely attempting to mine, that they would be better off packing up and heading home because the land had something else in mind. What was he thinking? The land didn't have a mind, yet it did mind, it didn't react well to this kind of mining. He was going to keep a good eye on what was going on here.

At the end of the day Andrew cleaned his machine thoroughly. He looked around the cab of the truck he had been using and noticing his wrench picked it up and returned it to its place on the leg of his painter pants. He saw Arnie about to leave and called over to him.

"Arne . . . Arne have you got a wee moment mate?"

Arnie, tall, lean, unshaven, and with a mop of blond hair any woman would pay her hairdresser handsomely for if she could obtain such a coiffure, signaled to Andrew that he'd heard him and would wait.

"Thanks man. I know you want to get back to your kids and family tonight. It's Joanie's birthday were you sa'ing?"

Arnie smiled, "Yah she's ten today."

"Well happy birthday ta her", Andrew smiled back.

"I was want'in to talk to ya. Have you noticed that we're not a gettin very far along?", Andrew asked.

Arnie's brow furrowed and he took off his cap and scratched the top of his head.

"Ya the hauls are still waitin' to be filled. And when you look around . . . well what have we done?"

"I was thinking this is a beautiful place. . . a special place", he paused to see what registered on his friend's face.

Arnie's brow cleared. The day was not yet over and the tall man looked up to the sky. The light played across white clouds. Sunlight touched the tips of the tall evergreens, shading some and highlighting others. Arnie smiled.

Andrew said, "That Bale is a bad character. When he realized that the haul trucks were still empty today he shouted and spat at Bill. Then he threatened him, I didn't hear what he said but Bill went white and fell back into his chair. You know he just came out of hospital from heart surgery and I didn't like the way he was sweating."

Arnie was looking at Andrew and asked, "What are you thinking?"

"I'm thinking that Bale is no good and that we should pack up and leave."

"Wha . . . What?", Arnie opened his mouth.

"I think that you and I should rally the guys and all leave", said Andrew.

"Wha . . . I don' know . . . I don't need the money that's right as Lorraine's dad left us enough for a while. We were talk'n about pack'n up ourselves and spending the rest of the nice weather with the kids in Brighton", Arnie's smile was broadening.

"Well that's exactly what you should do", Andrew encouraged his friend. "Now how do we get the other guys to come along with us?"

The next day the mining crew were three men short. Arnie had decided on his way home to pack up the wife and kids and head for the ocean. His wife was so excited that she called her friend Doris and she convinced her husband who worked with Arnie to join them in Brighton. Andrew called up Tom when he got home to discuss his idea and Tom said he would be happy to leave the job, stay home and take care of his garden. Andrew realized that unless he wanted a lot of trouble and soon, he'd better get organized and get the rest of the men to support him.

"Frank I need your help over here. Can you giv' me a wee bit of your time?", Andrew spoke to his mate as he walked over to his cab the next morning.

Frank was the social one among all the miners. He knew everyone and everyone liked him. He always had a joke, friendly jokes, to share and he liked people. He laughed with them and he listened. If Frank was behind leaving this job then the job was finished.

"Andrew how are you and what's up?", Frank said as he arrived at Andrew's truck.

"Frank I want to talk with you, I need your help', said Andrew. Just then at the top of the hill Andrew caught sight of Bale. He was moving swiftly down the hill toward the mine manager's office, Bill was about to get another blast. Frank followed Andrew's sight lines.

Frank's calm kind face changed. His jaw firmly set he said, "That man is a menace."

Andrew smiled to himself and nodded. "Do you think Bill is going to need some support?", he said.

"Come on, let's get there when Bale does", replied Frank and the two of them walked calmly but quickly to Bill's shed.

Frank was a man of six feet four inches and built like a bull. Having worked with his body all his life he was comfortable, very comfortable in his own skin. Arriving at the shed at the same time as Bale, Frank held the door for Bale getting an up close view of the man. Bale barely noticed the two men.

"Carter. Carter!", Bale shouted, "where are you?" Bale strode into the shed looking around him like an angry bull. From the back of the shed and around the corner came Bill Carter moseying along wiping his hands on an old tea towel.

"Good morning Mr. Bale. Would you like some tea? I've just made it", Bill said kindly.

Avaricis Bale spluttered, the vein in his forehead bulging, "No I don't want any tea. What I want is to know what the hell you are doing. Not one truck has come down the hill. How do you intend to get this job done?", he shouted.

Bill went slightly pink in the face and looked uncomfortable. Frank spoke.

"Good morning, Frank Snyder," Frank said, looking a tower standing next to a stovepipe as he addressed Bale.

"Who are you?", Bale demanded.

Having just given him his name, Frank smiled at Bale, then he said, "We've been noticing sir that the hill doesn't want to be mined. In fact . . .".

Bale cut him off. "Doesn't want to be mined!", the vein in his forehead bulged out even more, "What are you talking about!", he shouted ever more loudly.

Frank lowered his voice, "Have you ever noticed that the cow gives birth when the calf is ready to be born, that the bird sings when the morning comes, that the child begins to walk when it is time?"

Bale's face had grown very red and Bill and Andrew were waiting for an explosion. Frank however just smiled down on Bale. Instead Bale stood silent, perhaps trying to gather himself together to face an unexpected obstacle.

Andrew took his opportunity and said, "What we are trying to say is that the hill will not be mined and your resources Mr. Bale might be better used elsewhere."

Frank nodded, Bill looked relieved and calmer. Bale looked lost, and was speechless.

"Please sit down Mr. Bale", Frank said. "Bill's tea is very good", he continued as he went to get a cup for Bale.

Bale turned to look out at the hill from the one window in the shed. Whether Bale noticed the beauty before him or not, Andrew guessed that he did not, he was a pragmatic man. The hill remained unchanged, no mining was going on here. Bale could not mine it himself. Another way must be found. Bale took the tea cup offered him, still looking out over the hill.

Andrew was walking the distance to the launch that would take him home tonight. His concern about how to rally the men for support to stop the mining had been solved for him. As he walked he wondered at this place. He stopped at the stand of thick tall evergreens he'd seen from the top of the hill yesterday morning. He took in a deep breath and the fresh smell of pine filled his nostrils. He closed his eyes and breathed in deeply.

"Ahh", aloud he expressed his feeling of utter peace and appreciation.

He opened his eyes. He was standing in the center of the stand of trees and sunlight was coming down through the branches. As the light came from the sky to the earth it became beams that touched the ground at his feet. The particles of light within the beams twinkled and danced in mid-air. He watched the light play for some time. Andrew realized that the launch would soon be leaving yet he had no interest in meeting it. He turned around and began walking in the other direction.

He noticed the birds singing and smiled. At home the birds sang only in the morning or at least that is only when he had noticed it. He caught sight of a deer deeper in the forest.

He kept walking. He followed the stream for a few miles and then a path that led out of the forest. There ahead of him several hundred feet was a white house with a lovely porch surrounding it. He did not want to intrude yet the smell from the kitchen was so enticing and he was getting very hungry. A woman with reddy blond hair past her shoulders came out of the house with a pitcher of juice and placed it on the linen cloth that covered the table. She looked up,

"Ohh . . . hello . . .", she said pausing only a moment, "will you join us?"

Chapter Thirty Two

Destroyers' Entry

In the darkness Herd moved slowly along the path. Her small electric torch and the rough map seemed to indicate this was the way to the cottage in the forest. Snatch had stumbled and they had been delayed while Mally massaged his ankle which while not broken was definitely sprained. It was Tiny that was having the most difficulty. Being only five foot zero inches he could not maneuver unaided over the broken branches and downed trees that had been their initial path. And Herd, at five feet ten, had started them off at a pace she had been forced to slow.

"I tell you that root just suddenly appeared," Snatch complained with irritation. "I had my torch on the ground and it was not there and then it was."

Herd frowned at what she considered an idiotic remark meant as an excuse for falling.

"We'll have to dig out and broaden the paths, lay concrete and make this place civilized", grumbled Tiny.

"Did you hear something?", said Herd.

"No, what"? replied Mally.

"Everyone stop. I think I hear something in the forest", said Herd.

Bernard Yarnick who had been bringing up the rear barreled into Tiny and knocked him over.

"Watch where you're going!", Tiny snapped.

"Oh I'm sorry . . . I didn't see you", replied Yarnick as he stopped to help Tiny up.

"Well you should pay more attention", growled Tiny as he dusted himself off.

"Quiet, there is something going on in the forest", Herd was chastening them to listen.

When the five stood quietly on the path all around them a small and steady sound could be heard from the forest. It was a whooshing sort of sound.

"What is that?" Herd asked her companions.

No one replied. They did not recognize it. But if they had invested more time outdoors they might have. But then they had just arrived in the Other World and those whom they were about to confront had had the privilege of months or years here.

Terhaven moved briskly along the road she knew well and while there was no moon this night the stars twinkled brightly for her. She carried an enormous basket filled with the finest most nourishing foods and two ancient remedies Su Su had prepared along with Sarabeth's juice. The door to Fenfrew's home opened for her and she went immediately to his room. Paslan was sitting by his friend at the fire. They had moved his bed close to the fire to provide extra warmth and useable light at night. Although Fenfrew ate in bed the table was laid with linen and silver and china as Terhaven always laid it in preparation for the next meal. It was she said the only civilized way to properly appreciate food and company.

In a few moments she had laid out the food beautifully, a sight to see in color and proportion. And everything smelled so good. The wine she poured flowed into the goblet a deep rich red and released an aroma of sunlit vineyards of years gone by. Hepacorn meats juicy and so tender with their own scent of wild fields made one's mouth water. The herbal remedies Su Su had prepared were placed on either side of Fenfrew's plate to be eaten between portions of the broccoli eggplant casserole, the potato pomegranate souffle, and the meats. Fenfrew lay back on his pillows and smiled at her.

"You are a culinary wizard", he said. His voice while tired held his unique effervescent energy.

After offering him his plate she sat herself down beside Paslan at the fire.

"How is our patient?", Terhaven asked Paslan.

"Well he still has his appetite", Paslan replied as Fenfrew heartily addressed himself to the food before him.

Terhaven smiled watching Fenfrew enjoy himself. Noticing that Paslan looked hungry, in a moment she had prepared a plate for Paslan and she handed it to him with a smile.

Paslan said, "Thank you, you saw my mouth watering?"

"Yes", she said and laughed.

Fenfrew had just eaten the green bespeckled dollop on the side of his plate, "Now that was something new... to me ...it had a very old taste."

Terhaven laughed again, "You are right Bartholomew, it is very old, ancient."

Paslan looked left out, "Where is mine to taste", he said like a little boy missing his portion of dessert.

"There is only enough for Fenfrew", Terhaven said a little guiltily that she had not provided something that her friend wanted.

"Su Su prepared it for you Bartholomew from a

receipe she remembered of her grandmother's", Terhaven explained. "It requires grass grown on the south side of a hill with just the right amount of sunshine. We normally have so much sunshine here that I . . . well. . . I asked a stand of trees to move a little to help shade the grass I'd chosen."

Paslan tilted his head down and looking up at her asked slowly, "Did anyone notice the trees had moved?"

"Yes, I was surprised, Andrew noticed. The grass is growing near the hill where the miners were . . . Trying... to excavate", she replied.

"Ahh . . . yes Andrew would notice", said Paslan.

"Well what is this grass I'm going to be eating?", asked Fenfrew.

"It is a cross between Zoysia and Bent grass, they make quite a beautiful combination", Terhaven said.

"There is something else in it. . . what were the speckles?", Bartholomew was looking at his plate to see if any bit remained.

"Oh no you don't I'm not giving away all my secrets", Terhaven said flatly.

Fenfrew looked a mite chastened but said, "Well my palate thanks you for that which was previously untasted", and he made a little bow of his head to her.

"The forest is ready", Terhaven said looking at Paslan and changing the subject.

Paslan said,"Bale is not used to not getting his way. The miners packing up without gaining precious metals was a reversal for him though also fuel for his fury. He has recruited anyone who will follow him and is bringing them here."

"Do you mean other than Herd, Yarnick, Devolve, Tiny Turner and Mally Framer?", Terhaven asked.

Paslan replied, "Yes. He has easily recruited those who

have been following the movement of the day. It is a religion for some, fitting in and following the trend or what they consider to be progress. Rather than a true care and interest in where their time goes, it is the taking up of a banner that many seem to value, a banner under which one may feel an accepted part of progress. The proliferation in the world of laws and regulations upon companies and private individuals, the stamping down of the entrepreneurial spirit, and the penalization of profit and risk taking, mean the rewarding of mediocrity. Look carefully into the faces of their leaders and you can see, rather than elements of uniqueness and evidence of an individual mind, something is missing. There is a plainess, a mediocrity, and a desperateness. And there is fear. While hard to put one's finger on, it is there and because it shows up in the face it is deeply rooted. It includes a resentment of others' success, an empty void gluttonous to be filled with power, position, status of any kind. And of course the emptiness can not be filled by the route of pursuit. Like junk food or junk bonds, the easy way, the way without value, can give no value in return. If reality is avoided the value that is needed to nourish a life has been missed, and when all the value that was there is gone, they collapse inward upon themselves", Paslan concluded.

The light was dawning and three beams of light came streaming into the large window in Fenfrew's room. The beams met in a circle on the floor. Terhaven rose and looking at Fenfrew and Paslan in turn said, "I will be in the forest more of the time if you need me."

They smiled at her and Fenfrew said, "Thank you my dear", with a very sweet look in his eye.

An enormous number of oranges were piled high along the counter and Sarabeth was peeling them by hand.

"I thought it was you I heard in here", David said.

"Hullo, what's happening with your thesis?", she replied.

"It's ready, I'm seeing what can be done for publishing it", David said. "May I give you a hand?"

"Thanks, yes. I like to peel the oranges though there is no problem if some peel remains. The main peel goes in the bucket by the sink. With your help we'll be done in no time. If you like you could join me at the market which is where I'll be headed after the oranges are ready.

"You've got me for the market too", David said as he tossed the first peel in the bucket.

"I've had my nose in the books too long, this is my first time to the market", David said as he scanned the farmer stalls and merchant booths.

"It's crowded today", said Sarabeth as she led him down a narrow walk way between stalls to the vegetables.

"Terhaven grows most of her own vegetables but because she has been tending certain herbs and plant life needed by Fenfrew everyday, I've been coming here more often."

David nodded. Suddenly he stopped. Over by the potatoes he saw someone he did not imagine seeing, Donna Dreup. Sarabeth had stopped and was looking in the direction of David's attention.

"Do you know her?", she asked.

"She was in my philosophy class at Edinbridge", David looked at Sarabeth. "This means that Bale has brought many more here. No wonder Fenfrew is confined to his bed and Terhaven is caring for his food so closely."

Sarabeth took a good look at the face of Donna Dreup and said, "I imagine that her friends will be easy to recognize . . . there is a flabbiness around the face, indistinct character lines and what is it . . . an overall . . . ", her sentence was finished by David.

". . . resentment of life, of the personal responsibility required to lead one's own life", he said.

Sarabeth nodded.

Boris Belacuse was directing his crew from the top of the scaffolding. The cottage had been flattened and a building completely out of proportion to it's surroundings was being erected at an astounding rate. In the meantime large canvas tents had been erected to house Bale's key group and make shift pup tents to house the rest of the crowd that had followed him here and now deposited themselves on the landscape.

Boris was in a particularly belligerent mood today. He had ordered the trees cut in a large swath around the area. His superintendent insisted that they had been cut and Boris was pointing to the fact that there they stood. This was not the first morning for this particular argument. But today a decision had to be made on the final size of the building and therefore the area under construction. Though he resented changing his mind Boris decided that there were enough trees out of the way and his superintendent could move on to concern himself with construction of the edifice. At that moment the wind which had been a problem for the workers died down as did the rain to an easy patter. Even Boris's temper eased up a bit.

At the other end of the forest Terhaven had made plans for dinner. As the weather had cooled she decided that dinner must be indoors. Everyone was coming tonight. Fenfrew insisted that he would come and Paslan would bring him at the last moment. David and Sarabeth came home from the market loaded down. Jane and George were expected from Edinbridge. The dining room, the living room, and the parlor had tables laid.

CHAPTER THIRTY THREE

INDIVIDUAL COURAGE

That evening the house was filled with the wonderful smell of good food lovingly prepared. The welcoming aroma wafting out the windows readied everyone arriving for a very good meal. A family of deer poked their noses out of the forest and looked tempted to come nearer even with all the people around.

If you were there you would recognize Reginald Battersea, the lady who looked like Guenevere, Jean the french farmer, Jacques Chalafour with whom Paslan had had a conversation in the Toulouse pub, Princess Sophia of Sweden, the Count and his son who were the Count Karl Habstein von Schwartz Wald and Wilhelm Graf von Schwartz Wald. And there were others that each had brought with them after having spoken with Paslan. After reuniting, greetings, and finding their place at table, Paslan raised his glass in a toast, "Welcome. I bid you friends enjoy your meal and ask you a question for reflection and conversation, "Why are we here together this evening?"

After the main course had been thoroughly enjoyed by all it was the Count who began. "We are here to stop Herr Bale und alle his kind who would have us subjugated to their ideas und thinking", said the Count.

The lady of Merlin's time spoke, "If we do not stop

them some of us will be killed, I speak from experience, and the rest of us if not killed, will die to ourselves."

Reginald Battersea was nodding and had a sad and serious expression. Jean was looking anxious to speak and Paslan noticing his anxiety caught his attention, a smile and a nod brought Jean to his feet.

"Cette dame . . . this lady", and Jean indicated the Merlin madam, "understands well. If we permit Bale and his mauvais groupe de personnes to run us, to make the rules, we désigner ourselves to be apart from ourselves, to be another's puppet."

Jacques Charlefour was nodding and added to this, "One's rights are responsibilities. And so if we wish to be free we must stand up for freedom, for the rights Le bon Dieu has given us. If we will not we deserve what we get."

There was silence for a moment as Jacques looked around the room. The group assembled began to stand. Chairs were pushed back and standing in place the room of people took to their feet in full assent to Jacques words. It was Su Su Rong who raised the first glass.

"To freedom and the human spirit . . . may it soar like the eagle to the mountains and beyond", her voice resonated with strength, clarity, and courage.

Everyone raised their glass. A cheer went up, from George. Then Jane joined him.

Then to Nadine's surprise she heard Princess Sophia's voice and then the whole room became a chorus of cheering for freedom, for courage to fight. The voice became one clear and resounding 'Yes!' to life.

Paslan spoke, "I ask each of you to prepare a plan which you can envision personally putting into place. When you are ready please share it with me. This will help in coordinating the overall campaign. Now let us enjoy this wonderful meal together." He sat down and taking up his napkin daubed his eyes.

Over the next days the breezes seemed to flow in an irregular pattern. From the easterly part of the forest, where Bale's building was erected and where his recruits now resided, there was a cold slow wind that blew towards the west. If you stood at the western edge of the forest you would feel it and because it was slow it felt like it was enveloping you. However no one stood there. From the western part of the forest which edged onto Terhaven's property, the breezes were warmer, softer, and touched with the fragrance of stock, one of Terhaven's favorite flowers. For Su Su, who as she took her walks noticed these breezes, it was a present reminder of her mission.

George and Jane had arranged with Paslan to meet him in his study to share their plan. Being back at Edinbridge they were in the midst of the destruction. Professors were barely speaking with students, students were rude to staff, and staff often were not showing up to work. Once immaculate grounds, were now strewn with litter. The impact Bale's control had outside the walls of Edinbridge showed on campus. Trash was picked up only intermittently. This week the food service company neglected to come. So Jane went into town to shop and bring back a carload of food to provide for the students.

"What upsets me most Professor Paslan are the faces of people. Something is gone. It is as though their life blood has drained away. The purpose and zest for life has gone. It is a great tragedy", Jane ended.

"At first I didn't know how I was going to get my articles published", George said. "I thought that the staff would preempt the facts. But there is no one to stand in the way. Either they have quit or they are so consumed with their daily needs, given the gap created by others who have given up, that they haven't the energy to fight me", George said.

Paslan was listening. George turned to Jane who nodded indicating that he should share the plan they had decided to undertake together.

"We are going to pummel them with print, with the word. We are going to spell out who they are to their face. We are going to give voice in print to their corruption, laziness, and cowardliness. It will be direct unadulterated reality laid out before them", he finished.

Paslan smiled, "I think that is a very good idea."

The Count and his son were delighted and eager to be of service. When they arrived at Edinbridge to share their plan with Paslan, George, and Jane had shown them around the beautiful grounds and the old trees were a particular favorite of the Count's.

"Wir werden bringin sie the dachunds und Terhaven hast ein plan fir the garden of Bale und the group", said the Count.

The Count's son was bursting to share more but waited politely for his father to finish and for a sign from Paslan to speak. Paslan looked now to young Wilhelm.

"We have a hundred of our dachshund's ready. They can be very quiet, they vill follow my order", he said proudly.

Paslan laughed, his luxurious mane of dark hair sprang back from his head as he did so. The Count and his son stopped short, never having experienced anyone laughing at them.

"Please understand I do not laugh at you rather your wonderful idea has me laugh to imagine Bale's response when he awakes one morning to find the entire garden upended by the holes your hounds will furrow."

"Yes, yes you are right. We will starve them out", Wilhelm exclaimed with furvor.

Princess Sophia in taking a customary walk in the morning had met Ginbreste, who was out power walking.

He had slowed up to talk with her as they were walking along the river bank in the same direction. Whether in her royal finery or more standard civilian dress Princess Sophia was a beautiful young woman. She realized quickly who he was. Ginbreste was not a legal expert for nothing. Always eager to display his intellectual prowess he set about parading his peacock feathers for Sophia.

"You see I think that he will divulge all that he knows to me. My plan is taken from the Arabian Nights and my lure is the meals I will cook for him. My grandmother was a wonderful cook, my mother too, but my grandmother shared time with me through secret receipes she showed me how to prepare. These are receipes for food Ginbreste will never have tasted and he will want to come back for more", she smiled demurely her beautiful straight bright white teeth showing.

"Very good Sophia, you are calling yourself Sophia now"?, Paslan asked to confirm.

"Oh yes please. I am very happy to be useful, very happy", and her smile confirmed her words.

"We will set up a few different annoyances for them", said Jacques.

"The guillotine will be a fun trick", said Jean with glee.

"The guillotine"?, Paslan inquired with one brow raised.

"Mais qui", Jean replied with alacrity. "Madame Guillotine will appear one night, if moonlight, they may catch sight of her gleaming at them from the forest that surrounds their building. If they first see her in the mist of the morning that will be fine too. She has a way of stirring fear in the hearts of man", he smiled.

"We will broach them in the forest on their walk, in the market while they shop, and wherever they are, to offer them their chance to repent," said Jacques.

While the reason for their being in Paslan's home was a most serious one, Nadine, Will, and David were pleased to have been invited.

"I'd almost forgotten what your home looked like", Nadine said as they sat together in the study. "And I wasn't in this room, though the feel of it is familiar." Nadine continued, "This is just like your study in Edinbridge. There is one other place, or I should say there was one other place, that made me feel so beautifully comfortable and out of the world."

They were all listening.

"When I was about eleven I went walking by myself along the cliffs close to where we lived. Below the cliffs the river wound along the valley. I climbed down the side of the cliff where it ran beneath the golf course and where there were evergreen trees. I think it was early spring because I remember bits of snow and the green being so lovely. Hidden by the boughs of evergreen I found a shelf of earth upon which I could sit. I can still sense the feeling of sitting there where no one could see me and where I could enjoy the peaceful quiet and beauty of the river and the lovely fresh air and smell of evergreen, my secret place."

Will asked, "Is that place gone then, have they built it all up?"

"No they haven't built it up it's just that they have closed it off. One must be a member of the golf club to get onto the grounds now. And those who are there I imagine never dream of climbing down to the secret spots."

"Well my dear", said Paslan, "I am very glad that you feel similarly here."

"This is our first time here", Will said speaking for David and himself.

"Whether I am here or no you are always welcome," their host said.

Paslan stood and walking to the picture window which brought the outdoors indoors said, "It is time." The window, rather than a view onto the forest, had a view into the forest. As they looked where Paslan had directed his eyes they saw the trees swaying. No one had noticed a wind on their arrival. It struck them that the season was changing, fall would soon turn to winter. Why does the wind blow when the season changes? Is some part of nature fighting another part of nature resisting the change? Is struggle a necessity for us?

"Nadine will you use the Excelerator and go now to see what you may see at the Building?", Paslan asked.

Nadine stood.

Paslan said, "You will find your suit just outside this door."

The door opened. "Return as soon as you've seen what you need to see. We will be here," Paslan said to her.

He had been facing her and now turned back to the forest. Nadine left the room. She picked up the Excelerator from the chair by the door and put it on. The enormous push out windows of the dining area opened for her and she flew out. She sped above and into the forest directly east. Paslan and Will and David stood together now at the window looking into the forest, only Paslan could see her flight. Beneath her the leaves and branches of the trees were in motion and the sound of the wind was as rushing water. She was perfectly protected in Fenfrew's suit. Nadine was neither cold nor too warm, just right. The suit felt like a second skin. Initially she noticed deer below, squirrels and a couple of brown bears. As she moved east the squirrels disappeared and then the deer and then she saw not one animal. The tower room of the

Building appeared above the trees and she knew she was almost there. She slowed down and circled. The garden or what had been a large garden behind the cottage was torn up. The earth looked like a plough had gone over it with a broken blade. Dachshunds! Nadine smiled. Then she thought of Su Su and she felt badly.

The front door was open and she went directly in. Three people she did not recognize were standing in the foyer and she brushed one of them as she entered. Nothing happened. The woman kept on talking to the others.

"So I am not tangible to others in this suit", she said to herself.

She entered the main part of the Building which might have been a living room if this were a house. In the far corner sat Hil Gore and Ginbreste talking.

"Why were you out last evening again", Hil Gore asked Ginbreste in an accusatory manner.

"I've got to have some social life. For fifty years I have been studying, working, striving and now that I, we, have achieved all this I am going to enjoy some of it", he replied.

"We have not achieved anything until we are in control here", she snapped. "And who is this woman, what do you know about her?", Hil Gore interrogated.

"She is a lovely woman, a princess in fact, who has given up her title to live as we do", he said proudly.

"You are a fool", and she turned from him, got up and went to the window.

Suddenly she gesticulated to something outside and exclaimed ,"What is that?"

Nadine and Ginbreste arrived at the window at the same moment. There a little more than thirty yards into a clearing in the woods was a vertical wooden structure and

near the top a horizontally shaped flat piece of metal glint-
ing in the sunlight. Hil Gore's hand flew to her neck as
she yelled, "A guillotine! Who put that there?"

As though in answer to her question suddenly a voice
rang out from somewhere in the forest as though through
a megaphone,

"Ye fools beware. . . Madame Guillotine awaits your
foolish dreams of power. N'oubliez pas . . . pride cometh
before a fall . . . and when this razor falls it gives a very
close shave."

Hil Gore screamed. Ginbrete's mouth hung open.
Nadine turned away and stifled a laugh.

Bale stormed into the room. "What is going on here!",
he demanded.

Hil Gore pointed to the gleaming blade. As Bale
turned to look a beam of sunlight burst through the clouds
and beaming upon the blade almost blinded Bale. His arm
flew up to shield his eyes. Then he commanded, "Call
Boris and get him to take it down. I'm surprised that Paslan
would allow such a ridiculous prank."

Hil Gore seemed to become more composed and
went off to get Boris. Just then Su Su Rong came into the
room and said, "There are no vegetables for cooking. The
garden has been torn up."

Bale sneered at her and moved to the back of the
Building where the garden could be viewed. Nadine followed behind.

This time Bale frowned and looked a little strained but
in a moment said, "Well get to the market and get all you
need."

"Today the market is closed", she said.

"Closed, why?", he bellowed.

"It is Sunday today," said Su Su.

"Sunday? I don't understand", and as he was about to

storm off he noticed something in the trees. It was a large printed banner. It read,

"If you will not fight for the right when you can easily win without bloodshed; if you will not fight when your victory will be sure and not too costly; you may come to the moment when you will have to fight with all the odds against you and only a small chance of survival. There may even be a worse case: you may have to fight when there is no hope of victory, because it is better to perish than to live as slaves." Winston Churchill

"What is . . . Who put that there?", Bale asked angrily. He looked around almost accusing Rong and Ginbreste. He looked back at the banner and under his breath said, "Too bad they didn't pay more attention to their history", and smirked to himself. Then he barked at Ginbreste, "Get a hold of Herd, Framer, Turner, Yarnick, Devolve, Dreup, and get them to my study. Make sure Hil Gore is there", he spat out his orders and their names like prefabricated pieces of metal coming off an assembly line.

"Why are you waiting? Get to the study", he rudely commanded Rong. Suddenly remembering that she had been missing the other night for a few hours, a malevolent glint beamed off his eye and Su Su caught it. As he was leaving the room Nadine saw him catch another look at the banner.

In a moment Nadine was beside Rong, "Su Su", Nadine whispered. Su Su stopped. "Su Su it's Nadine. I'm right here beside you in a suit Fenfrew made."

There was a pause as Su Su collected herself. Then she said, "Come to the kitchen I'll get something to drink for the group."

In the kitchen Nadine stayed as close to Rong as possible without stepping on her. "Paslan sent me to see what was happening here. To confirm what is happening I probably should say as he always knows what is going on." As she said this a thought came to her. I think it is happening now. It is time", she repeated Paslan's words.

Su Su paused as she placed the coffee pot on the tray.

"I think that you should come with me, I think it is time for you to leave them", said Nadine.

"How?", is all Su Su could say.

"I'm not sure except that we've got about one minute to decide", Nadine finished.

It took Su Su three seconds to decide. "Let's go."

Out the front door they went.

They ran down the path to the forest. In a moment they were under cover of the trees and stopped running, keeping up a brisk walk. The white stag was waiting for them. He nodded to them to follow. Nadine and Su Su followed the stag walking on either side of him. As she walked Nadine registered how very large he was, his back was above her shoulder and his head a few feet higher still. They walked in silence for many minutes and then he spoke,

"They will have discovered you absent now", he said to Su Su. "And they will set out to find you. While we walk together in the forest they will not find you. I will lead you to Paslan."

They walked together some time longer and then found themselves at the edge of the forest. They stopped. The white stage turned to them and said, "You must follow this path on your own now. Paslan will meet you. Do not stop", he said looking directly at them, the Excelerator did not seem to hinder his seeing Nadine. He gave them a nod, turned, and bounded away into the forest.

As the two sped along the path Nadine said, "Don't worry Su Su, Paslan will meet us and we will be fine."

"I'm not worried for myself. I'm concerned about the trouble I'm getting all of you into. And in particular you at

this moment. . . although can they harm you in that suit?",
Rong said.

"I had forgotten I had it on. I don't know," replied
Nadine.

"Keep it on", she said.

They heard a whirring sound overhead which grew
louder and louder. It was a helicopter and suddenly
through a megaphone,

"Rong! You have betrayed us. Look at you! . . .
running to Paslan. . . what are you thinking? Your only
hope is to come with us and try and explain yourself to
Bale."

The helicopter had circled lower and was landing
nearby in the field.

"Keep walking Su Su, don't engage them", Nadine
urged. "I'm going to fly over to see how many there are
and will be back by your side in a moment. Remember
don't stop."

Nadine was up and off flying towards where the helicopter was landing. The pilot was Boris and the man with
the megaphone was Tiny Turner. There were only two of
them and Nadine knew they could take them on. In
another minute she was back with Su Su.

"There are only two of them, Tiny and Boris." We
have the advantage they don't know I'm here."

"They may have weapons", said Rong.

"I didn't see any", said Nadine. "Here they come."

Boris was striding out toward them and Tiny was
running along beside him trying to keep up. Nadine
zoomed up into the air and then down to the ground
behind the two men. She picked up a large stick and struck
Boris on the back with it.

"What are you doing?!", he turned on Tiny.

"What do you mean?", said Tiny.

"No funny business we've got to bring Rong back."

This time Nadine struck Boris on either shoulder with the stick.

Boris turned and seized Tiny by his lapels, "Cut it out or I'll carry you back to the copter", and he thrust him backwards as he released the lapels.

Tiny stumbled and fell. Looking angry he shouted, "I don't know what game you are playing but I won't have you pushing me around."

Boris was out ahead of Turner. The delay had been enough for Su Su to get out a distance ahead of Boris. The stag knew something they did not, once Tiny had stopped he could not move forward again. The earth beneath his feet seemed to give way and every step he took seemed to bring him two steps back.

"Stop right there Rong, I'm taking you back to Bale", Boris shouted.

Su Su slowed her pace and turning sideways said, "No thank you Boris. I have found someone here who appreciates my work, whom I respect, and with whom I intend to work. Bale has no interest in my work."

"What do you mean?", he called out after her for he was dropping further and further behind.

"Ask him", she replied her voice wafting back to him on a breeze.

He stopped apparently thinking about what she had said. But when he went to move forward again it was too late.

Nadine flew back to Su Su's side, "We're alright they can't touch us now."

Chapter Thirty Four

Deadly Sins

"Turner and Boris could not harm you", said Paslan.

"But Bale can?", asked Nadine.

"Bale is fired with pride, greed, envy, and now anger", said Paslan.

"Do you mean that Nadine's thwarting Bale's attempt to bring Su Su back has caused him to be angry?", asked Will.

"Yes, that, and in combination with the garden being torn up, the guillotine, the voice in the woods, and the banner," said Paslan.

"Was he not an angry man before"?, David asked.

"He was not angry, until now. Bale was used to getting his way in everything. Suddenly others are willing to stand in his way, to fight", Paslan said.

"What is Bale envious about?", Will asked Nadine as they sat together on the porch after the others had gone.

"Paslan", Nadine said.

The guillotine stood in plain view of the Building and every time one of them stood by the window it winked at them.

The blade always seemed to be gleaming in either the sunlight or the moonlight.

"Why can't we get rid of that", Hil Gore said irritably.

Ginbreste looked up from his desk. He seemed to be the only one who did not notice it. "We've tried but the roots of the trees seem to have formed around the scaffolding and they can't topple it."

"They could hack it down", she replied.

"They've tried that too but after an hour of such a racket and not getting anywhere I asked them to stop", he ended and went back to his work. She frowned at him.

Hil Gore was getting tired of being stuck in the woods. The truth was that she had little to do and no one with whom to interact. Now that Rong was gone . . . Why had she left?

Bale was in a fury. He was harder to take these days. But the point was that unless Bale succeeded and quickly she was wasting her time because she was not furthering her career here. She should make her own plan and get on with it. There might be bad blood with Bale but she'd have to lump it. If they had brought Rong back what would Bale have done she reflected? She was sorry they had not caught Rong then she could have learned from Bale's actions towards Rong what to expect. Bale was in such a fury now she was certain that he would act.

The work on building the tarmac, as part of Ginbreste's plan, was a worse failure, if that was possible, than the mining operation they had attempted. Every tree they cut down seemed to be replaced overnight by another. While Bale refused to believe the construction foreman's stories that this was the case, he could see for himself that they were getting nowhere. As he had no intention of losing time he changed the plan. Instead of the weapons being brought in cargo planes they would have to be brought by helicopter. Boris was an excellent copter pilot and knew others who could pilot.

That night the copters flew in in droves. Hil Gore had her hands full ordering the worker crews about and at one point her arms were literally full of ammunition boxes. She had handed off the organization of where the pilots and new fighter recruits were to sleep to Herd who was deftly managing the responsibility. Vladamir Pravdan had provided the army of fighting men. Hil Gore wasn't sure about Pravdan's ambitions but at the moment he was exactly the right connection for this job. Pravdan had been a general and had run the Russian plot for the smashing of Ukraine's independence. At the moment he was planning the strategy and the positioning of the men in the forest and all the way along to the community where Paslan and the rest lived. Tomorrow was the day.

Terhaven had moved into Fenfrew's house as he was now strictly confined to bed. And besides preparing all he ate, she was now administering to him by layering his skin with poison absorbing herbs made into lotions and poultices alternately applied. Old doctor Fernbrody had been called in though he had long been retired. His advice was rest and relaxation. The rest had been firmly imposed of late and Fenfrew was very tired so he was not fighting the order. The relaxation was far harder to achieve. With all the Intrusives colliding with the atmosphere, the Other World was out of balance and Fenfrew's system was suffering for it. Fenfrew was most upset about not being able to work with Will and Su Su. The three of them would have had the Time Differentiator perfected by now. Up until the last two days Fenfrew could think things through with them, now they were on their own as he slept most of the time.

Su Su and Will were working furiously. Nadine had volunteered as a guinea pig. At first they both refused her offer. Then when the droves of helicopters arrived they agreed to a mini trial.

"The idea is to send them to the time gap so that they will be in a nether land unable to bother us any longer and at the same time we are not foisting them on others in another world", said Will as he tightened the plate of the dial on the purple cylindrical box. Rong was looking through the myriad of light filters that she had been refining for weeks, holding them up to the sunlight and examining them. After she placed them down carefully on the purified cloths lying along all the tables of Fenfrew's lab she said, "We are not going to attempt to send you to the gap. There will be no trials for that, when the time comes we will just do it", her eyes met Will's.

"We will try a . . . little trip", said Will cautiously. "Remember how we got to the other side of the door of McLellan's office?", he asked her.

"Yes. I'm ready Will. Try it", Nadine said with a firmness and confidence that made them both pause, and made all three ready.

Will put the bracelet attached to the little purple cylindrical box around Nadine's wrist. "Stand straight ... what am I saying ... your posture is perfect", Will said nervously.

"Don't worry Will, I have full confidence in you", Nadine said and then she added, "And in Su Su. "We've all got to do our part to pay the price of being free, to support Paslan and help Fenfrew."

As she expected, Fenfrew's name had it's effect. Will lost his hesitancy.

"Center yourself, feet shoulder width apart", he said firmly as he watched her spread her feet a little further apart. Remember we will send you there just for a few moments and then bring you right back. Are you ready?"

"Yes I'm ready", she said.

Will slid the dial a fraction of a miliimeter to the left. There was a whoosh of wind and Nadine disappeared.

She found herself on a quiet track of land. It looked like a farm. There were a couple of idle tractors, a barn, and a little house. Where is this she thought and when? While I don't know much about machinery I don't think I've seen tractors like that. It could be sixty years or more ago. Was this the Yorkshire moors? The land was rolling in every direction. A long loose stone wall maybe three to four feet high ran a good distance along the crest of one hill. Nadine noticed that the air was very fresh. She breathed deeply. This is marvelous air she said aloud as she breathed in through her nose and out through her mouth in the most approved fashion. She stood in one spot. She wondered why she did not want to set off for a walk. Something told her to stay put in the same spot where she had arrived.

She had quite a view from this position. How exciting to be able to flick a switch and arrive in another place and time. Will was going to be rich she predicted. Just at that moment she felt a soft wind whoosh about her, the moors disappeared and she was back in Fenfrew's home with Will and Su Su standing in front of her.

"It worked she cried!", hugging Will and then Su Su who looked startled with the show of emotion. A little smile appeared on Su Su's face and Will looked wholly relieved.

"Please tell us everything", Su Su's voice sounded light and happy.

"I'm pretty sure I was on the Yorkshire moors", she began but was interrupted immediately by a burst of clapping. Both Will and Su Su had broken into spontaneous simultaneous applause.

"That is where I decided to send you", Will said happily. "The probability was good that you'd arrive in the middle of a field and not in the middle of a street."

"Thanks", Nadine said patting Will's shoulder.

"Did you see anyone?", Su Su asked.

"No but I saw a couple of old tractors, maybe sixty years old", Nadine replied.

Su Su and Will looked at one another with happy smiles, "That sounds about right", Will was beaming.

"The air was lovely, so fresh you could smell the earth growing", she said with a lilt in her voice.

"Let's tell Fenfrew", Will said excitedly to Su Su.

"You go and tell him", she said kindly.

Will paused and then said, "Thanks", and left the lab.

"Any ill effects?", Su Su was giving Nadine the once over.

"No I feel fine", she said.

"I think that Paslan will wait until the very last moment to use this", Su Su was speaking slowly and her eyes held steadily to Nadine. "He will give everyone, including Bale, a chance to change their minds and leave."

"Do you think any of them will?", Nadine asked Su Su.

"I don't know. Most of them are followers and without Bale they have no direction. It might be harder for them to leave on their own than to follow Bale to. . .."

"Yes I see", said Nadine. A number of minutes passed as both women reflected on what was about to happen. Then Nadine asked, "How do you feel?" It felt a little awkward to ask that of Su Su. Prior to this it would not have crossed Nadine's mind to ask how Su Su felt about anything.

Su Su went to the huge window and looked out over the meadow that spread like a beautiful carpet in front of the house. In a calm voice she said slowly, "For the first time since I was a child . . . I feel alive. I feel life all around me. For years and years I have not felt life. I have only pushed myself to achieve. I have only heard my ambitions, instead of the birds and nature, as my grandfather taught me", her voice cracked. Silent tears came streaming down her cheeks. "Paslan has reminded me of my grandfather, of life. I feel love for life again." Su Su turned to Nadine and smiled, letting her friend see her tears.

Nadine stepped forward and joined her at the window. Quietly, gently, she put her arm around Su Su's shoulders and they stood together looking out onto the meadow and the sky. In the distance a large bird flew onto the plane of the horizon. It was quite a distance yet as it flew at an angle to them they could watch it's flight. Very quickly it came closer. It was the largest bird either had seen, with a wingspan of likely seven and a half feet. It was an eagle.

CHAPTER THIRTY FIVE

TWO WORLDS

"There is something I had not thought about. How stupid can one get?", Will was chastising himself as he paced up and down Fenfrew's lab.

"What is it?", Nadine asked with impatience. She had not ever seen Will so discomposed.

"For the Time Differentiator to move someone to the Gap the bracelet has to go on them. How am I going to get the bracelet on Bale?", he asked her with his mouth hanging open in disbelief at his own stupidity.

"Well . . . what does Su Su say?", said Nadine.

"I don't know. She hasn't thought of it either yet", Will said distractedly as he randomly moved about the lab.

Rong burst into the room. "Will I just realized we've organized the transmitter around connection to the bracelet. How are we going to get a bracelet on Bale?!"

Suddenly Will burst out laughing followed in a moment by Nadine. Rong stood staring at them.

"I just thought of it too", Will said. "You make me feel so much better as I thought myself such an idiot."

"Don't speak for yourself as you make me one too", said Rong.

They had stopped laughing. Following the quiet, Su

Su said,

"What are we going to do?"

Paslan sat eating his breakfast in the sunroom off the kitchen. Outside dark grey clouds filled the sky and the wind was whipping up the tops of the trees. Inside Paslan's sun room it was bright as a glorious summer's day. There was a knock at the front door. Paslan put his napkin on the table, rose and went and opened the door. There stood Ginbreste.

"Good morning Libby. Won't you come in please?", said Hale Paslan.

Ginbreste stepped inside and the the door closed behind them.

"It is not a matter of pushing you aside", Ginbreste was saying to Paslan. "Avaricis wants progress. He is a very bright man you know", Ginbreste was looking over the rim of his glasses at Paslan seemingly trying to understand why Paslan had not joined them.

"Intelligence you say? Well . . . it is not the whole kettle of fish", said Paslan as he offered his guest a plate of haddock.

Ginbreste took the plate and with a frown said, "Well what is it then? Why won't you join us?"

"Because more important than knowing who we are given to be for which freedom is required, is . . . nothing", said Paslan.

Ginbreste stopped eating, his face set in an uncomprehending grimace.

"I like you Hale. I have always respected your intelligence

and you have always had a listening ear. However when progress is at stake I can not go along with having any . . . thing stand in the way", he said.

"What is progress?", asked Paslan.

Ginbreste replied, "What do you mean?"

"You have a very high regard for exact language. And so I ask you, what is progress?", Paslan repeated himself.

Ginbreste, still frowning, wiped his mouth with the linen napkin, cleared his throat and said, "Progress is to develop in a positive way, to advance. As time marches on so must we. It is the build up of knowledge over time, the steady accumulation of improvements, it is growth, goal achievement and change. Thinking collectively we can have peace and harmony, thinking separately acting individually, we can not have peace."

"And what is thinking if not the creation of an individual mind and therefore the best guide to a life?", said Paslan.

"The thought of the day, of any culture, is an accumulation of thinkers, intellectuals, academics. One person does not a community make", replied Ginbreste.

"Is the essence of time a day? Is a community a mass of people?", Paslan said.

"Well . . . community is a group of people who come together with common interests", Ginbreste said.

"I would suggest to you that a community is a group of individuals who choose to live in close proximity to one another in order to share some simple basics of life; time, wares, support, and perhaps, yet not necessarily, friendship. In other words without individual choice which presupposes individual thinking, a community would be without foundation, meaningless. I would hazard that you do not bother to think about this. That you prefer to think that those who do not share your intelligence and have not applied the kind of discipline you have applied to your education and work are those with whom you like to have little to do. And that you go on to assume that therefore they are incapable of or without the foundation for making the right choices for themselves and therefore for society. And that therefore the community or society, of which I believe you privately more narrowly define as yourself and those like you, is better equipped to make decisions or in other language, direction for all", Paslan finished.

Inadvertently Ginbreste pushed back his chair. He coughed and appeared for a moment to be choking on the last of a scone. He was speechless. Paslan leaned slightly towards him and taking up the water pitcher poured more water into Ginbreste's glass. Ginbreste continued to sputter but did not take up the glass. The color had risen in his cheeks and he looked angrily at Paslan but said nothing. There was really nothing he could say.

Chapter Thirty Six

Courage and Freedom

R ong walked up the path to the Building. The
picture window in the main room was shuttered
so she could not tell whether Ginbreste was there
working. She knocked on the front door. As she waited she
pulled the collar of her coat up around her neck as the
wind was cold and blowing. It was always colder here on
the northeast side of the forest. An intercom system acti-
vated at the door and a woman with a Russian accent said,
"Who is it?" Rong was sure that there was a hidden video
at the door and that they could see her. Nonetheless she
responded to the question, "It is Su Su Rong. I have come
to see Avaricis Bale."

The woman's hard cold voice said, "Wait there." The
intercom system cut out.

The wind was picking up as Su Su stood on the landing.
After a few minutes the door was opened by an aged man,
his back bent over with years of being tired. He looked at
her with sad yet intelligent eyes.

"Come in please", he said, his politeness not suiting
the atmosphere of the Building. "If you will wait in this
room", and he opened a door off the foyer into a large
room which in a house would have been a parlor but in the
Building was more of an office lobby waiting room.

Su Su entered the inhospitable space and while there were a number of chairs and a large sofa she went to the little window which faced the back. The garden had been laid over with cement. There was a large commercial waste barrel and some pieces of plastic and paper refuse blowing about the ground in the wind. The door behind her opened.

"I thought you might want some water", said the old man who brought in a tray with a pitcher of water, a glass, and a little plate with two wedges of lemon. She smiled at his unexpected kindness and walked over to him.

"Thank you", Su Su said warmly, looking at him and hoping to encourage him to say what apparently was on his mind.

He looked at her and his sad eyes seemed to say you come from a better place. In a barely audible voice he said, "Thank you for coming here perhaps you can help us", and he turned and left the room.

He had barely gone when the door swung wide and Bale entered. "I am surprised to see you again - here", Bale said rather cryptically. He looked different. The somewhat cynical twist at the mouth was there but something was different. Su Su kept her eyes on him, though it was difficult. His energy was so aggressive, and peculiarly negative.

"Why are you here?", he demanded.

"I thought we should finish the job we began", she said simply.

He paused a moment and said, "Sit down."

Bale pointed to a chair near the small window. She sat down and he sat directly across from her. "I'm sure that you realize you are in a dangerous position. I no longer trust you. What can you do for me?", his black eyes were boring into her.

"I can give you the technology you have wanted from the beginning", she replied.

She thought she heard a slight intake of breath. But she could not be sure as the wind was now howling outside.

"Well then give it to me", his voice was coldly excited.

"Do you have a room at the top of the building? To show you properly we need to avoid any interference from electrical waves", said Su Su.

He stood up and went immediately to the door. He stood back and let her go through first to be able to watch her. Then he led her up the narrow staircase to the top of the building. They walked to the end of the hall and Bale pushed open the door. This room had a large window that looked out upon the sky. She pulled open her bag and reaching in drew out a small purple cylinder. She sat down at the table in the middle of the room. Bale sat down close beside her. She pressed a small button on the side of the cylinder and light seemed to fill the room. Bale looked up to the window seeking the source of light. Dark clouds, whipped by the wind, sailed eastward. He looked back down to the cylinder and took it in his hands.

The room disappeared and Rong and Bale were sailing with the clouds to the Gap between the worlds. Just as they ascended Rong caught a glimpse of a large bird soaring above them. She recognized the eagle. She could have sworn that she saw him looking at her. The Gap was just that, a space in space and time with no particular characteristics, a neutral ground. A bit she thought like the waiting room in the Building. She wished the old man would come through a door in the clouds now with some water with lemon.

"What is this? "Where are we? "Why have you brought me here?", said Bale sounding belligerent and a little less sure of his ground.

"This is the Opposites Magnet technology advanced, Time Differentiator technology", said Su Su Rong.

"Okay let's get back. How are we going to use it against Paslan?"

"We aren't", she said.

He looked at her grasping her meaning.

Suddenly she felt herself falling through the clouds. What was happening? This wasn't planned. She and Will had planned that she would reverse the Time Differentiator and bring herself back with the small companion device in her pocket. There was the possibility that it would not work and she wouldn't be able to come back. But she had made the choice. Just as suddenly as she had felt herself falling she felt herself lifted up, supported. She was moving horizontally and descending at a much more comfortable rate. The eagle had come to get her. And now she was flying with him.

The bird soared up on the updraft and floated in a wide spiral downward. He continued the motion a dozen or more times and each time Su Su relaxed a little bit more. She could see the ground now though they must be very high because she could not make anything out. Quickly that changed as she began to make out trees, lakes, and rivers. The eagle was circling around a house. It was Paslan's house. Su Su realized that he was flying as slowly as he could, getting closer and closer to the ground and that he could not land on the ground and that she would have to jump off. The bird was trying to give her the best landing spot. It's now or never she thought and gently laying her hand on the bird's back she said, "Thank you", and then let go.

She fell on soft grass and in a bit of a crumpled heap. In a moment she got to her feet. She looked up to the beautiful bird who was still circling though much higher.

She waved and could have sworn the big bird tipped his wing before soaring off.

"How are you?", a warm familiar and most welcome voice asked her.

"Oh Paslan Bale is gone. We did it", she said almost in a whisper. She reached out to Paslan. Taking her arm and then putting his own arm around her, Paslan lead Su Su into the house.

"You were very brave", he said as they sat together by his fire.

"It was the only thing to be done", she replied.

"Perhaps it was", he said.

She looked at him, wondering.

CHAPTER THIRTY SEVEN

TIME AND LIFE

The wind was whipping up the last air pockets of thick grey clouds, collecting them all as before a cataclysm. The storm clouds dark grey and heavy with rain moved across the sky at an alarming rate. Paslan buffeted on the air managed to stay close to the eye of the storm and remained relatively dry. Bale still a few miles further on was tossed upward through the heavy clouds and turned about every which way and then fell hundreds of feet before the brewing storm of wind, and what was now sleet, tossed him upward again.

"Bale", Paslan's voice resonated through the clouds.

Bale, beside himself, alone, confused, and fear filled, heard a voice. For a moment he could not collect his senses to respond.

"Bale it is Paslan, can you hear me?"

"I can hear you", came Bale's voice muffled by the tossing and turning.

"Will you consider what I am about to say?"

"What . . . where are you? What is happening? Can you get me out of here?", came a frightened and desperate reply.

"I can not get you out of here in the way you mean", said Paslan.

There was a silence but for the whipping of the wind.

"Are you willing to listen?", asked Paslan.

There was a groan and then Bale said, "Yes, . . . yes I will listen," the desperateness was increasing.

"You can remain here in the Gap or you can return to earth as a boy and try and make different choices", said Paslan.

There came a sound of a deep groan that continued and rolled off the clouds and swirled in the wind, a groan within groaning. Paslan waited.

"I don't understand", came back a mournful cry.

"I can send you back to your childhood and once there you can make different choices. You can honor your parents, make friends, have more fun, and look at life as a gift rather than as a race", said Paslan.

The groaning continued many long minutes and then slowly grew quieter.

"Are you offering me a chance then . . . on earth?", asked Bale in a small voice.

"Yes", said Paslan.

"Yes," replied Bale.